AF429257

The Art Of Letting Go
(Opus Magnum)

by

Rhonda Hanson

The Art Of Letting Go
(Opus Magnum)

by
Rhonda Hanson

ISBN 979-8-218-52625-2

Copyright 2024

by

Grace Under Pressure Publishing
P.O. Box 337
Bell Buckle, TN 37020

*All rights reserved. No reproduction of any kind
without expressed written consent from
Grace Under Pressure Publishing*

graceunderpressure.com

Dedication

To Louis Bartet, a man of God who greatly influenced my walk with God, and who had a great part in establishing the foundations of my faith by teaching me about the Abraham walk. To a man whose consistency and integrity have been a source of comfort to me and who once preached a sermon with a simple title that has stayed with me, all these years. It is with his permission that I have the honor of naming this, my ninth work of fiction, "The Art Of Letting Go".

While I don't necessarily expect Louis Bartet to ever read this book, as he might rightfully suspect that it's a romance, I still owe him a debt of gratitude for the inspiration I've always received from his own walk with God.

Rhonda Hanson

The Art Of Letting Go
(Opus Magnum)

Cora had tugged at the nasty blue carpet until she thought her arms were going to fall off. She'd started at the far end of the room and began pulling it away from the wall, thinking she'd just keep rolling it toward the front door and then lug it out, but that wasn't happening. Finally, she gave up and resorted to what Clyde Murray, at the hardware store, told her to do in the first place, and used the sharp carpet knife he'd sold her to cut the carpet into manageable strips.

She was glad Clyde wasn't around to gloat, when his advice turned out to be exactly what she should have been doing all along. Now she backed out of the door of the little house, pulling another ugly section of carpet with her and almost falling down in the process. She stopped to roll it tighter, and then gathered it up to drag it around to where she was piling it all.

She almost felt good about her progress, until she remembered that the smelly padding would be next, after this.

"Oh, great," she breathed. She stood looking back at the pile of offensive carpet and wondering if she could burn it, or if she'd have to rent a trailer and haul it off. Tucker Mills, the area fire warden, had told her that if she'd have a section of land cleared of debris first, she'd be okay to burn much of what she threw out of the house, since she had streams running around the front and side of the house and a big pond in the back.

He'd asked her to take certain items to the landfill, rather than try to burn them, but she'd forgotten to ask him about the carpet. She was just itching to throw gas and a match on it.

"I'm starving," she suddenly realized, out loud.

She'd gotten to the little house just after daylight, and had been working for hours, without even thinking about eating, but now that she'd stopped for a breather, she realized that she'd left this morning without breakfast.

She was temporarily lodging in a beautiful upstairs section over Sandra Birch's very nice restaurant, Ingleside Fare. Sandra stopped her on her way out and made her take a sack lunch.

She protested at first, but now she was glad Sandra placed it firmly in her hands and patted her cheek in a motherly way, and wouldn't take no for an answer. Cora had left her food in her Jeep, since she had no idea of what kind of creepy crawlies she would encounter in the house.

She began making her way a fair distance out to where she'd had to park it, stepping gingerly over the little makeshift footbridge that made accessing the house possible. She kept her head down as she stepped over the carpet of fallen autumn leaves, just in case snakes were still active.

She had learned to be alert, coming and going out here all alone, but she was unprepared for the danger she now walked into, squarely slamming into a hard wall of red plaid flannel.

"What are you doing here?"

Cora staggered back and looked up at the man who stood blocking her path to her vehicle. He was glaring down at her, his arms crossed and a dark scowl resting on his face.

She continued to stare up at him, trying to remain calm, even though she realized that her breathing was much too shallow. She did have a small pistol in the inner pocket of her lightweight trench coat, but she desperately hoped things wouldn't escalate to that point.

"I asked you what you're doing here," he reminded her, coldly intimidating. He was regarding her with so much obvious anger that Cora wondered if he was mistaking her for someone else. He persisted in riveting his gaze on her, not missing the quiet way she continued to look up at him, her clear, green eyes seeming to analyze him.

"Why? Are you a journalist?" she asked, sounding much more nonchalant and sarcastic than she was actually feeling. She hid her fear of this strange, hostile man who had appeared out of nowhere, with an outward calm that masked the truth.

He took a step closer and Cora admirably stood her ground, refusing to back up.

"Where's Jane?"

She drew her brows in confusion. "How would I know?"

"I'm not playing around with you," the man advised her, clenching his jaw and evaluating her with his dark, unreadable eyes. "I want to know where my sister is, and I want to know who you are, and what you're doing at her house. I don't recommend making me ask again."

Cora continued to express bewilderment. "I don't know anything about your sister, or anyone else's sister, but I do know that this is *my* house."

Her claim caused the man to narrow his eyes and, although he hadn't touched her, she had the odd sensation that he had just grabbed her and shaken her.

"Do you think I don't know my own sister's house?" he demanded, in a low voice that displayed his mounting irritation.

Cora raised a hand, subconsciously signaling for him to stop, then swept her long, dark blonde hair back over her shoulder, before crossing her own arms defiantly.

"I don't know what kind of scam you're trying to run on me," she said evenly, "but I bought this house and this property and I have the papers to prove it."

"Produce them," he countered.

"Do you think I carry them in my pockets?"

Cora had begun to exhibit her own anger, as her eyes flashed and she set her chin firmly. "This property came up for auction and I bought it. If you don't believe me, you can just go back to town and talk to the bank. They have my money, and I have this property. If anyone's trespassing, it's you!"

The man slowly advanced and looked down at her, silently appraising her and attempting to determine if this woman was deliberately lying, or if she really believed that what she was telling him was true.

Cora returned his scrutiny, taking in his dark, unruly hair and grudgingly admitting to herself that he was handsome, even if he was a potential axe murderer.

"Your sister is Jane, then?" she finally asked, when it became apparent that he wasn't planning on leaving.

"I made that clear. I suppose you're now going to try to convince me that you bought this house with her blessing?"

"Since I have no clue who she is or who you are, I have absolutely no reason to try to convince you of that."

Cora studied him quietly. "You don't like the answers I'm giving you, and I'm not going to start making stuff up just so you'll be satisfied. The best thing you can do is to go back into town and talk to Ned Frazier, at the bank.

"All I can tell you is that the bank auctioned off the house and property as is, it was an online auction, and I bought it. I don't know how to be more simple than that."

"I'm sure you could find a way," he muttered, looking around into the trees and flexing the muscles around his mouth, frustrated that he hadn't found a man on his sister's property so that he could beat him to a pulp until he confessed what he knew about Jane.

Instead, he had to encounter this vexing creature who was either a proficient liar, or really hadn't been given any details about who the house belonged to.

She seemed to be reading his mind. "When's the last time you saw your sister?"

He lowered his head and raked his fingers through his hair in a way that implied stress, then absently began to knead the stiff muscles at the base of his neck. He took a moment before reluctantly answering her question.

"It's been a while," he admitted, in a dull voice. He turned his back to her and slowly paced a short distance toward both their vehicles, before stopping to retrace his steps back to where she stood waiting.

"She brought me out here when she was trying to buy this place. I didn't even go in, and I tried to talk her out of it."

Cora thought about that and turned to look more closely at the little house, trying to view it as someone's protective brother might, and finally nodded.

"I guess I get that," she said softly.

He followed her gaze and studied the house with a tidal wave of emotions hitting him all at once.

Something was wrong. Something was very wrong. His sister loved her odd little house and she wouldn't have just abandoned it.

"Do you live near here?"

He heard her quiet question as she looked back toward him, and merely shook his head.

"Are you staying in town, then?"

He abandoned his deliberations and lowered his eyes to inspect her curiously. "Why do you want to know?"

"Because I can show you the papers if it'll help at all, but they're not here. I don't live out here, yet. I just come out during the day to work on the house. I'm staying in town, in the upstairs room over Ingleside, in the meantime."

"Ingleside."

"It's a restaurant; the main one in town."

He continued to read her, and it created an awkward silence that she felt compelled to fill.

"I'm Cora Hartmann," she offered. "Not that you care, but it was one of your questions. So, now you know."

When he nodded slightly and looked away she continued, managing to hide a smile. "Do I get to know your name, or do I just call you the axe murderer?"

The irony of her description of him caused a faint smile to hurry across his face and Cora drew in a quick breath at the transformation, however brief.

"Morgan Roberts," he murmured, still unwilling to accept that the person in possession of his sister's home had no knowledge of her, at all.

She tilted her head and considered him.

"It's a good name," she decided.

"I'm relieved to hear that," he returned dryly.

"It is, though. It's sort of like..." Cora broke off, trying to come up with the right word.

"Try pirate," he suggested, with a dour expression.

"Yes!" she exclaimed, before checking herself. "Oh, I guess you've heard that before, then."

"A few times," he admitted, as he let out a weighty sigh, and deserted his negative assessment of the house.

He began to move toward his vehicle, then stopped to address her. "I'm staying at the inn, which I imagine is still the only one in town."

"So far," she informed him.

"You seemed to be going toward your Jeep, before."

"I was. I'm hungry, and there's a sandwich in there."

"Is there also something to write on, in there?"

She motioned for him to follow and led the way.

Morgan watched her as she buried her hands in her pockets and strolled toward the Jeep, glancing up at some leaves that were twirling down and smiling at them like a delighted child, while the filtering sunlight lit up her hair, changing the color to resemble honey.

She opened the vehicle's door and reached into its side liner, pulling out a small notepad and a pen to give to him.

Morgan took them, while briefly resting his eyes on hers, then glanced down and scrawled a phone number and room number on the pad. He turned the pen and noted the bank's advertising on it and simply shook his head, before handing it to her along with the notepad.

"When you're back in town, I'd like to have a look at the papers, if you're serious about showing them to me."

"I insist," she replied. "It's possible that you may notice something that wouldn't mean anything to me, but might give you a clue about what's going on."

She patted the top of a small cooler.

"If you're hungry, I can hook you up."

He allowed another rare but fleeting smile, something that she could tell didn't come easily to him.

"Thank you, no. I need to get back and try to see what else I can find out in town."

"I'll call you when I'm back, then."

Morgan offered a slight lifting of his hand and returned to his Land Cruiser, making an attempt to organize his thoughts.

Cora watched him drive away, then lifted the cooler from the car seat and headed back to cross over the footbridge.

She stopped and raised her eyes to look at the little house in the woods, seeing it differently now.

"What secrets are you hiding, little house?" she whispered.

✳✳✳

Sandra Birch pulled out a chair and settled down at the table Cora was sitting at with a loud sigh.

"This is the first time I've taken a break since after the lunch rush," she admitted.

Cora glanced up at her curiously, then looked around the cozy, but loud dining area.

"Where's Debra?"

"She had an OB appointment, and I told her to go ahead and have the rest of the day off. Her poor ankles have been so swollen, I don't know how she's walking."

The owner of Ingleside Fare returned a smiling nod to a customer across the way, before focusing her attention back on her beautiful, young boarder.

"That slouch of a husband of hers should be the one in here working," she declared hotly. "Disability! He's not too disabled to spend all day up in a deer stand, and most of the night playing pool, I've noticed!

"Meanwhile, his sweet wife is carrying his child and doing all she can to keep the bills paid and the lights on. I'd like to knock *his* lights out."

She waved away her own words impatiently. "Well, that's enough of that. I'll keep on until I say too much and work myself into a fit, the way I always do."

Sandra peered at Cora's left hand and reached for it to examine it closely. She'd managed to get a fairly long and deep scratch in her palm.

"What did you do, honey?"

"I was pulling carpet away from the wall and rolling it and there were some old staples in it. I was expecting carpet nails.

"I grabbed it just right, I guess." She looked down at it and cautiously pressed around it. "It's still a little tender."

"Did you boil it out with some peroxide?"

Cora grinned up at her. "Yes, ma'am. You made me take enough first aid stuff with me to start my own clinic. It'll be alright. But this was just me in the very first room so hopefully, I don't keep escalating my injuries the further into the house I go. I've pretty much just been focusing on the living room."

"But you've been through the rest of the house, right, to see what you have ahead of you?" Sandra was still inspecting her hand, looking for signs of infection.

"All but the attic," Cora admitted. "I'm sort of putting that off until I finally have to go up there.

"I keep imagining bats and rats greeting me at the door. I don't even know if there's a light up there."

Sandra had to laugh at the look on her pretty face. "You may want to get someone to go up there with you, when the time comes. Someone who's not afraid of bats and rats."

She noticed the pile of papers Cora was resting her hands on, with a question in her eyes.

"Am I interrupting something you're working on, honey?"

Cora twisted her lips into a grimace. "I have to prove that I own the house and land I just bought."

Sandra wrinkled her brow. "Who's asking? The IRS?"

She shook her head. "I ran into some man while I was out there working today, and I mean I literally ran into him. I was looking down and slammed into him like a tree, which he might as well have been, to be honest."

Sandra stared at her with her mouth open.

"Cora, you know good and well, that I haven't been too happy with you going out into those woods all by yourself, and this is not making me change my mind. I wouldn't be surprised if some old hobo has been squatting in that old house. Did he threaten you, or anything like that?"

"He's not a hobo," Cora said, with a little smile for her friend. "He's a little too refined for that, and you can tell that he's not exactly destitute. He's also not congenial."

Sandra sat thinking for a moment, then reached a finger to tap the pile of papers.

"He's the one you have to prove all this to? What business is it of his?"

"He claims that the house belongs to his sister," Cora replied. "The more I tried to convince him that I don't know anything about that, the angrier he got."

"Who's his sister?" Sandra wondered.

"Jane. That's all he said."

"Jane." She repeated the name softly.

"There used to be a girl around here called Jane. Well, not a girl, a young woman. Very pretty, with lots of curly dark hair. She didn't come into town much though, and I only saw her in here a few times. Then she just stopped coming. I haven't thought about her in a while. I wonder if she's the same one?"

"She could be," Cora said slowly. "That man... well, his name is Morgan Roberts. Anyway, he has dark, curly hair. It sounds as if she might look like him, a little."

"Morgan Roberts, with dark, curly hair?" Sandra raised her brows and smiled mischievously. "Refined, and not exactly destitute? Please tell me he's a pirate!"

Cora twisted her lips into a little grin. "That's what I said, but he didn't seem to appreciate it."

"Jane Roberts." Sandra tested the name for recognition, but shook her head.

"I can't remember what this Jane's last name was, but it wasn't Roberts. It was a short name, one syllable. When I see Debra again, I'll try to remember to ask her. I saw them chatting every once in a while, so I imagine they became friends."

She stopped and seemed to remember something else.

"I think this Jane was an artist. I don't remember ever seeing her work, but I'm pretty sure Debra said she was an artist and she was thinking about opening a shop in town.

"Now that I think about it, it seemed to fit her. She was a little bit of a hippie. I guess Bohemian is the word.

"You never knew what she was going to come in here wearing, but no matter how strange her little combinations might be, she was always beautiful. I wonder what ever happened to her?"

Cora nodded ahead, drawing Sandra Birch's attention toward the dark-haired man who stepped into the restaurant and stood tall, letting his eyes search the room.

"You're not the only one," she said.

Chapter Two

ora wasn't surprised when she looked up from where she was sitting on the front porch of the house, and saw Morgan Roberts making his way toward her. Even from a distance, she could see the way his face was lined with tension.

She'd gotten a late start this morning and was just sitting quietly, smelling the damp leaves and listening to the birds and their early morning frenzy with a feeling of contentment, when she realized that she'd heard a car door close. She simply knew that it would be Jane's brother and readied herself, hoping he was in a better frame of mind today than the one he'd been in when he left the restaurant, the night before.

She'd handed the papers over to him and he read through them in a way that revealed his familiarity with legal documents. She'd actually asked him if he was an attorney, but he'd only shaken his head and continued to pore through the pages, finally laying them down and leaning back in his chair with an expression of disappointment and defeat. His sister had lost her home then, for whatever inconceivable reason.

Cora's purchase of the house and property was completely aboveboard and, after staring for a long moment into the flames crackling in the large fireplace that gave the restaurant its name, he abruptly rose from the table and left without a word.

She watched him now, as he crossed the footbridge and steadily approached her in a way that warned her not to expect any improvement in his attitude toward her, and he didn't disappoint her.

"What did you do with her things?" he demanded in an impatient tone of voice.

Cora drew her brows in confusion and he cut her off before she had a chance to deny knowing what he meant.

11

"I saw you carrying things out to a burn pile yesterday. Have you burned any of her things? What did you do with them?" He stepped up onto the porch and stood next to her chair, staring down intently at her.

"Morgan, the only thing I've removed from the house so far, has been the carpet and padding in the front room, and the curtains, and some old Christmas wrapping paper and empty boxes I found in the front closet."

Cora could see how agitated he was, and kept her voice soft, deciding that she should dispense with sarcasm and try to help this man, who was using anger to control his fear of what might have happened to the missing sister that he clearly loved.

She reached a hand to gently press against his leg, indicating that she wanted to stand and he moved to one side, but remained close.

She raised herself out of the chair and looked up at him with a sadness washing over her face, as she clearly saw a flicker of pain in his eyes.

She moved toward the door and turned to look back at him. "Why don't you come in and search the house for anything that might give you a clue about what's going on?"

He registered mild surprise, mixed with relief and simply nodded and followed her into what he still identified as his sister Jane's little house.

Cora paused in the living room and watched Morgan's expressive eyes travel around. He hadn't bothered to come into the house when Jane dragged him out here to convince him that she was meant to have it. The living room was empty, but he could see that the rooms beyond appeared to be furnished.

"What was in here?" he asked quietly, noting that she had removed the carpet and padding just as she had claimed, and that the curtains were gone.

"A small loveseat and a couple of chairs and a table. I put them in the next room, so that I could pull the carpet out. So that room is a little crammed, right now."

She walked through a door into what was apparently a bedroom, but now had the living room's furnishings stacked in one corner.

Morgan stood in the doorway, his alert, brown eyes slowly moving around the room, as he took note of any items that he could recognize as once having been in his sister's apartment.

"I haven't touched any of it, Morgan."

Cora thought he hadn't heard her, until he breathed out a sigh and murmured, "Thank you."

Morgan flexed the muscles in his face, seeming to struggle with his emotions as he fought back his fears regarding his young sister's fate with a visible effort.

He moved around a chair to get to the dresser and reached for the small, ornate box he had once given Jane as a birthday present. He lifted the lid, staring hard down at it, as strains of Beethoven's Für Elise began to waft into the air.

As the music played slower and slower and began to lag, decelerating into stark silence, Morgan could see his sister's lovely face fading away from him, gradually dimming, until she was completely gone.

Cora was dismayed to witness this big, strong man suddenly shut his eyes tightly and begin to tremble. Without stopping to think, she hurried over to him and gently took the music box from him, returning it to its place on the dresser, then clasping his hands in hers.

"Morgan, are you sure you can do this?"

She felt a stab of compassion for him.

He continued to stand still with his eyes closed, but she saw the hint of tears on his lashes. After a moment, he lifted his head and looked up at the ceiling, blinking rapidly and drawing in a deep breath.

"This is all wrong," he whispered. "She wouldn't do this. She wouldn't just leave and not tell me."

Cora made no attempt to offer any sort of explanation, and speculating was pointless. There was simply nothing she could say that would give him any hope, at this point.

She saw him drop his gaze down to their hands and quickly released his, with a delicate blush.

"Was Ned Frazier able to tell you anything at all, when you went to the bank?" she asked softly.

He cleared his throat and folded his arms, moving over to look out the window.

"He told me that she had taken out a second mortgage on this property, and then stopped making payments and wouldn't respond to any attempts to contact her."

He spun around and gave Cora a look of disbelief.

"I bought this place for Jane. There was no mortgage on it, at all. I can't understand what she was thinking. If my sister needed money, she could have just called me. She knew that!"

"When's the last time you did talk to her, Morgan?" she asked, watching him grapple with her question.

"It's been a few months. Sometimes, we would talk every week; sometimes she couldn't reach me if I was out of range, and sometimes I'd have trouble getting in touch with her, but sooner or later, we'd connect. I at least checked my messages and I certainly would have tried to call her right away.

"I've been so swamped lately and I hadn't stopped to realize that we hadn't talked in a while, then when I made it a priority to reach her and couldn't, I packed a bag and flew out to come check on her.

"I came out here before yesterday, but of course, she wasn't here and neither were you. I waited around, then finally drove back into town."

Morgan stopped and drew his brow and Cora turned to try to discover what he was seeing across the room. He stepped rapidly past her and then reached down to pick up something from the floor.

He was practically glaring at what appeared to be a man's cigar cutter. Cora approached him and once again touched his hand, as she lifted it up to be able to see what he had found against the baseboard.

"Is that a thing you clip cigars with?" she asked, looking up at him and drawing his gaze away from it. He rested his eyes on hers for a disturbing instant before nodding.

"Why does it have MAT engraved on it?" she wondered out loud. "I guess that's the brand name."

"Or initials," he speculated. A grim severity settled around his mouth. "There's a man involved in all of this."

"You don't think it could have been dropped by someone the bank sent out to inspect the property, before the auction?"

"I doubt it. This isn't a cute little hidden gem, with a white picket fence, rose bushes, and potential curb appeal," Morgan returned dryly, again wondering what it was that Jane had seen in it, and thinking that Cora Hartmann had no idea what she was up against.

"There's not even a road, let alone a curb. For all intents and purposes, this is just a shack in the woods. The real value is in the land. I wouldn't expect that the bank even bothered about an inspection."

"I guess I would have received a copy of it, if they had," Cora acknowledged. "and I don't remember seeing one in the closing packet. It was a foreclosure, and since it was sold as is, I can't see why they would have paid for one."

Morgan pressed his lips together and gave her a slight nod of agreement, pocketing the cigar cutter and searching around for anything else that might have belonged to someone other than his sister.

"Cora."

She was flooded with a sudden awareness that he had never said her name before, which made his doing so now arresting in some way. She looked up at him and waited.

"It's very important that you don't dispose of anything here, unless it's very obviously not personal, such as curtains and carpet. Please, I'm asking you to not get rid of any personal items. If you need the room, I'll arrange to have everything gathered up and stored, but please be careful about what you toss out. I just need some time. Can you give me that?"

He had moved closer to her and was gazing intently at her in a way that revealed his sense of desperation.

She simply nodded, then offered a little smile, and he surprised her with one of his own.

"Thank you."

"Sure."

Morgan moved back out into the living room and Cora followed him to show him through the rest of the house. The only other items they managed to come across that might have belonged to a man, and that Morgan was certain hadn't belonged to Jane, was a fishing lure and a cigarette lighter.

He explained that not only did his sister absolutely not smoke, but that Jane objected to fishing.

She felt sorry for the fish and he had never been able to talk her into going with him, because she insisted that the hooks hurt the fish, and she wouldn't be a part of what she called "piscis abuse".

Cora lifted one brow, which gave her a comically cute expression and he almost managed to laugh.

"My sister loved to flaunt her Latin and piscis is, of course, Latin for fish."

"Well, of course it is," Cora said, widening her eyes. "Who doesn't know that?"

He couldn't help smiling at that, then gave the room another sweeping glance. "This is all, then?"

"Not exactly," she admitted, with a bit of dread.

"Either it is, or it isn't. What does not exactly mean?"

Cora let out an exaggerated sigh and motioned for him to follow her back through the kitchen and into the little utility room off to one side.

Morgan came in with a look of confusion. The room was absolutely bare, so he couldn't understand her unwillingness to include it.

"So, that *was* all, then?"

"I'm afraid not," she confessed. "There's one more place to search, but I've never even gone in there. I've been putting it off, but it looks like today's my lucky day."

She said this with a little grimace and he continued to wear an expression of confusion.

"Are you afraid?" he finally asked.

"I'd like to say that I'm not, but my father's a retired minister and a professor of theology and somehow, I just know that he'll find out, if I lie," she replied with a sour expression.

"What are you afraid of?"

"Bats and rats."

He had the suggestion of teasing in his eyes.

Cora gestured for him to follow her to the far wall, where he was surprised to find a recessed area off to one side, containing a switchback staircase. He looked down at her and a slow grin began to steal across his normally austere countenance.

"So, the attic, then."

"Yes, and it's probably full of things that will get in my hair and crawl in my ears," she said miserably.

She held up her left hand with the deep scratch where the carpet had attacked her. "Apparently, I'm a walking target."

Morgan furrowed his brow and took her hand, holding it next to the window they had stopped in front of, and giving it a close inspection.

"Cora, this is getting infected," he said in a quiet voice. "This has to be treated."

"It's not really hurting," she protested.

He looked at her with a fair amount of doubt.

"Well, not a lot," she amended.

"Let's finish up here, and then get back to your hand," he said, overruling her objections with just a look.

"Fine," she sighed. "But you go first. I'm right behind you," she added, breaking into a slight giggle when he tossed a pointed look over his shoulder at her.

Morgan mounted the stairs, having to duck when he encountered the landing, and then stopped at the door to make sure Cora had made it up safely. He had turned on his cell phone's flashlight feature, since the stairwell was getting darker as they went up, and he hadn't noticed a light switch at the bottom of the stairs.

He tested the handle and the door opened easily enough. He was able to see a light switch just inside the door even without his phone, which seemed odd to him. He flipped it and could tell that lights had actually turned on, then glanced back at Cora, who was still managing to look slightly terrified.

"No bats, no rats." He seemed to take pleasure in needling her. "Cats, hats and gnats, maybe, so watch yourself."

She pursed her lips at him and lifted a harmless fist, causing him to give way to a gentle laugh, before he opened the door all the way and stepped into the attic.

Cora followed him in, and they both stood in complete silence, unprepared for what they'd found.

To begin with, there was enough natural light coming into the attic to flood the room from windows that Cora had never even noticed when outside the house, which was unexpected.

But it was what the light revealed to them that held them speechless, Cora with simple amazement, but Morgan with an overwhelming, ominous premonition that seemed to hit him directly in the chest.

He raised a fisted hand and covered his mouth, as a stark realization caused devastation to bear down on him and the tears that had been threatening him downstairs suddenly broke free.

Cora had been staring at all of the beautiful paintings displayed on easels, leaning against the walls, and resting on table tops, but it was the sound of a soft moan that caused her to look up at him. Her beautiful eyes filled with alarm.

"Morgan, what is it? What's wrong?"

He continued to stare wildly all around him, completely unaware that tears were coursing down his face, and made no attempt to speak.

Cora had never seen so much grief in a single moment before, and it broke her heart.

"Please tell me." She laid her hand on his arm.

She was shocked when Morgan suddenly pulled her close, holding onto her tightly, and burying his face in her hair. She could feel his heart pounding against his ribs and realized that he was too distraught to answer.

She wrapped her arms around his waist and just stood quietly, letting him draw whatever comfort he could from his impulsive, desperate embrace.

Cora gently lifted a hand to rest on his back, caressing it lightly and whispering little words of comfort, but feeling helpless to do anything else. She had no idea why he was having such a strong reaction to seeing these paintings, until she slowly began to recall Sandra Birch telling her that the Jane she remembered was supposed to be an artist.

Cora gasped softly and raised her face to examine Morgan carefully, reaching her fingers up to touch his cheek.

"Your sister was an artist," she breathed.

He opened his eyes and stared into hers for a long moment, before breaking his gaze and looking away toward one of the windows with a nod.

"She wouldn't have left her paintings," he said, in a hoarse voice, that shook with uneasiness.

"She would never do that! Her art meant everything to her. She wouldn't have just taken off and left all of her beautiful paintings stuck up in some attic to eventually be ruined."

He looked back into her eyes, seeming to plead with her to help him make sense of everything.

"Something's wrong, Cora. Something's happened to her and I can't continue to just wait around, wondering. I have to find my sister. She's the only family I have, and I can't lose her."

Neither of them seemed to remember that they were still being held in each other's arms, until Morgan drew in a deep, cleansing breath and finally became aware.

He looked down at Cora, suddenly self-conscious and mildly embarrassed. Both were sensations that he despised and this, coupled with his fear, caused him to become infuriated.

"I'm sorry," he said brusquely, releasing her all at once, not realizing that she was feeling the brunt of his anger. He walked away from her to approach the windows and stood staring out through the tree limbs, returning to his former cool detachment and leaving her with an unpleasant blend of uncertainty and humiliation.

Chapter Three

Cora quietly watched him, trying to work out what had just happened. As far as she was concerned, Morgan became very distressed when seeing all of his sister's artwork, and reached for her because it overwhelmed him. Did he think she was confused about that?

She approached him and simply stood beside him, sharing the window's view, before she finally spoke.

"I can tell that you're planning to frost over again," she began, concentrating on the falling leaves and missing his slight reaction, "and that's fine."

She was speaking softly now, in a low undertone. "I think you're more comfortable being combative with people, and since I don't understand what you're going through and what you're feeling, I'm not going to try to change that. But I won't be guilty of ever being a source of sympathy for you again, especially since it makes you so uncomfortable."

She knew this was hardly the time to make it all about her, but an undercurrent of resentment began to surge in her. After all, he was the one who pulled her to himself and held onto her. She hadn't offered, and she didn't appreciate his making her feel badly about it, as if she had taken advantage of him.

Cora turned her back to the window and rested against the sill, folding her arms and sizing him up candidly.

"You're welcome to come and go, and look and probe, and do whatever you need to do. Take anything here that you want, Morgan Roberts, and when you're done then I'll gut the place, which I planned to do anyway.

"But you go first, and I'll stay in town until you tell me that you're done out here."

She made a move to leave, then paused to look back at him. "There's a big rock under the front door steps, left, as you're approaching. I'll leave a key under it."

She was almost out of the room, when he called her name.

He came over to her and stood regarding her in a strange manner, wanting her to stay, but not knowing how to ask.

"Did you move here from somewhere else?"

His random question caused her to look at him oddly.

"You seem far too enamored with these woods than I would expect a local resident to be," he continued. "I think that was the thing that drew Jane. She wasn't from here and she'd never been in a place like this, until she stumbled on it and fell in love with it. Is that what happened to you?"

"Not exactly," she answered, disappointed that he hadn't stopped her to apologize, and not necessarily wanting to sweep everything under the rug of small talk. "I just needed a place to be alone to work on something, where I wouldn't bother anyone and they wouldn't bother me. That's pretty much it."

Morgan expelled a deep breath and gestured around.

"I guess this is the place for that, then."

Cora nodded and made another attempt to leave.

"Why?"

She halted and turned around, not bothering to mask the look of bewilderment on her beautiful face.

"Why what, Morgan?"

"Why do you want to be so isolated?"

"I have aspirations to be just like you, apparently."

She considered his surprised expression, and shrugged.

"It's not important, but thank you for trying to be interested. I guess that counts for something."

Again, she walked away and again, he stopped her.

"Cora, don't go."

When she turned around this time, she treated him to a cool, reserved countenance.

"But, I am going. I'm going back out to sit on the porch, which is where you found me, and make a list of things I can do in town, to keep this day from being a total wash.

"I'm not going to stay up here with you, and witness what this room does to you, and be expected to have no reaction at all to that. I'm not a freakin' tree, Morgan!"

He seemed taken aback by her words.

"Why would you use that expression?"

"What?" She looked and sounded put out with him.

"Why would you tell me that you're not a tree?"

"Because I'm *not* a tree and I'm also not ashamed of it!"

With that, she flounced down the stairs and left him completely at a loss, heading straight for the porch and throwing herself into the rocker. She carelessly flung one leg over its arm, blinking back hot tears. She had no idea why she felt like crying, but she did, and she decided to just get on with it.

Morgan stepped out onto the porch and paused to observe her. He pulled a straight chair over next to her and angled it so that he could face her, then sat down, leaning forward to convince her to look at him.

"Yesterday, you asked me if you could know my name or if you should just call me the axe murderer."

Cora had been making a point of looking anywhere but at him, but now she raised her eyes to his and gazed at him steadily.

"Now, today you tell me that you're not a tree," he continued. "I can't tell if you've been running my name through search engines, or if you're just incredibly perceptive."

"I did run your name through a search engine and it turns out that you're an axe murderer," she muttered, with a dark, little scowl that she had no idea was beautifully charming.

He recognized that she was being facetious and rested his eyes on hers with a faint smile.

"Well, I *have* murdered my share of axes, I suppose."

"Am I meant to guess what we're talking about?"

He seemed to find it amusing that she had become so aggravated with him.

"That's not necessary. It's just that I own a large amount of timberland and forests, especially in the pacific northwest.

"I found your accusing me of being an axe murderer and then announcing to me that you're not a tree to be ironically humorous, if not coincidental."

Cora widened her eyes in astonishment, in spite of her intention to stay mad at him.

"So, are you actually trying to convince me that you're a timber baron?"

"Are people still using that terminology?" he asked, with mild surprise. "Then yes, I suppose I am."

Cora merely shook her head, and flung her arm out toward the trees around them.

"Then why do you act like this is the forest primeval, wilderness lost, and Bigfoot's hideout, all rolled into one?"

Morgan leaned back against the chair and rested his ankle on one knee, crossing his arms and laughing quietly, in spite of feeling so crushed only moments before. This strange, beautiful, contrary woman made him angry, made him suspicious, made him grateful, and made him laugh.

"The land is beautiful," he conceded, with a smile still lingering in his eyes.

"This house, on the other hand, leaves a lot to be desired, but you seem to be undaunted by that. I suppose I admire your determination, if I'm being honest."

She glanced away and shook her head, and he felt compelled to win her over, not only because he needed her help, but because he didn't like this aloofness between them any more than she did.

"You're angry with me."

"You were being a jerk."

"I know. I'm sorry." He reached over and took her hand when she declined to respond. "Cora, I'm very sorry."

She pulled her gaze away from the trees and rested her lovely, green eyes on him guardedly, before finally relenting and giving way to the very faintest ghost of a smile. "Forget it."

"Is 'forget it' the same thing as 'I forgive you', then?"

She lifted her slim shoulders in a little shrug. "I guess."

He studied the slender hand he was holding and a frown creased his brow.

"Come with me out to my vehicle to get the first aid kit. We need to do something about your hand."

He released it and stood to his feet, claiming her other hand and giving it a slight tug. "Come with me."

She rolled her eyes but let him lead her down the porch steps, noticing the way he laced his fingers into hers, as they walked toward the road where they were both parked.

Morgan pulled the kit out of the Land Cruiser and Cora seemed to actually notice it for the first time.

"This is nice," she decided.

"I'll let the dealership know you like it," he replied lightly, laying the kit on the passenger seat and opening it to find what he needed.

"I flew here, so I leased it from the closest dealer to the airport. I already knew I'd have to drive almost an hour to get here and then need transportation to get back, and since I had no idea of how long I'd be here, it just seemed logical, I guess."

"You could have leased a soccer mom car, but you went for a manly SUV, so points for that," she returned, causing another grin to flash across his face.

"You should do that more often," she added, wincing as he used an antiseptic wipe on her hand.

He glanced up apologetically before responding to her comment. "I should clean your wounds more often?"

"No, smile. It changes your face."

He lifted one brow and fixed her with a challenging look.

"Does my face need changing, then?"

"Your face is a masterpiece," Cora said melodramatically. "But it wants more smiling and less scowling."

"Does it?" He wrinkled his brow and began to gently apply an antibiotic ointment along the length of her scratch. "What good would that do?"

"For one thing, you could become known as the smiling lumberjack. People could tell their children stories about you."

Morgan paused before applying a bandage to her hand and gave her such a look of perplexity that she laughed.

"What I lack in affability, you more than make up for," he observed dryly.

"That only benefits people, if we come as a set," she pointed out. "But we don't, so you'll have to carry your fair load of congeniality. I can't keep picking up your slack."

He checked the bandage, then fastened a gaze on her that seemed to be investigative in nature.

"What is it, that you want to live out here alone to work on, where you won't bother anyone, and they won't bother you?"

He refused to let her get away with another one of her little shrugs. "I have you hemmed in between the door of this vehicle and myself," he pointed out. "I'm waiting for an answer."

"Why, so you can make fun of me?"

"It depends on what it is. If you're out here splitting the atom, I may be impressed. If you're out here sewing little outfits for bats, rats, and cats, I may have to mock you."

She rolled her eyes and leaned in toward him, lifting up her dressed wound. "So, we're done here?"

"Not even close."

They stood eying each other, like two gunfighters at high noon, and Cora finally realized that he was in no hurry.

Her sigh was theatrically loud. "Fine. I'm a composer."

Her name began to register with him, but he didn't say so.

"Are you seriously, or are you just messing with me?"

"I guess the world has to have its fair share of composers," she returned, "and I just happen to be one of them."

"What are your instruments?" He continued to regard her with genuine interest, instead of simply humoring her.

"Piano, cello. Violin, on a lesser level. Guitar, on an even lesser level, and a smattering of miscellany."

"A smattering of miscellany," he repeated, seeming to view her with a bit of fascination.

"You wanted me to say I was out here splitting atoms," she accused him blandly.

He shuddered and waved her words away. "Not another physicist," he protested. "That's the last thing the world needs. But we could do with a few more composers."

Cora tilted her head and seemed to be assessing him.

"I wouldn't have taken you for a music lover."

"But an axe murderer, you had no trouble with."

"You were scary."

Morgan laughed and gestured for her to step out of the space between the Land Cruiser's door and frame.

"I hardly think so, Cora. You were as cool as ice."

She moved out of the way as he shut the door.

"I'm also a good actress, but I went with music."

They both began strolling back toward the house without being conscious of it.

Cora watched the ground as she walked, which was her habit. Morgan noticed, and stopped to reach over and lift her chin with his finger.

"Staring down at the ground is exactly how you happened to run smack into me, yesterday," he reminded her.

"I'm watching for snakes," she explained.

"I believe that I have proven to you that there are much more dangerous things to look out for than snakes."

His warning came with sarcasm, and she laughed.

He paused to let her cross the little footbridge first and remained on his side, analyzing it critically.

"This thing could collapse any day. It's the same old piece of junk it was, the very first time I saw this place, and it hasn't improved with age."

"It's on my list," she sighed.

He came across it and propelled her toward the porch with his hand on her back.

"I have to be going, but let's sit a minute," he requested.

"Dibs on the rocker!"

Cora broke into a run and Morgan stood watching her with an expression of something very close to joy on his face.

He softly laughed and proceeded to follow her, but at his dignified, steady pace.

"Too slow," she criticized.

"I would never take your rocker," he said with a little grin.

He reclaimed the chair he'd been sitting in earlier and gave Cora a serious look.

"You won't be afraid to live out here all by yourself?"

"I don't believe in Bigfoot," she informed him.

"Stop it. I'm seriously asking."

"Nope, me and God. Or is it God and I? God and me?"

She screwed up her face and thought about it.

"Anyway, I have an impressive arsenal of weaponry."

She actually managed to amaze him, and it showed.

"So, you're saying that if I want to come out here and fire off a few rounds at some old metal cans, you won't get all girly about it?"

"If I outshoot you, you won't be all macho about it?" she countered, raising her brows up and down suggestively.

"Is that a challenge?" he asked.

"It's not a invitation to dance."

He looked out across the trees in front of the house with a little smile, seeming almost at peace. Cora watched him, but not so furtively that he wasn't aware of it.

"Right now, you remind me of Jane," he surprised her by saying, as he shifted his position in the chair.

"She used me to practice sketching for her art classes when she was in high school, so she spent a lot of time staring at me. Not that you literally do that," he amended. "But you do seem to aim some expressive looks my way, although I expect you can't help being expressive with those eyes."

She was stunned by his remark but recovered smoothly.

"You make me dizzy with your popcorn personality."

Morgan shook with silent laughter, then stood up.

"I have to go. I'm going to meet with law enforcement and file a missing persons report on Jane."

Cora stood up with him and laid her fingers over her mouth, those expressive eyes he was just talking about beginning to mist over with emotion.

"Will you be okay?"

She stopped herself abruptly and lifted a hand.

"Never mind. I said I wasn't going to do that anymore."

"I'm sorry I made you feel that way," he said, pausing before he moved past her to leave. "Because I couldn't have coped today, if you hadn't been with me, Cora."

"This is awkward," she said, crossing her arms and looking up at him with a little frown, "because I'm naturally wired to lean toward empathy but apparently, you don't like that."

"No, that's not true. That wasn't it, at all."

The man who yesterday, made her think he might very well snap her into pieces, now slipped an arm around her and gave her a gentle squeeze, then reached a hand to ruffle her hair.

"Don't ever let me change the way you're wired. You're exactly who you're meant to be and that's who I need you to be."

He stepped off the porch and turned back to look at her.

"Don't use that hand today, Cora. There's no rush here. You need to go back to your room and keep that hand slightly elevated and put some ice on it. I noticed a little swelling."

He waited, giving her a long look. "Will you do that?"

She indulged in a bit of eye-rolling and heavy sighing.

"I guess so. Besides, I need to heal up so that I can astonish you with my ambidextrous marksmanship."

Morgan continued to hold her in his gaze, then flashed her a soft wink and turned to make his way through the trees.

Cora watched him walk away, as the sunlight filtered through the leaves and washed across him, and the wind lightly played with his hair. By the time he reached his vehicle, he was out of sight and she suddenly felt alone for the first time, since buying the little house.

Chapter Four

Sandra Birch stopped by Cora's table and nodded toward her hand with approval.

"I see you finally let the doctor take a look at that hand of yours. I'm glad, because last night, I didn't have a good feeling about it."

Cora lifted it up with a little frown. "I'm supposed to be keeping it elevated and use ice, but I keep forgetting."

"Well, I can hook you up with the ice, but I can't force you to keep it elevated. Which doctor did you see?"

Cora smiled softly to herself and Sandra drew her brows, wondering which of the old white-haired doctors in their little town could possibly generate that kind of reaction.

She pulled out a chair and plopped down onto it, then held out her palm, curling her four fingers toward herself repeatedly, silently instructing her young friend to come forth with the details about whoever it was, who had put that Mona Lisa smile on her face.

Cora opened her mouth to speak, then stopped and gazed toward the doorway.

Sandra followed her line of vision, then shook her head with a shout of laughter, pushing herself back from the table.

"Well, I see there's a doctor in the house," she quipped, standing up and catching Morgan Robert's eye, then indicating Cora by resting a hand on her head.

He smiled and came their way.

"So, the pirate moonlights as a man of medicine."

Sandra uttered this only loud enough for Cora to hear, and laughed again. "The plot thickens."

She gave the blushing Cora a playful little swat and moved away to check on her customers.

Cora watched heads turn, as Morgan Roberts passed by tables and approached her.

He slid into the chair beside her and rested his arms on the table, acknowledging Cora's attempt to make him believe she'd been sitting there the entire time with her hand elevated, by lifting a brow and giving her a fierce scowl, tempered with a little wink.

"Has it been throbbing?" he asked, reaching for her hand and loosening the bandage so that he could inspect it.

"Only since you wrapped it up," she declared, causing him to pause and rest his brown eyes on her skeptically.

"Stop it," he murmured. He pulled the bandage away and glanced up impatiently at the dim lighting, suitable for ambience, but not for purposes of evaluating an injury.

Morgan lifted her hand to the light and seemed satisfied that it wasn't continuing to swell and certainly wasn't any redder.

He glanced up as Sandra returned to the table with a zippered plastic bag of ice.

"I see the doctor is in," she said, giving Cora a pointed look. "I'll just leave this in his capable hands, then."

She let him take the bag of ice, as he continued to simply look up at her with a question on his face.

"Sandra, this is Morgan Roberts," Cora offered, before glancing over at Morgan.

"Sandra Birch owns Ingleside Fare, and she's also letting me live upstairs, for now."

"Forever, if you need to, honey."

Sandra smiled down at the man she'd just decided really was a pirate, after all, and maybe even the captain of his ship.

"It's nice to meet you, Morgan. Have you eaten? Can I bring you anything?"

He wrinkled his brow and looked over at Cora.

"I don't believe I've actually remembered to eat anything today. Have you eaten?"

Cora shot a look over at Sandra, who clearly wanted to know the answer to that question, herself.

She crossed her arms and planted an appraising look on Cora, then rolled her eyes and lifted both hands dramatically.

"If I didn't make this girl eat, she'd fall out in the floor," she declared.

She pulled a menu from a nearby cart and laid it in front of them. "I'll come back and find out what you want, but can I get you something to drink, in the meantime?"

"Would there still be coffee?" Morgan asked hopefully.

"I can guarantee fresh, hot coffee," she assured him.

She held up a hand to stop him from saying anything. "No need, you take it black."

He looked over at Cora with an odd expression, trying to remember if she knew that about him.

"She can just tell. It's one of her talents," Cora informed him. "She can usually decide, just by looking at someone, if they even drink coffee and if they do, how they like it."

"You're easy," Sandra told him, with a dismissive flick of her hand. She gave Cora a meaningful look.

"No coffee for you, sweet girl. Water with cucumber."

She moseyed off to give them time to look at the menu, and Morgan watched her go with a thoughtful expression, before turning his attention to the menu, that he pushed over to share with Cora.

"So, why aren't you allowed to drink coffee?" he asked quietly, glancing over at her. "And be careful with your answer, 'sweet girl', because if you tell me that you don't drink coffee, we can't be friends."

"That's actually the problem," she admitted dismally.

"Sandra cuts me off around this time, every evening. She says I don't drink enough water and that I don't eat enough either, to be allowed to have as much coffee as I want. She gives me this tiny little thermos of coffee to take with me out to the house every morning, and then I stop by a convenience store on the way, and buy enough to fill up my real thermos."

"That's my girl," Morgan commended lightly, continuing to read through the menu. "And how do you take it?"

"Like any good pirate would, I guess." She grinned at his hushed breath of laughter.

"My first day here, we had an argument about it," Cora informed him. "She doesn't believe that when you drink coffee, you're drinking water."

"And how did you defend your position?" he wondered, lifting his eyes from the menu.

She made a little face. "I asked her, if I eat a coffee pod, and then chase it down with a cup of water, have I not had any water, but her argument is that coffee is a diuretic and that I cancel out my water consumption, by drinking it."

She rested her cheek on her good hand and breathed out a sigh. "We're at a stalemate."

"I may feel just a bit badly about ordering coffee then, if you can't have any," Morgan admitted.

"Don't feel bad. I intend to move closer and pretend to like you, when I'm really just breathing in your coffee steam," she said flatly.

She kept a straight face when he laughed quietly, as if she had no idea why he assumed she was kidding.

Morgan tapped the menu suggestively. "You have to eat."

"Potato soup and corn muffins."

"I'm in," he agreed. "Two, then."

He pushed the menu to the side of the table, as Sandra arrived with his coffee and a glass of sparkling cold iced water, with thin slices of cucumber in the bottom of the glass and one riding on the rim for garnish.

"Now, you know you want this," she told Cora, with a wink. "You just like to give me a hard time."

She approved their very simple orders with a little nod and headed off to make it happen, as Morgan picked up Cora's glass and inspected it in the light.

"Very pretty, Miss Hartmann," he admired. "You have exquisite taste in the very water you resent having to drink."

"When it's like this, I actually like it," she confessed. "Cucumber does amazing things to plain water."

"I actually like it this way, myself," he admitted.

He wrapped his hands around his hot coffee cup and simply sat looking at her.

"Do I have cucumber on my lips, or something?" she finally demanded.

He deliberately lowered his gaze to her lips, before raising his eyes again to meet hers.

"I need to thank you," he said, in a low voice.

"For which gloriously wonderful thing do you need to thank me?" she challenged. "For telling you that you were being a jerk, or for telling you that I wanted to be isolated, so that I could be like you?"

He allowed a slight wrinkle to draw his forehead as she surprised him by immediately reaching back for those two examples, then lifted her hand to very gently begin rewrapping the bandage around it.

"When you wake up in the morning, wash your hand with some warm water and antibacterial soap, then pat it dry. If you can't bandage it again, perhaps Sandra can help with that."

"It sounds as if you're giving me discharge instructions."

She drew his attention by looking steadily at him, her beautiful face solemn. Morgan could read the question in her unhappy, discerning eyes, and pressed his lips together.

"Not here, not tonight," he whispered.

"Something's up," she concluded softly.

"Let's wait," he said.

She continued to look for the answer in his eyes, before finally relenting.

"So... you need to thank me?" she reminded him, allowing them to return to where they were before.

"Not so much for any one particular thing, Cora," he said, slowly releasing her hand and resting the bag of ice on her palm.

"When I was so mean to you yesterday, you remained calm and kind. For the most part," he added with a little grin.

"I implied that you were some kind of squatter or even worse, and I demanded all sorts of things but you ended the day by offering me a sandwich."

He absently stroked her wrist above the bag of ice.

"I stormed onto your porch this morning and practically accused you of throwing my sister's things out or burning them. You gently explained which items you had taken out, and then offered me a tour of the house.

"I was so impacted by the discovery of Jane's artwork in the attic, that it almost broke me in two and you steadied me, just by allowing me to claim you for support."

His soft brown eyes were filled with emotion as he settled them on her face and seemed to be trying to memorize it.

"Yes, but I also fired off some shots at you, Morgan, so don't make me sound nicer than I am," Cora protested mildly.

He waited to reply until Sandra had brought their food to them and checked on their drinks, then watched Cora carefully, as if he were waiting for something.

When she very briefly and discreetly bowed her head, before lifting it and glancing up at him, he gave her a slow smile.

"I believe I've cracked your code," he claimed, continuing to appraise her.

"My code?" She lifted her brows. "I have a code?"

"In a way. I'm beginning to see what makes you..." Morgan searched for the right word. "Wonderful."

"I'm not wonderful," Cora argued lightly. "So, if I have a code, it remains intact. You have discovered nothing!"

She lifted up her spoon and tapped his chin with it.

"You said your father is a retired minister and a professor of theology," he remembered, relieving her of her weapon.

She tilted her head and narrowed her eyes, with the faintest of curious smiles. "Where are we going?"

"You're a Christian," he stated simply.

"Does that worry you?" she returned evenly.

"Not at all. In fact, it makes you fascinating."

He toyed with stirring his soup, looking down at it, while he thought about his discovery.

"Morgan?"

"Hmm?"

He continued to watch his spoon move slowly around in his soup bowl.

"If you really want to thank me, then please don't leave without saying goodbye."

He smiled sadly and drew in a deep breath.

"So, I learned something today," he murmured.

She laid her hand on his arm. "About Jane?"

He nodded and after a moment, gestured toward their dinner. "It seems that neither of us are very hungry, after all."

"I think you're right."

"Can we go find a place to talk?"

"I think we need to," she answered calmly.

"Where's your coat? It's a clear night, so it's cold out."

She patted the chair on her other side. "I never made it upstairs, when I got here."

Morgan stood and took it from her to help her into it. He pulled out a pen and scrawled a hasty note on a napkin to Sandra Birch, letting her know that their food was very good, but that the two of them had to leave, and left a generous payment with it, before leading Cora outside.

He helped her into his vehicle, then came around to settle in behind the wheel.

"I don't know this town, so I'm not sure where to go."

"Morgan, if we're just looking for a quiet place to talk, you don't have to drive around. We can just sit here," she said.

He seemed relieved at her suggestion, and nodded.

"Did you file the report?" Cora asked, when it seemed that he was unable to begin.

He shook his head. "There was no need."

She drew in her breath and a look of alarm rushed to her face. "What does that mean?"

"She's not a missing person."

A cold feeling of dread washed over Cora and she closed her eyes and raised a hand to her lips.

Morgan looked over at her face, illuminated by the street lamp and saw fresh tears beginning to appear.

"It seems that the items we found in the house, that we regarded as clues, belonged to her husband."

She took on an expression of shocked disbelief.

"She got married, and never told you?"

"Apparently, she did," he admitted, "to some lowlife dope dealer. Michael Tewks," he added, with a clear look of disgust. "Michael Alan Tewks."

"MAT," she whispered. "So, initials, then."

She glanced off down the street, then shook her head in bewilderment.

"But you said that Jane would never leave her paintings, Morgan."

"She wouldn't."

She looked over at him quickly. "She's not..."

"I guess she is," he said, in a dull, tired voice. "They were evicted from the house last year, according to the sheriff. It sounds like he got her pretty messed up on meth."

Morgan took in a labored breath.

"My kid sister was always a free spirit and a little bit of a hippie. She was always having her head turned by some guy. The sheriff said that Tewks was picked up a few months ago for an outstanding warrant and that he was drunk and ranting about his wife drowning. I guess they had been living in a tent by a riverbank, after being evicted, according to him."

"Morgan..." Cora broke off and felt an intense wave of compassion almost take her breath. She reached over with her bandaged hand and touched his fingers with hers.

He looked down at her hand and then reached to raise the armrest between them and lifted his arm, making a place for her beneath it and silently inviting her.

Cora deliberately abandoned her resolve to never be a source of sympathy for this man again, and moved across the seat to be close to him, and he gave her shoulder a light caress.

"Did they follow up on what he told them? Did someone try to confirm any of that?"

"No body was recovered, but her things were found in the tent and her clothes at the water's edge. I recognized them."

She glanced up and saw his jaw clenched and a silent, pulsing anger in the way he glared straight ahead at nothing.

After a moment, she spoke to him tenderly.

"You don't have to finish this. I can see that it's painful for you and I also realize that it's personal, and I'm a stranger. You've only known me a couple of days."

She flashed him a bittersweet smile.

"Can you believe that?"

"No, Cora, I can't believe it and I can't accept it. Surely, I've known you all my life. I just hadn't met you, yet."

She couldn't pull her eyes away from his, even though she was embarrassed by tears that she couldn't control.

Morgan had gone to the sheriff's office a little before noon. When he left, he had driven straight over to the hotel, then got into a hot shower and sobbed like a child, for what seemed like hours. He cried, and he cursed, and he shouted, until he emptied himself out, then everything just went quiet.

Now he sat with his arm around this beautiful, forgiving woman who possessed some sort of divine ability to share suffering and pain with him. She was his lifeline.

He reached a finger to wipe her tears and brushed her cheek with the slightest whisper of a kiss.

She looked straight ahead and smiled.

"This is messed up. You're not supposed to be making *me* feel better."

"Well," he sighed. "I'm the one making you sad, so it's the least I can do."

She rested her head on his shoulder and he laid his cheek against her hair.

"I actually tried to speak to someone yesterday at the sheriff's office, and I sat there for over an hour. It literally seemed that no one worked there. I finally stopped a woman who strolled by with a radio on her hip and a bunch of keys she was jingling, and she said most of them were out on a call."

He glanced down at her, noticing the way she was watching him and just listening.

"I just wanted to be certain about what she was saying and, sure enough, they were all out on the same call. They say the smaller the town, the more cops who show up at anything interesting, and I guess there's some truth to that."

In spite of her recurring tears, Cora found that funny and a little giggle escaped her. She hurried to clamp a hand over her mouth and stared up at Morgan in dismay.

"Oh, I'm sorry," she whispered.

He took in her flustered state.

"Don't be sorry. The sound of your laughter has been like music to me, today."

Cora was worried bout his stoic, apathetic demeanor and studied him with soft, sad eyes.

"Do you think you may be in shock, Morgan?"

He flexed the muscles around his mouth. "Maybe a little numb now but trust me, I had my moment earlier."

A blanket of silence settled over them, and they sat nestled beneath it for a while, before she raised her face to look at him.

"There are so many questions, but I can't seem to do that to you, tonight. It feels mean, somehow. But at the same time, I know you're leaving.

"I don't understand why Jane married that man, or why she kept it from you, and I may never fully know what these past two days we've shared have been about, Morgan, but I somehow feel blessed by them."

She swiped at her tears impatiently.

"I'll always treasure you as a special friend, instead of just some angry guy I crashed into, while I was looking down at the ground." She glanced down at her bandaged hand then looked back up at him oddly.

"How, Morgan, were you able to come into Ingleside tonight and be so nice about my silly little scratch, and so willing to just sit there listening to me drone on about coffee and cucumbers, when you had just found out what happened to your sister?" She was genuinely baffled.

"I just needed to be with you, I guess," he said quietly. "I needed to hear you drone on about coffee and cucumbers."

"Before you leave," she finished.

He made no reply but nodded slightly.

"Is tonight goodbye, then?" Cora asked, almost choking on the words.

Morgan struggled with composure and pulled her into a tighter embrace. "Cora, I thought about coming by the house tomorrow, but the longer I take to say goodbye to you, the harder it's going to be."

"But Morgan..." Her troubled eyes continued to regard him with uncertainty. "I don't know what to do. I mean, where did you want me to put Jane's things, and her paintings?"

She could see that her question startled him and he drew in a breath and blinked, trying to focus.

"I never stopped to think about that," he confessed, in a tired voice. "Once they told me about Jane, it felt over, and I didn't seem to be able to plan beyond that, since there was no funeral to arrange. It seems as if it's been a year, since we found her paintings in the attic. This has been a surreal day."

He had been staring blankly at the dashboard, but now he rested his eyes on hers. "I won't leave you with any of that, Cora. I'll take another day and see to it."

"If you don't want me to be there, I'll stay away," she offered in a small voice.

"Did you slip a key under that rock after all, then?" he asked with a little smile.

"No, but I can give you one now. If you want me to."

He let his eyes linger on hers for a long moment. It was all he could do not to lean in and kiss her, but if he did that, it would create more problems than it would solve. Leaving her was going to be hard enough as it was, although he couldn't understand why she was able to make him feel this way.

Morgan Roberts was a highly successful, very recognizable figure in his industry. He was a handsome man who met beautiful women daily and was never without one of them on his arm, for whatever social function he was obligated to attend.

But there was something about Cora Hartmann that completely arrested him and held him captive. She was intelligent but quirky. She was beautiful, but seemed to be unaware of it. She was a deep thinker but could switch gears in a heartbeat and say something completely off the wall, leaving him equally bemused and charmed.

In two short days, she had managed to do what no other woman had even come close to doing, and commanded his thoughts, as he lay in bed trying to fall asleep and immediately, as soon as he began to stir.

His feelings seemed to be spilling from his eyes, and Cora reached a finger and touched his chin, as her own eyes mirrored what she found in his.

"So, that's a no, on the whole key thing, then?" she asked, twisting her beautiful lips into a little grin.

He smiled down at her and traced his finger around her mouth. "That's a no, on the whole key thing."

He opened the door and slid out, then reached a hand to her. She took it and stepped down beside him, and he put an arm around her and walked her back to the restaurant's entrance, pausing and moving off to one side, into a shadowed area.

They stood facing each other and Morgan swept his sad eyes over her face and lifted a strand of her hair back with a finger. After a long moment, he wrapped her into a secure hug and laid a kiss on her forehead.

"Don't forget to keep that hand elevated," he whispered. "I'll see you tomorrow."

Chapter Five

Cora had arrived at the house just after daylight. She'd remembered to bring some bubble wrap and packing tape and was now being very careful with each of Jane's paintings, taking the time to study each one and occasionally blink back tears at the realization that hers had been an extraordinary talent that was tragically cut short.

She was securing each one in the bubble wrap, then taping it and laying it onto a stack near the door. She heard Morgan call for her, and answered to let him know that she was in the attic.

He mounted the stairs and stopped in the doorway to realize what Cora was doing for him, and gave her a tender smile. "How long have you been here?"

She seemed to be thinking about it. "Three cups of coffee ago." She smiled down at what she was doing.

"I guess around daylight. That's pretty typical."

"You're an early riser, then?" He made his way over to her and stood looking down at the painting she had laid on the table in front of her.

"All my life, I guess. I've never been able to lie in bed, once I wake up. I feel as if the day is leaving me behind."

Morgan seemed impressed, but he wasn't surprised to learn this about her. He nodded down at the painting.

"Cora, would you want to keep any of Jane's art, or would that be too weird for you?"

She looked up at him. "Weird, how?"

"Maybe you'd rather not have any reminders in the house about its not so warm and cozy history."

"She was your sister. That wouldn't be weird, at all."

He laid a hand on her back and continued to study the painting, with a grateful smile crossing his face.

"Have you seen anything that stands out to you?"

She glanced around. "There are a couple that are very similar, almost as if she had been unsure and had tried it again."

She hoped she hadn't wrapped those already, and felt relieved when she spotted them underneath the table, leaning against its leg, ready to be next.

She pulled them out. Jane had painted the view she had from the front porch of the property, and since the season was autumn, they would be at least a year old.

"This is how it looks now," she said, again blinking away the sensation of tears.

Morgan looked down at them, with a firm set to his jaw and nodded. He returned his hand to rest on Cora's back and looked down at her in a way that connected him to her.

"Why don't you hang one on your wall, and I'll hang one on mine? Maybe, if our imaginations are fertile enough, we'll be able to see each other."

That was her breaking point. Cora slipped her arms around his waist and buried her face in his chest. He could feel her trembling and heard the soft sound of weeping.

"Cora, don't cry." He held onto her and rested his face against her soft hair. "I'm sorry. I wasn't trying to upset you."

He coaxed her to look at him.

"I feel like an idiot," she mumbled.

He frowned, as he traced her cheek with his finger. "Why would you say that?"

"Because I barely know you! This is so stupid! Why am I acting as if I'm losing the love of my life?"

He felt a check in his heartbeat when she said that.

"Is that how you feel?"

She gently tried to press against his chest to step back, but he tightened his arms around her and waited.

"In case you've forgotten, I'm not a tree, Morgan. I feel things. That's probably all this is, so don't let me creep you out."

He had to smile at her attempt to sound indifferent.

"So, that's a no on the twin paintings, then?"

She looked back at them with longing.

"I'd really love to have one, if you're sure."

"I'm very sure. And I'll have the other one."

He reached for her bandaged hand, and lifted it to kiss her fingertips. "I'll want to look at this again, before I leave."

She nodded. "I guess I'd better keep moving then, and get the rest of these wrapped."

"But are you feeling any effects of it in your hand?"

"No, it seems fine."

"I'll set our paintings over in the corner by themselves, so they won't end up in storage. If you're good here, I'm going to go break down Jane's bed and begin getting the big pieces together. I have some movers arriving in a little while to take everything to a storage facility."

She nodded and turned her attention back to wrapping the painting in front of her.

Morgan carried his sister's paintings over to a corner, and then flashed a smile at Cora as he passed by her again, on his way out. She was unaware that he paused in the doorway and stood silently watching her, and battling the same sort of strange feelings she had just confessed to having.

He didn't understand it, either. Cora was certainly not an idiot and neither was he, but they were both being strongly drawn toward each other in a way he had never experienced before. He longed to continue postponing his return, but his absence was already being felt by his employees and he had responsibilities that he couldn't simply abandon for a woman he'd only known a few days.

That was what his mind told him, but his heart would have him remain.

He breathed out a silent sigh, and headed downstairs to get down to the business at hand, the way he'd always been taught to do, but feeling as if he'd left his heart in the attic.

By the time the movers arrived, Morgan and Cora had brought everything down from upstairs and had it all stacked in the living room.

Morgan had advised them of the need to bring ramps, if they had any, because of the stream.

They had laid them to one side of the rickety bridge and had slowly backed their truck over them and up to the porch.

Cora came over to stand by him and they watched the loading process, each feeling that it was suddenly happening too quickly, but not speaking.

Morgan had given special instructions about the paintings and advised the men that he would come by the storage building on his way out to check on things. He'd given them a temporary lock for the door, and they went on their way, leaving nothing but two twin paintings in the little house.

"I guess you have a clean slate, now," Morgan said, taking Cora's hand. "Come over here, and let's have a look."

He brought her over to the edge of the porch to catch the sun and gently removed her bandage. She suddenly felt the need to look anywhere but at him, so she stared down at her hand and held her breath.

He studied the scratch and glanced at her.

"If you promise not to do anymore work here today, and just take it easy, I think we can dispense with the bandage."

"Whatever it takes to be rid of it," she replied.

"Which is your way of saying..."

"I promise. I vow. I swear. I pledge."

"You left out guarantee," he said, with a little wink.

"All of the above," she conceded.

"Now that the movers aren't likely to take our paintings by mistake, I'll go up and bring them downstairs," he said, giving her chin a little stroke.

She watched him go, then looked out across the property, leaning against a post. She told herself that the moment for Morgan to leave had come. She needed to be as upbeat about it as she could manage, so that she wouldn't be pulling on his emotions, on top of everything else he had to deal with.

When she really tried, Cora could be disciplined and she made herself accept that today was the day for self-control.

Besides, she was already disappointed in herself for being so foolish upstairs and crying in front of him.

He brought the paintings out into the daylight and rested them against the back wall of the porch.

"I want you to have the one that resonates the most with you, Cora." he instructed. "It's not like trying to second guess which flavor of donut I'm hoping you'll leave for me. If one of these captures you more than the other, then there's a reason for it, and that's how I want you to choose."

"I keep being drawn to the way the sun filters through the trees in that one," she said quietly, as she indicated it with a nod.

"Then you shall have it," he said lightly.

He picked it up and returned it to what had been the front bedroom, then came back out and lifted its mate away from the wall. He reached for Cora's hand and she hesitated, looking up at him and seeing his reaction.

"You didn't want to just leave it here?" she asked softly.

He wrinkled his brow. "The painting?"

"The goodbye."

He studied her. "Would that be better for you, Cora?"

"I think so." She didn't want to just stand and watch him drive away. She wasn't that disciplined after all, apparently.

"Let me go put this in the Cruiser then, and I'll be back."

He tried to be nonchalant about it and she appreciated the effort. She wandered over to her rocker and watched him stride through the trees, until she couldn't see him, and hurried to do some deep breathing and make sure she was ready to get through this.

She heard the door on the vehicle shut and immediately felt the familiar constriction in her throat and the difficulty in being able to breathe.

She couldn't stop herself from watching him walk toward her and the same grim, stern expression she had seen on his face the day she met him was back.

Morgan was furious that he had to leave. He was angry at Jane, because if she hadn't been so reckless, he'd never have met Cora and he wouldn't have to be leaving her now.

He had intended to be pleasant and wish her the best with her new house, but he was more enraged and bitter right now than he could remember being in a long time, and he wasn't able to pretend to Cora that he wasn't. He stepped squarely up onto the porch and gestured for her to come to him.

Cora rose up out of her chair and slowly approached him, waiting and watching.

He immediately captured her face in his hands and kissed her with every rampant emotion he was battling coming to bear on their kiss. He would not be prudent, he would not be careful, and he would not be rushed.

She completely yielded to him, and was blindsided by equal portions of pain, grief and exhilaration. After a long while, they clung to each other, both reeling from the impact of what only three days together had done to them.

Morgan raised her chin and looked at her, then finally spoke, with an urgency in his voice.

"We're wasting our time, trying to make sense out of this. It's never going to make sense. That would make it common. If it could be easily explained, it could be easily dismissed.

"One year. I'm coming back, whether I ever hear from you between now and then, or not. I'm coming back here, one year from today. We are going to meet together, we are going to talk and we are going to see if this is still alive."

She was unable to do more than gaze up at him, with a flicker of hope in her beautiful eyes, and silently nod.

"I'm sending a construction crew out here, Cora."

He frowned impatiently when she opened her mouth to argue with him.

"Stop, I don't care. You can be mad at me after I leave. I'm sending them out here. You don't have the kind of time that it would take, to waste on this decrepit house, if you have to try to do it all by yourself. You're not created to swing a hammer or pull out carpet. Maybe some women are, but that's not who you are. You are created to write beautiful music, to be heard by the masses."

His eyes were burning with conviction. "When I come back here, if you haven't been working on your music, you'd better be ready to explain yourself."

"Will you at least let me pay the crew?" she asked quietly.

"I will not," he answered curtly. "That's a detail that you and I can work out between us later. You could be an heiress with limitless funds, but all that's beside the point.

"I want this done right away, and if I leave it up to you, you'll continue to try to manage it yourself, a little at a time." He lifted her injured hand. "I won't let you keep damaging hands that were meant for more excellent things than this! Look for someone to be out here soon to begin putting a culvert in at the stream and paving a road over it, so the renovation can begin."

Cora was overwhelmed. She didn't know how to respond. She wasn't sure how she felt about all this. She reached her hands to grip his arms and examined him closely.

"I have questions."

He glanced back out toward his vehicle, and she tightened her grip on him. "Morgan Roberts, I have questions, and they need answers. Are you seriously in that big of a hurry?"

He traded a long look with her, then something in his face began to soften.

"Ask your questions."

"You're angry with Jane," Cora stated calmly. She lifted a hand to be allowed to continue. "I understand that, and I'm not saying it as a rebuke. I'd be angry too, I think. But I also think that you may be trying to do damage control, now. Morgan, I'm not damaged. I'm just heartbroken.

"You don't have to pledge to come back to me, or assign yourself the responsibility to take care of me."

"Do you not want me to come back?" he asked.

"I don't want you to leave in the first place, so yes! I want you to come back, Morgan! You're not understanding me."

She felt helpless and he could tell. He took her hands and raised them to his lips.

"Help me understand, then. I'm listening to you."

"Take a moment," she said softly. "Look at me and take a moment and tell me the real reason that you want to put all these things in motion, right now. But talk to me, not to Jane."

He looked at her strangely. "Do you think I'm confused about who you are and who Jane is, Cora?"

"I think you're upset that your sister wouldn't tell you that she needed help. You feel that you could have saved her, but you had no idea she needed saving.

"It's easy for you to look around this place and see, rightly so, that I could use some help, and so you very generously and lovingly, if not forcefully, want me to take it. I'm not proud, Morgan, and I know how to receive, as well as how to give, but I think you're being motivated by a false sense of responsibility."

He drew in a breath and looked down at the porch floor, wrestling with her words and wanting to engage in mild combat, but recognizing the truth of what she was saying. He looked at her with much less anger in his eyes and the tenderness that he kept reserved for her had returned.

"Is there any room for compromise, Cora?"

Morgan pressed her hand over his heart and seemed to be pleading with her.

"I want to hear your music. Please let me help you get to a place of being able to write it, instead of just coming out here every day to yank out ugly carpet and burn stuff."

She was visibly moved by the yearning she could hear in his words and she saw his heart behind them.

Cora moved closer to him and he welcomed her into his arms and continued to search her face expectantly.

"I can afford to pay the crew, Morgan, but I don't know a lot about how to make contractors actually show up, or how to be certain that they're not ripping me off. I don't believe that a pirate and a timber baron such as yourself could have become successful without knowing these things, and I would be grateful if you would be my project manager and represent me."

He had grinned at her referring to him as a pirate and now laughed gently and leaned down to give her a soft kiss.

"Will you promise to call me, though, Cora, if things become more costly than you're budgeted for?"

"Only after I've made an effort to adjust the budget," she replied, with a little smile.

"Am I invited back in a year?" He waited, with a light of hope in his eyes.

"If you don't show up, I'm gonna come get you," she threatened, trying to look fierce. "You have one year to fall in love with me and get back here."

She brushed his chin with her small fist and he caught it in his hand and looked at her with eyes beginning to brim over with emotion.

"I know you don't want to walk out with me, and I get that. So I guess we'll say goodbye here."

"Are you flying back or driving?"

"I'm gonna drive. It's a long way, but I did lease the car, rather than rent it. I may as well run up the mileage on it."

He smiled at the way she rolled her eyes and looked away.

"Thank you, Cora, for walking through all this with me. Thank you for sharing pain with me. Thank you for just sitting and talking with me about whatever we found to talk about.

"I'm going to go ahead and tell you, here and now, that I love you. I don't know much about love, and I'm not sure what kind of love this is, but I do know that I'm not confusing it with gratitude. Against all reason and logic, I do love you."

She reached up and caught his handsome face between her hands and smiled through fresh tears. "I love you, too. I already knew that I love you before you kissed me into oblivion, so I'm not shocked by it. Still, if I've ever prayed about anything in my life, I'll be praying about this.

"I'll be right here waiting, a year from now. We are going to meet together, we are going to talk and we are going to see if this is still alive."

They made their pact and sealed it with one last kiss, then Cora stood watching, as Morgan Roberts walked away, the sun trying to catch him, and the autumn leaves seeming to escape from their limbs to try to follow him.

Chapter Six

Debra Gregory wasn't nearly as naive, or as willing to put up with nonsense as people in town may have believed her to be. She deliberately allowed Ben Gregory or, as Sandra Birch referred to him, "that slouch of a husband of hers" to think that she didn't know the gender of the baby she was carrying.

When word finally spread that she had just given birth to a healthy seven pound boy, and Ben finally took some interest and actually came to the hospital to see his son, and to take selfies to send out to his buddies, Debra very gently but firmly laid down the law to him.

She let him know that if he couldn't "man up" and be a provider for his wife and son, that she was confident that she'd have no trouble finding someone else who would.

Whether she was serious enough to follow through or not, Ben decided that he didn't want to risk it. He miraculously recovered from his disability and took a job working for Walt Emmons, a gentleman farmer who secretly approved of Debra's methods and very willingly provided her husband with a means to earn a paycheck.

Cora sat at her usual table and peered up from her project to watch Walt Emmons and Sandra Birch grinning at the way Ben Gregory came out of the kitchen with Debra and handled the baby carrier while he escorted his wife out to their car, at the end of her shift.

She took note of the muted conversation between Walt and Sandra and didn't need any more evidence than that, to realize that those two had been behind Debra's ultimatum and, if any doubt remained, their celebratory high five took care of that.

Cora smiled to herself and focused her attention back on her notebook and the ledger.

Morgan had told her she should maintain one, in order to keep up with the kinds of hours various crews were working, as well as bid amounts, wages, and materials. He was tracking it, but he thought it would be good for her to be armed with hard numbers, if she needed to be.

She had balked at first, not at all feeling confident that she could handle it but, at the same time, even though Morgan had stepped into the role of being her project manager, she wanted to make the effort to learn.

A driveway had been paved from the main road, across the stream and to the house. That, alone, was enough for Cora to begin to feel energized and to once again see the potential in her investment.

Morgan had never expressed any enthusiasm for the rundown house, and had made it clear that he would have been far more favorable of the twenty-three acres of streams and beautiful hardwoods, if there had been no house at all on it.

This had caused Cora to wonder if she'd made a mistake, since Morgan's business was built on his ability to recognize land values and to know real estate as well as anyone, and she entered into a period of buyer's remorse.

Morgan had a lot of time to think, on his drive back up to where he lived, and admitted that even though he had given Cora his honest opinion, he could have been kinder about the way he'd done it.

Almost immediately, after he'd returned to his home, he called an architect friend of his and sent him some photos of the house, asking him to see what he could do about turning a sow's ear into a silk purse.

When Morgan received the drawings and blueprints back, he was excited but also a little nervous about showing them to Cora. He wanted her to realize that he was trying to tell her that he saw potential after all, but at the same time, he didn't want her to think that he didn't believe her to be capable of coming up with her own ideas.

He was surprised at how much he struggled before he finally emailed the plans and overnighted hard copies to her at Ingleside Fare, and waited to see how she would respond.

When he finally did hear from her, she was so excited that he regretted not being able to see her eyes light up and watch her animated gestures that he so quickly had become familiar with, and could anticipate.

They chatted about the next phase of construction and Morgan told her that since she approved the drawings, he would also provide them to the contractor so that they would all be on the same page.

They tended to linger on these calls, even when there were periods of silence, and Morgan finally asked Cora if she would agree to video calls with him in the future.

She had simply never thought about it, but she wanted to see his face as much as he told her he wanted to see hers, so it soon became their habit to have a set time, at least weekly, to relax in their respective rooms and talk about anything and everything.

Cora had brought Jane's painting to hang in her room at Ingleside and Morgan had hung his copy of it in his own bedroom, so when they made their video calls, each could see the other's painting.

Morgan pointed out to Cora that since their paintings were their backdrops, and that they could indeed see each other, maybe his whimsical comment about the possibility of this hadn't been so farfetched, after all.

Their common goal of finishing the renovation quickly in order for Cora to begin focusing on writing her music had helped to ease the pain of parting, and had created the opportunity for them to continue to interact regularly. It calmed the fear that each one fostered that the other would allow time and distance to create uncertainty about the future.

However, what was an ongoing project was now rapidly nearing completion, and Cora was already making arrangements to visit her father and have her piano and other instruments brought to her new home.

Morgan was relieved to hear this, but at the same time, he knew that she would soon be giving more and more of her time to working on her compositions, and they would speak much less than before. He was torn. It was what he wanted for Cora, but not what he wanted for himself.

Still, he had a great number of issues that needed his time and focus as well, and he had put several things on hold, not only to take the necessary time to search for his sister, but in order to fulfill his commitment to manage Cora's renovation.

Obligations wouldn't continue to be held at bay indefinitely and although he had a large team of employees who were capable of looking after the day to day management of logging activities, transportation, processing and marketing, new potential buyers were asking for meetings and Morgan, alone, handled negotiations.

In addition, he had acquired two new mills and had yet to come onsite to inspect operations. This was, again, something that Morgan never trusted others to do.

Still, at the end of a particularly grueling day, when he was finally able to go home to relax, the minute he entered his bedroom and saw the mate of Cora's painting on his wall, he longed to be able to climb inside it and be where she was.

Cora had so many decisions demanding her attention and arrangements to make so that she could move into her house, that she found her days to be taxing as well. She had similar stirrings, when she would return to her room over the restaurant, and see the painting. She would stand in front of it and wish that she could see Morgan come walking toward her, through the trees, and it sometimes seemed as if she could.

Both of them stubbornly clung to their memories, even though life seemed determined to dissolve them.

Paul Hartmann glanced up from his reading and gave his beautiful daughter a contented smile.

"You must have smelled the coffee," he teased.

Cora gave him a sleepy-eyed grin and groped her way over to the pot. It was only a little after five in the morning, but both Cora and her father had always been early risers.

He liked to have his morning devotion before even giving thought to the rest of his day, and Cora liked taking an interest in whatever he was studying and quietly sipping on her first cup of coffee, as he highlighted verses that particularly spoke to him.

It had been their custom for many years, especially after the passing of Paul Hartmann's beloved wife, Cora's mother. Now, it was just the two of them, but Cora had slowly been moving out on her own.

Her father encouraged her to pursue her dream of writing what she intended to be her opus magnum, that would hopefully be the culmination of a body of work that she had already managed to achieve, despite her young age.

Cora had not only been offered musical scholarships at very prestigious conservatories, but had been actively playing with orchestras and was sought after for studio sessions for the past few years. Her absence, while she took the time to find a place where she could live quietly and focus on her music, created a stir among some of her colleagues, who continued to seek her involvement in various projects.

She'd asked her father not to tell anyone that she was coming back this week, in order to stay on track for getting her things moved to her house, and he was glad to grant her request and have her all to himself, which was a rare pleasure.

She'd thought of Morgan this morning, as she was stirring to wake. After she'd gone to bed the night before, she couldn't fall asleep, and she finally turned on the lamp by her bed and dared to video call him.

He'd been lying awake himself, staring at the ceiling.

Morgan had to travel halfway across the state to meet with suppliers and had declined their invitation to have drinks at a nearby club, afterward. Instead, he'd returned to his hotel room and grabbed a shower, before falling wearily into bed.

He couldn't seem to dial down, but when he heard the ringtone that he had assigned to Cora, he smiled to himself in the dark and turned on the lamp to answer.

Each of them was surprised to see no painting behind the other. He wondered why she was obviously not at her room over the restaurant, and she told him that she was at her father's house, while she arranged to have her things moved.

Morgan was glad that things were on track for her to move ahead with her music but something about her progress seemed to threaten to put even more distance between them.

She recognized that he was in a hotel room, and he shared a little about his meeting and why he still insisted on overseeing certain aspects of his business himself, rather than trust anyone else with them.

There had been a moment, just before ending the call, when she seemed not to hear a question he'd asked her and just stared longingly into the screen at him, forgetting that Morgan could see her sad face. When he pressed her to tell him if she was alright, she gave him an emotional, teary little smile and just waved it all away.

"I know, Cora," he had said softly. "Me, too."

He told her that he loved her and she immediately responded, just as she had on the day he kissed her.

Cora quietly informed him that even though he promised to return in a year, if he were to just show up before then, out of the blue, she probably wouldn't run him off. He'd laughed at that and told her that she had no idea how many times he'd already considered doing just that.

It was comforting for them to talk, and then finally be able to go to sleep, but as they said goodnight, both of them sensed changes coming that neither of them felt good about.

Now, as Cora brought her first coffee of the day over to the table and sat down across from her father, he eyed her in a way that let her know she could never hide anything from her dear old dad, and she flashed him a guilty smile.

"It's such a long story, Dad," she admitted.

Her voice shook just a little and he reached forward to lay a hand on one of hers and give it a comforting squeeze.

"Well, my first lecture isn't until the afternoon, so there's plenty of time."

Cora slumped down slightly in her chair and hugged herself, looking off toward the window to see hints that the sun was thinking of joining them soon.

Her father resisted the urge to study her face or try to make any guesses, and simply rose to go top off his coffee, and give her a moment.

When he returned, he settled back down and gave her a questioning look, prepared to frown if the situation called for it.

"Warren didn't follow you off down there, did he, Cora?"

She raised a brow. She's actually forgotten about Warren Abernathy, who was the most persistent man she'd ever met and who was forever trying to convince her that the two of them could "make beautiful music together", a lame sentiment that never ceased to annoy her.

She shook her head.

"No, thank God. I know I have you to thank for that too, Dad, since I'm sure there's no way you ever would have told him where I was."

"You got that right," he declared blandly, making her smile and then returning it.

"Well," he said, studying the steam wafting up out of his cup. "I was so certain that what I'm seeing in your eyes this morning surely concerns a man, but you don't know any men where you are now, and you haven't had time to meet anyone."

She raised her beautiful eyes to his and flushed, and he gave in to a little sigh.

"Honey, I know you're a grown woman, and I'm not going to fuss at you, but I think it might help if you tell me what's going on. It can't be too long of a story, since you've only been down there a few months."

"It's complicated," she murmured.

"It must be," he said, after a long moment passed and she was no closer to explaining, than she had been when she walked into the room.

When her father now saw a single tear slide down his daughter's face, he was taken aback. He had never known Cora to allow anyone, even as all of her high school and college friends were rushing headlong into romance, to affect her to such a degree as he was witnessing now. He knew that whoever this man was, he was very special to her.

He quietly said as much now, and a few more tears broke free. Cora came around and knelt down by her father and laid her head against the side of his leg, as she had done all her life when she was troubled. He stroked her hair, and then rested his hand on her shoulder.

"I won't judge," he encouraged softly. "I'll just listen."

It took a while, but Cora haltingly told her father about the man she collided with, who suddenly appeared on her property, demanding to know about his sister.

She told him that his name was Morgan Roberts, and her father failed to make the expected pirate comment, but he did draw his brows, in obvious recognition, while she continued to talk about him.

She told him about their time together going through Jane's things at the house, about finding her paintings, and that the sheriff had told Morgan that there was no need for him to file a missing person report, along with the tragic reason why.

When she finished with those details, she raised her face up to him and bit her bottom lip.

"Dad, do I strike you as stupid, or irresponsible?"

"Neither of those things, Cora."

"Then please tell me how I could fall hopelessly in love with a man I only spent three days with."

She was struggling for composure, and trembling with emotion and hearing herself say this caused a fresh longing for Morgan to sting her.

"I'm not going to ask you if you've prayed about it."

Her father's face was solemn.

"I'm certain that you have. Morgan Roberts is a very high profile man," he added, mainly to himself, not missing the way Cora quickly looked up in surprise.

"He owns vast amounts of timberland and forests and is at the helm of a huge milling and production operation."

"How do you know all this?" she asked, clearly startled.

"I'm an old man, honey, I know things." He smiled down at her, but she continue to stare up at him in bewilderment.

"He wouldn't remember, but I met him once. Of course, he was just a young fellow then. His little sister was there too, a tiny dark-eyed beauty who kept grinning up at Lydia and grabbing hold of her," he said, referencing his late wife.

Cora raised straight up and her eyes couldn't hold any more shock than they were flooded with at the moment.

"How? What are you talking about?"

"It was when your mother and I were at a conference in Washington state, just below the Canada border. Morgan's father, Evan Roberts and his wife Candace were staying in the same hotel that many of us were staying at, since the conference was being held there.

"Your mother and I shared a breakfast table with them one crowded morning, and we enjoyed the company so much, that we kept looking around for each other the rest of the week.

"They lived not too far from the hotel, but Evan said that the only way to keep from having to answer his phone every few minutes was to be able to truthfully tell others that they wouldn't be at home. Besides, they wanted to enjoy the entire conference experience, rather than just come to listen to speakers, so they booked a room there.

"Before we flew back, they asked us to come to their home for dinner, and that's when we met Morgan and his little sister, who had both stayed with their live in housekeeper.

"He must have been all of ten or eleven, then. Before you came along," he added, with a little wink. "But, as I said, there's no way he would have made the connection between your name and mine, since he wouldn't remember us. His parents met a lot of people."

Cora lifted herself to stand and returned to her chair.

"Was it a Christian conference? Were Morgan's parents Christians?" She seemed to be holding her breath.

"It was, and they were, indeed. Very lovely people. They're both with the Lord now, although their parting wasn't so very long ago. It was a two car accident, maybe a couple of years back. I did fly out to attend the service."

Cora remembered Morgan saying that Jane was his only family but she had no idea that he had been dealing with the stress of only having recently lost both of his parents. As much as they talked together, he'd never told her that.

Her father cut into her thoughts.

"Well, Cora, would you agree that Morgan Roberts looks as much like a pirate, now that he's a grown man, as I thought he did when he was a lad?"

He made her smile.

"When he first showed up glaring at me, I guess he could have been mistaken for one. I asked him if he wanted to tell me his name, or should I just address him as 'the axe murderer'. When he did tell me, I zeroed right in on the pirate thing, but he wasn't very amused. I guess he hears that a lot."

They both sat with their own thoughts a moment, before Professor Hartmann leaned back in his chair and studied his only child with discerning eyes.

"Cora, are you trying to discover if you really love him, or are you only questioning the logic of it?"

"I love him more, every day," she said softly. "But I have no idea how that happened."

"Well, honey, sometimes when two people share a highly emotional experience, whether that experience is a positive one or, in the case of poor Jane, a tragic one, it can create a bond between them. One person may confuse love and gratitude, and the other may confuse love and tender compassion, and if there's also a physical attraction between them, it really muddies things up. Is there any chance at all, Cora, that this could be the case, here?"

Paul Hartmann counted on his daughter's practice to look at things from every perspective, but her heart was involved now, so he wasn't sure how honest she was willing to be.

"Well, Dad, if it was just compassion, then once Morgan seemed to be coping well, and he does seem to be, wouldn't I have begun to give my time and attention to other things, by now, instead of feeling so empty without him?"

Her father raised a brow, mildly surprised. He had no idea that Cora was feeling that way.

"Has Morgan told you that he loves you, Cora?"

"He was the one who said it first. He was honest, though, Dad, and admitted that he didn't know much about love and that he wasn't sure what kind of love this is, but he also said that he was certain that he wasn't confusing it with gratitude.

"We talk at least once or twice a week and he always takes the time to tell me very clearly that he loves me. He doesn't just rattle it off to me, as an afterthought, and he's always the one who speaks of love first."

Professor Hartmann said quietly, pondering that.

"We have a standing date," Cora said, with a sweet smile resting on her face. "One year from the date he left, he's coming back. He says we're going to meet and talk, and decide if what we believe is love is still alive."

"I didn't realize that young man was given to such poetic gestures," her father said, with his own smile.

He started to rise from the table, then checked himself and looked at his daughter questioningly.

"Do you have any idea if Morgan is a Christian?"

"I don't know," she admitted, her smile fading. "I mean, he was upset about his sister, and he was angry because he thought I was squatting in her house, but once that was cleared up, he ended up being a very kind man.

"I'd kind of ripped my palm open," she said, indicating it with a finger, and tracing the scar. "He was upset when he saw it and insisted on cleaning it, and dressing it, and checking it every time he saw me. He made me keep it elevated and iced.

"Then he tried to make me let him finish the house, because he said he wasn't going to allow me to keep damaging hands that were meant for excellence, not for swinging hammers and pulling out carpet."

She couldn't hide a rush of pleasure, remembering the moment he said those words to her.

"That makes him a remarkable man, Cora, but it doesn't make him a Christian. Does he know that you are?"

She nodded. "He recognized it, when I bowed my head before eating. I asked him if that bothered him, and he said that it made me fascinating to him."

He thought about that. "Well, his mother was a gracious, lovely Christian woman, so I believe Morgan was sincere, when he said that to you. I would think that there are many women who try to make themselves available to powerful men, but a man like Morgan Roberts would more than likely become jaded to that, very quickly. You would certainly be unique to him, and you would probably remind him of his mother, who I do know he loved very much."

Cora looked down at the floor and began blinking rapidly, and her heart sank. She knew her father hadn't meant to upset her by what he'd just said, but what if that explained Morgan's belief that he loved her? What if she just reminded him of his mother, and he hadn't realized it?

"I didn't mean for what I said to hurt you, honey," her father said regretfully.

"No, it's okay," she said in a low voice. "I probably need to consider that, I suppose."

She stood up and her father also rose, picking up his Bible and notebooks, and coming around to give her a big embrace.

"What's your day like?"

"I'm going to move my instruments into the room with the piano and then see what else I have here, that I could use at the house. Then, I guess I'd better call the movers about getting it loaded up. I'd like to be on the road tomorrow, Dad, if that's possible. Are you still going to be able to come down and see the house and stay a few days?"

"If I'm still invited, after the talk we just had," he grinned, giving her back a little pat. "Let me see your scar."

She held her hand open and he shook his head.

"Has the pirate seen this? Is he impressed?"

She laughed and gave him a light punch.

"He has, but now his new worry is that it might generate some sort of tendonitis in my left hand, which he knows is my fingering hand. He's even concerned that it might affect my intonation and articulation which, I have to tell you, Dad, completely took me by surprise. The man knows music."

Professor Hartmann stood thinking about this with a sober expression.

"Cora, listen to him. I hadn't even stopped to think when you said you ripped open your palm, but Morgan's absolutely right. You need to see either a doctor, although the wound is healed over now, or at least a physical therapist. You don't want to mess around with something like that."

She nodded and silently agreed, then gave her father another hug before heading off to get dressed for the day and begin to prepare for moving into her house, and once again playing her music.

Chapter Seven

Sandra Birch glanced up at Walt Emmons with a shrewd expression, as she refreshed his coffee, and caused him to laugh quietly. Cora decided it was some kind of private joke between them, and smiled down into her own coffee that she was surprised Sandra brought her, without a side of nutrition advice.

She glanced up as Sandra pulled a chair out and dropped into it with an exaggerated groan.

"Every other week, I think about selling this place," she confessed, as Cora shook her head.

"No, you don't," she returned, giving her a deadpan look.

"Well, you're moving out today. Walt just told me he's going to be in Colorado the rest of the week, and now that Ben Gregory's acting halfway human, and 'Tall, Dark and Handsome' has gone back home, it's going to be tumbleweeds around here."

Cora smiled at her reference to Morgan and closed her notebook to look around the restaurant.

"This really is a beautiful place though, Sandra. It's sort of unexpected, for such a small town, I think. Most small places have the usual diner or the meat-and-three, but it's so cozy and nice in here, especially with this amazing stone fireplace, and the music you play is so subtle that you can easily talk over it and even string a few thoughts together, when you need to."

"What kind of thoughts?" Sandra wondered. "Thanks, by the way. What kind of thoughts?"

"Not what you think," Cora insisted, when Sandra raised her brows up and down suggestively.

"Then, what?"

"I've had an offer to tour with an orchestra, that I've played with before. I do enjoy working with them, but it's for three months. I really wanted to focus, especially now, when I'm beginning to feel music coming to me. I believe I can capture it.

67

"I'd have to be gone a long time if I accept their offer, but then again, touring with this orchestra is pretty lucrative, and I'm almost tapped out after finishing the house."

"So you stuck to your guns and wouldn't let Morgan help you at all with the budget?"

"I wasn't trying to prove anything, Sandra, and if Morgan and I had known each other for years, I might have considered letting him make me a loan. But as it was, it would have just been too awkward."

She expelled a breath. "Anyway, that's my answer to your question about what kind of thoughts. Now you know."

Both of them looked up as Walt Emmons approached the counter, and began pulling out his billfold.

"He never lets me bring him the ticket and then have him sign it. He always strolls up to the counter," Sandra complained. "Tell me again, how classy this place is."

She met the handsome farmer over by the register and after a moment, Cora heard the same words she heard every time Walt Emmons was leaving.

"When ya gonna marry me, Sandra?"

"How 'bout next Thursday?"

"If I get all my chores done, then that might work."

Cora laughed as Sandra rolled her eyes and waved him out the door. It was more reliable than the sunrise. Every parting netted Sandra Birch a proposal from Walt Emmons, and they set the date for the next Thursday, but they never seemed to satisfy the conditions.

Cora got up and began loading her arms with some last minute items she'd left upstairs, and was getting ready to take them out to her Jeep.

"You too?" Sandra gently griped. "Everybody's runnin' off, just when it's time to do the dishes. That's about right!"

Cora held up her scar and Sandra belted out a laugh.

"I think you can give that a rest."

She giggled and pulled Sandra over for a tight hug.

"Thank you so much for letting me live upstairs," she said, suddenly fanning her eyes with one hand.

"Stop," Sandra said roughly. "You're not leaving town, you're just right down the road a piece. You won't be able to stay away, and you know it."

"Well, that's probably true," Cora admitted. "Okay, so not goodbye, then. See you around."

"See you around, sweet girl!"

Sandra shot her a playful wink and began absently bussing tables as Cora stopped at the door with one more look around, before heading out to her Jeep and pulling out onto the road that would take her to her music.

✳ ✳ ✳

Morgan leaned back in his office chair and rested the tips of his fingers together, regarding Blake Jenkins, his Chief Forester, with an unreadable expression.

Blake was used to his boss's taciturn nature, and knew that whatever his reservations were, they had more to do with the situation itself than with him, so he didn't feel uncomfortable. He merely waited for Morgan to finish considering what he'd just come into his office to relate to him.

"That's going to keep me tied up for several weeks, at the very least, and maybe even months," he said, with a frown of displeasure clearly settling around his mouth. "For crying out loud, Blake, I'm still trying to deal with my sister ending up face down in a river, and hoping every day to be told that they've at least recovered her body, and I'm supposed to now just pack up and take off out of the country?

"How desperate do these people think I am to acquire a concession I've never even asked about? And why are there no bidders, apparently? That's suspicious, for a start."

Blake raised his brows, but made no comment. He knew that Morgan was simply giving vent to his overall frustration, but that he'd eventually do what was best for his company.

He sat quietly and made no attempt to convince him, one way or another.

69

"My first inclination is to flatly decline," Morgan muttered. "In fact, just pass that on to them."

Blake risked a quiet comment.

"They know that your reputation is to ensure sustainable forest management, Morgan. They're only now beginning to recover from the effects of deforestation that occurred decades ago, not to mention the illegal logging they constantly fight.

"They're trying to develop a government endorsed conservation agenda and they believe you are the man to help them achieve that. They haven't asked for bids, because they specifically wish to deal with you."

"So, they can put their guy on a plane and fly him out here to me, then!"

He spoke sharply, feeling that he was being put upon by this small South American country he had never even considered traveling to, and had never expressed an interest in dealing with, and he didn't appreciate it.

"Do they have any idea at all of what sort of expense they're looking at?" Morgan's brown eyes flashed with his irritation. "It would be far most cost effective for them to offer this concession to one of their own private entities."

Blake surveyed him thoughtfully, only pointing out that those private entities were actually the problem. He waited for his boss to table his final decision, as he knew that he would, and after another long moment of glaring straight ahead, Morgan stood and reached for his coat and looked around for his keys.

"I've hired a private company to drag the river in search for my sister's body, as well as investigators. I'm not going to be dealing with this concession offer right now," he announced, impatiently. "Tell them I'll call them by the weekend and give them a yes or no. If yes, it'll be within my own time frame."

Blake Jenkins got up from his seat and proceeded Morgan out of the office and into the wide hallway.

Morgan locked his door and turned to give him a pointed look. "If no, then it is to be recognized as a firm no. I won't continue to be coaxed."

He strode toward the direction of his private elevator and entered it with a hard set to his jaw, and a desire to do nothing more than simply get in his vehicle and drive as long as it took him to get to Cora. If he had been a less disciplined man, given over to being led by his emotions, he might just have done so.

He drove through the sluggish traffic almost automatically, his mind racing in several directions at once.

There was a time when Morgan would have at least patiently listened to the kind of proposal his head of operations had just presented to him.

He did have a desire to help struggling populations implement the kind of sustainable practices that would give them the ability to maintain their own forestry efforts, and learn to balance that against protecting their resources.

He had learned from his own conversation with one of that country's government officials, that they had been battling illegal logging and that blood had actually been shed when the battle took on armed clashes, since many of those engaging in the practice had formed alliances with organized crime. He had challenged the country's decision to not seek permission to appoint an ambassador to the United States, but as far as he knew, no such attempt had ever been made.

He knew why this small, overlooked country that was able to boast of vast tracts of tropical rainforest was seeking him by name, and he appreciated their recognition of his efforts, but this could not have come at a worse time, he felt.

Morgan hadn't talked to Cora about the conflict warring inside him, regarding his inability to accept that his sister was really dead. The more he had tried to work through it, the harder it was for him to just let it be over.

He longed to talk to her now, but he needed to be able to look into her eyes, rather than at her video image on a computer screen. He needed to watch the subtle nuances in her lovely face, and listen to her inflections and feel the clasp of her hand.

He did have business where she was, since he had hired an investigator to determine if Jane had actually been trying to put distance between herself and Michael Tewks.

It wasn't that he didn't believe she had married him. His sister was a hopeless romantic and he had no doubt that Tewks might have swept her into a rash, impulsive marriage.

Still, Morgan wasn't sure why that would have benefited Tewks in any way, and he wanted to know the answer to that.

He had also hired a private company to drag the river near the location where Tewks claimed that he and Jane had been camping, and where law enforcement confirmed the discovery of Jane's personal belongings.

It wasn't that Morgan felt that he was deliberately being deceived by the small town's inadequate sheriff's office, but he did suspect that they were too willing to simply believe everything Michael Tewks was telling them. He was not.

He pulled his vehicle through the gates of his residence and on into the garage, turning off the engine and sitting quietly, trying to settle his thoughts and wondering where Cora would be this time of early evening.

He factored in her time zone, and let himself in through the door of his home, tossing his things onto an antique storage bench and heading straight for a shower, which was his method of dealing with stress.

After he had spent some time trying to decide if he would be burdening Cora with everything he wanted to tell her, when she had enough of her own concerns to deal with, he tried to look at it from her perspective, which caused a tender smile to come to his face, and created a sense of calm for him.

When she answered his call, he tilted his head and inspected the screen with an amused look in his eyes.

"Well, that's a new look," he observed lightly, causing her to wrinkle her brow in confusion before blushing and yanking a pencil out of her hair.

She had gathered her long hair up, giving it a twist, and using the pencil as a sort of clip, pushing it up and through, then back down to hold her beautiful golden locks out of her eyes while she was working. Now she hurriedly pulled it out, and the length of her silky hair fell free from its constraints and caused Morgan to draw in his breath.

He hid his reaction well and simply laughed at her lack of poise, before taking in the rest of what he was seeing.

"It looks like a recording studio, Cora. You've been busy."

"Well, I have been, but I think describing it as a studio at this stage, is a little generous. You should see all the junk I brought from my dad's house. It's all piled up in the guest room. I won't take you on a tour just now, since I'm not willing to continue to be embarrassed in your presence."

He laughed again, and then she saw an expression of longing in his eyes that she felt he could see in hers.

"So, I was thinking," he began quietly, "and you tell me if this is a bad idea, or just bad timing..."

Cora began to tremble with a rush of adrenaline and broke in, before he could finish.

"Are you coming here?"

He saw her face light up with hope and suddenly, it was no longer just a thought. He had to get there.

"I am, if you're agreed."

"Oh, my goodness, yes! Are you kidding me?"

He sat witnessing her joy with an unexpected sensation of belonging to someone, although that seemed to be an odd way of describing it. He wondered if he had been feeling more alone than even he realized, because her blissful response seemed to feel like an embrace in the doorway of a place he loved.

"I actually have some business there," he explained, "but that's something I'd rather talk to you about in person, since it's a bit involved. It does bring me to your door, although not with the same hostility I brought with me that first time."

She laughed and instinctively reached a finger to the screen, and he imagined that he could feel her touch on his face.

"So, you don't plan on positioning yourself in front of me like a brick wall, and then demanding that I explain myself?" she teased, causing him to flash her a grin.

"Well, not like a brick wall, anyway," he murmured. He nodded toward the screen.

"Are you taking care of your hand, Cora?"

"Between you and my father, I have no choice," she said. "Apparently, he's on your side."

"Good man," he replied lightly.

"You used to think so," she returned with an air of mystery. He drew his brow and tried to follow that.

"Dad knows you. Actually, he and my mother knew your parents," she amended. "He said they met at a conference when you were around ten or eleven."

Morgan widened his eyes, in recollection. "They came to our house," he breathed, in wonder.

Now it was Cora's turn to display wonder in her own eyes. "Dad didn't think you'd remember, since it was so long ago."

"I do remember."

He smiled, recalling the way his little sister thought that Cora's mother was an angel, or a fairy, or whatever it was that her childlike imagination had conceived, and wouldn't keep her little hands off of her.

"Jane was enchanted by your mother," he said, causing her to smile, unconsciously fingering a strand of her hair.

"A lot of people were," she answered.

After a silent moment between them, she asked him how soon he would be able to come, and he offered her a couple of choices, not surprised when she pounced on the earliest one.

"Alright, then, my little squatter," he said, referencing the joke that had taken on a life of its own between them. "I'll be there by the weekend. I'll text you my travel details."

She offered to come to the airport, but he declined.

"I have to meet with people, so I'll need transportation for that. I'll rent something and let you know when I'm headed your way. Hopefully, it will be during the day, so that I can see the place and judge it against the photos."

She traded a long look with him.

"You just turned my whole day around, Morgan."

"You just did that for me, as well."

He kissed his finger and touched the screen and she returned it, before they ended the call, each smiling for the same reasons.

Morgan waited a moment then lifted the phone and gave Blake Jenkins a call.

"Have you already contacted your man in South America yet, Blake?"

His Chief Forester looked up from his report, wondering why he wanted to know.

"Not yet, Morgan."

"Alright," he returned smoothly. "I'm going to pad my response time until next week. I'll be flying out Thursday, to meet with the people I've hired to look into my sister's reported death, and I doubt I'll return before Monday. If anything comes up during that time that only I can see to, then you can let me know. Otherwise, I'd appreciate it if you would just deal with it.

"I realize I could have just told you all this when I see you tomorrow, but I wanted to speak to you about it now, before you placed a call to your guy."

Blake furrowed his brow. "Why do you keep referring to him as mine, Morgan?"

"Because hopefully before it's all over, he will be, along with that entire operation."

Blake was startled at his response, but covered it well.

"Okay, boss. I'll sit tight, and if he calls again, I'll let him know that it will be next week before you decide."

Morgan hung up and raised his legs onto the ottoman in front of his leather chair and rested his head back into its soft support, closing his eyes and smiling to himself.

He brought back the recent image of Cora pulling the pencil out of her hair and the way it tumbled down, giving her the appearance of some beautiful, mythological wood nymph, and wondered if it was too soon to think about packing.

Chapter Eight

Cora had been sitting on the porch ever since Morgan called her to say that he was on his way from the airport. It was a long drive, almost an hour, but that didn't matter.

She was too restless to sit indoors and although it was cold outside, she had come out to watch through the trees for the first glimpse of a car, blowing on her hands to keep them warm.

She'd been hoping that it would still be daylight when he arrived, so that he could see some of the outside work that had transformed her old house into a lovely cabin, but already the sun had pierced through the trees, as it slowly began to set. It reached its fingers through them now, just as it was doing in the painting that Morgan had given to her.

Of course, even though she had imagined it so many times, when staring into Jane's painting, she realized that she wouldn't see Morgan walking through the trees to come to her.

A very nice driveway had been paved from the road to her house and she knew he would simply drive up to it, but she was resolved that he would find her waiting for him, when he did.

When at last, she saw the car approaching, her breathing became shallow, and her pulse threatened to knock her down. She suddenly seemed to have lost the use of her legs and could do little more than sit there and shake.

Morgan had glanced up through the windshield and flashed her a glad smile, then proceeded to extricate himself from the vehicle. He shut the door and turned to look up at her, his brown eyes filled with happiness and a grin lighting up his handsome face.

Cora pushed herself up from the rocker and came to the edge of the porch, still doubting her ability to walk. She smiled down at him with a helpless shrug.

He seemed to understand, and came to the edge of the porch, simply reaching his arms up to her and lifting her down and into his embrace, wrapping her up tightly and wordlessly holding her for a long, intoxicating moment.

They both shivered from the heady rush that washed over them and Morgan took a moment to steady himself.

"My little popsicle," he murmured, regarding her lovely face, pink from the cold. "What are you doing out here, silly girl? You're freezing!"

Sudden tears appeared on her lashes and revealed how desperately she had missed him.

He let his gaze travel over the lines of her face, with a sense of quiet joy. He had cautioned himself to exercise restraint and not overwhelm her, but he was losing himself in her eyes.

"Let's see if I can thaw you out," he suggested softly.

He secured her into a more snug hold and kissed her in varying degrees of intensity, clearing away any lingering nervousness between them, and causing her to raise her eyes to his in the sweet, trusting way that he had grown to love, and that he had longed for so deeply.

Finally, he gave her chin a soft stroke and then let his observation take in the property, reaching to catch her hand and move slowly around, assessing the many improvements.

What had once been a dull, dirty white shack, badly in need of leveling and painting, had been transformed into a rustic cedar cabin that seemed to merge seamlessly into the woods that surrounded it.

Cora scanned his face, watching his expressions and Morgan didn't disappoint her as he smiled with contentment, silently approving the changes and telling himself that he could be very comfortable in a little place like this.

He looked down at her tenderly. "Are we happy?"

"We're delirious."

Up until then, she still hadn't spoken but her first words were said with her playful, dry inflection and he laughed and pulled her back into another hug.

"You're right, we are," he confirmed.

They strolled toward the back and stood looking at the pond that had been cleaned up and had become home to a few stray ducks that apparently didn't realize that it was winter. Morgan smiled at the idyllic scene.

She gave his hand a little tug and he let her lead him back around to the front of the house and into the door.

They stood close together, as Morgan appreciated the fact that taking out the wall opened what was a small living room into a large open space that Cora's baby grand piano had now found a home in, as it sat beautifully grouped with other instruments, including her beloved cello.

Morgan turned his eyes to hers and looked at her with a startling awareness that this was who she was. She wasn't just some beautiful woman yanking out carpet, or standing her ground in a confrontation with an irate stranger.

These instruments were there for her, not the other way around. They were there to accentuate who she was at her core, and to call that beauty to the surface.

She returned his look with a question in her eyes, and he stroked her brow fondly and then forced himself to focus on the rest of the house.

He laid a hand on the stone fireplace that he had insisted the contractor put in, since there had to be an alternate heat source in the event of a power failure. No gas lines ran near the property, but Morgan intended to bring in propane tanks and have them filled. He flashed Cora an 'I told you so' wink.

She grinned and moved toward the front bedroom, then stood at the doorway so that Morgan could see the painting hanging across the room from her bed. There was a little cushioned glider and a small table and lamp beneath it and he recognized it as the place she sat to share their video calls. The room was lovely.

"Were the bats and rats upset with all the construction noise?" he asked her with a little laugh, and Cora widened her eyes in excitement.

"Oh, come here and see it," she begged, catching his hand and leading him toward the attic.

They passed through a pretty, nicely furnished kitchen and into a utility room that had been fitted with new appliances, before going up the staircase that was now very efficiently lit by tasteful fixtures.

When they reached the door, Cora turned the handle, then moved back to let Morgan go in first.

He stepped inside, then stood quietly astounded at what had been transformed into the room where Cora's vision could be realized.

This was what he had observed to be a recording studio, the last time the two of them had shared a video call. He hadn't recognized then that it was the upstairs portion of the house.

He remained still, taking it all in, as it became even clearer to him that Cora was not just a music enthusiast, or someone who merely had some talent and perhaps had aspirations toward excellence, but that she was, in fact, an accomplished musician, as well as a professional one.

It wasn't that he had doubted her claim to be a composer; he knew who Cora Hartmann was, but he hadn't stopped to become aware to what degree she was able to apply that title.

She watched him, feeling a little self-conscious, since this room had once been filled with his sister's art. She hoped that he wasn't feeling that she had been trying to erase all that by deliberately making it all about herself.

He seemed to pick up on her concern and reached a hand to slip around her waist, as his eyes continued to appraise the efficient layout and the complexity of the recording equipment that she very obviously seemed comfortable with.

"Cora, this is your dream," he breathed quietly. He turned to rest his eyes on hers. "This is why you bid on this house to begin with, and now you can do what you were born to do."

Morgan made himself push back against small anxieties that were trying to surface, that wanted to suggest to him that this would eventually separate them.

He told himself that he was being ridiculous, and that she could entertain those same anxieties about *his* career, if she wanted to be as unreasonable as he felt he was being.

Now, he pulled himself out of his solemn reverie, and responded to the touch of her finger on his chin, looking down to see her unspoken question.

"This is wonderful," he assured her, not missing the relief that seemed to wash over her. "Did you expect that I wouldn't think so, Cora?"

"It's just that Jane's art was in here."

"I see," he said in a hushed voice.

He moved behind her to pull her to rest against him, encircling her with his arms and breathing in the scent of her hair. He felt her release a sigh of relief.

"No, sweetheart, I'm not at all upset to see what this room has become. If you're feeling any sort of vibe coming from me, that's not what it's about."

She looked up at him closely. "What is it about, Morgan?"

"It's about all the things that you and I have to sit down and talk about together, this weekend. There's a lot to be said."

She thought about that and gently stepped out of his embrace to wander over and look out the window.

"Am I gonna cry this weekend?"

Morgan smiled at that. "I would expect so, not because you'll have any reason to cry, but because you so naturally possess the ability to cry, for whatever reason."

She considered his answer. "But you haven't come all this way to give me a reason, have you, Morgan?"

He frowned, and drew his brow.

"You seem to be proactively preparing yourself to be hurt, Cora. Why is that?" He came over to stand beside her.

"I guess I've just been feeling that life has plans to pull us away from each other."

He looked at the treetops and pressed his lips together in a firm line, as she put into words what he had also been feeling.

"That's part of what we need to talk about," he conceded.

A slightly bitter smile rested around her mouth, and she wondered if he was trying to gently let her know that this would be their fate and then continue to tell her how much he had really cared about her.

"I remember back in high school, when one of my friends met her 'summer love' and fell head over heels for him, and then, of course summer left and so did he, and I was tasked with the chore of talking her off her emotional ledge."

She looked at him steadily.

"Are we going to talk about the fact that all good things must come to an end, Morgan?"

Disappointment settled on his face.

"Are you saying that you believe that I came all this way, took you into my arms, kissed you until I realized it was too risky for us to continue kissing, and gave you every indication of what I feel for you, just to tell you that we're done here?"

He allowed a hint of anger to flash in his eyes.

"You don't have any fears?" she countered.

"Not about our feelings for each other."

"You're sad, though. I can see it."

"I don't deny that, Cora, but don't automatically connect it to you and me."

She saw the look of disapproval on his handsome face, that reproached her for reaching her conclusions without talking to him and lowered her eyes. "I'm sorry, Morgan."

He breathed out a heavy sigh and gently collected her back into his arms.

"Listen to me."

He drew her attention by the intensity in his eyes and she returned his gaze.

"Let me say these things plainly, and then keep them all where they belong, and don't keep messing around with them later, when I try to talk to you about other things that may be upsetting, and mix it all up into a hot mess. The things that I'm about to say to you now are separate from that. They belong to this moment and you are not to misunderstand them, or to forget them, or disregard them, or to question them."

He waited, holding her with his eyes until she nodded.

"I love you." He didn't allow her to say it back to him, but rested his finger on her lips to keep her from speaking.

"I love you," he repeated. "I know that, because I live and work and function in a high pressure world of success that seems to bring with it no shortage of women who go out of their way to convince me and men like me of their desirability."

When she dropped her gaze, he lifted her chin.

"There is no other woman in this world, Cora Hartmann, who has ever commanded a second glance from me, an afterthought, or anything else. You own me. I may be a fool for admitting that to you and you may one day feel your own worth and decide that you have no further need for me, but I'm saying it, anyway. You own me.

"Rather than have time and distance do what I feared it might do, it has only served to deepen my love for you. I no longer try to explain it away, or get it to make sense. I just accept it for what it is.

"I tried to reason it away by telling myself that you and I had simply formed a bond from everything we shared when I was here before, looking for Jane.

"While there might be some level of truth to that, I don't believe it disqualifies our love but I think it enriches it.

"I don't know if God is involved in any of this. I haven't really talked to Him since my parents were killed and then this thing with Jane didn't exactly help.

"But He might be. I just don't know. I haven't asked Him. I only know that you are a gift to me and I cherish you."

He saw a steady stream of tears finding their way down her cheeks and wiped them away with a faint smile.

"I guess the answer to whether or not you were going to cry this weekend has been answered," he lightly teased.

She threw her arms around his neck and buried her face against it, slightly trembling.

"Cora, there are serious things that you and I need to sit down and talk about this weekend, but whether or not we have a commitment to each other is not one of them."

He was absently flexing the tips of his fingers against the back of her neck and now persuaded her to look at him.

"Don't be afraid," he whispered. He smiled softly at her and she rested her head against his chest.

"I don't mean to be," she murmured, in a small voice.

Morgan simply held onto her for a while until she began to feel more composed, then she lifted her face and offered him her own little smile.

"You called me sweetheart," she reminded him.

"I did."

"It was nice."

"You've been called pet names before." He tapped the tip of her nose with his finger.

"But not by a man I was in love with," she said, causing him to look at her with a light of banter in his eyes.

"Oh, you mean me?"

She sighed. "No. Tchaikovsky. But you're okay, too."

Morgan laughed and gathered her just a little tighter, then released her with a light groan.

"What does a man have to do to be offered a cup of coffee, around here?"

She nodded toward the kitchen downstairs.

"I hear you take it black."

Morgan gave her an engaging little grin and covered one eye with his hand. "Aye."

Cora giggled her way down the stairs, and he followed her with leftover humor leaving the trace of a little smile.

organ glanced up, as Cora brought their coffee into the living room. She handed a hot cup to him, before settling down beside him on the leather sofa, and tucking her bare feet up underneath, to get comfortable in front of the fire he had built.

He gave her a light swat on her leg and nodded toward her lack of footwear. "If you end up with a splinter walking around barefoot on these hardwood floors, I guess that's your business, unless I catch you walking on your hands. And then, I'll be making it mine. That reminds me."

He set his cup on the end table and reached for her to surrender her left hand. She obliged him and he opened it and studied her palm, gently inspecting the scar and slowly flexing her hand, opening and closing it.

"You felt that?" he asked, when he saw her slightly react.

"It's not pain," she assured him. "It's just sort of tight."

Morgan drew in a deep breath and expelled it in a sigh of frustration. "You need to see a physical therapist."

"That's what Dad said, too," she confessed.

"But, of course, you've not looked into it."

She shook her head and twisted her lips into a remorseful little scowl. "I keep meaning to."

"We're going to pull up some options online while I'm here and you're going to get a consultation," he informed her.

"You're not the boss of me," she said, showing him her very scary little fist, and a playful grimace that made him smile.

"We'll see about that," he returned, reaching over for his coffee and settling back into the sofa contentedly.

"Cora, will you play music for me this weekend?" he quietly requested, surprising her.

"Be careful what you ask for," she kidded, blushing a little.

"You play for the masses," he persisted. "Would it really be difficult to play for just me, here in your home?"

She started to reply, then stopped and looked at him.

"You once charged me with running your name through a search engine," she said, with a slow smile working its way into her eyes. "Morgan Roberts, you accused me of what you have apparently done yourself. What we have here," she continued, leaning to whisper next to his ear, "is projection."

She was too close not to kiss, so he took advantage of the opportunity, then relaxed into his comfortable position again.

"I did," he admitted. "I missed you and I wanted to see your beautiful face, and learn everything about you that I could. I also watched a few video clips of your performances and they were amazing, but I'd love for you to play personally for me. I can only assume that you will, in no way, refuse me."

He grinned to himself at her reaction to that.

"This weekend," she finally agreed. She tilted her head and seemed to be analyzing him.

"I plead guilty to running your name through a search engine as well, but only after you went back to your house," Cora confessed. "I wanted to see your handsome face again, and I guess I was pining for you."

She teased him with her lovely eyes. "Pining. See what I did there, Paul Bunyan?"

"Yes, you're very droll," Morgan said with a little laugh.

He put his cup on the table and reached for her hand, lifting his feet to rest them on the coffee table and kissing the top of Cora's hair, after she snuggled into a relaxed state and laid her head against his shoulder.

"Okay, honey," he sighed. "I have some things that I want to talk to you about and I also have some questions about things that concern you. I feel that we both have decisions to make that are career related and it might be helpful for us to share any concerns that we have and clear up any potential for misunderstanding."

Cora simply nodded and waited.

"Before we get to any of that, I need to tell you why I'm here," Morgan said.

She looked up at him curiously, still waiting.

"I'm not satisfied, Cora, with what the sheriff's office told me about Jane."

"You don't think she drowned?" she asked softly.

"That's just it. I should be able to have confidence in what law enforcement told me but there's just something about it that's not right. It's not so much that I believe any of them are lying to me, but I feel they have been lazy about this whole thing and wrote Jane off as just another druggie that didn't have to be accounted for.

"I feel that they were too willing to simply accept Michael Tewks' story about what happened, especially in light of their own admission that it was the ramblings of a raving drunk.

"Yes, her clothes were found on the riverbank according to official photos, but that raises more questions than it answers. Who's to say that she had been wearing those clothes, the day she went missing? Even if she had been, why were they there on the ground, and not with her body, regardless of where her body is? Why were there no footprints near the clothes?"

Cora looked at him quickly, mildly shocked. "There were no footprints? Not even hers?"

"That's what I'm told," Morgan said.

"Staged?"

She rested a hand against her throat, in alarm.

"That's how it seems to me. The photos confirm it."

"The sheriff's office missed all this?" She was stunned.

"I've hired my own investigators," he told her. "They've been all over that riverbank, within five miles in every dry direction of where their tent had been set up and there were no footprints. It's definitely not a boat launch area and no one would go there to swim or for a picnic. It's pretty grown up.

"I'm surprised that Tewks put his tent there to start with, unless he was just looking for an isolated place to smoke his crack pipe."

Cora continued to examine him. "Morgan, do you think there's a chance that Jane is still alive?"

"I realize I may be coming across as simply being in denial, Cora, if that's your worry," he began.

"No." She stopped him. "I'm not discounting anything you're saying or even feeling. In fact, to be honest with you, I've had my own doubts about whether or not Jane is truly gone."

Morgan looked over at her and seemed to be at a loss for words. "This whole time?"

"Not too long after you went back home, I spent a day here just walking through the empty house and thinking about Jane and trying to imagine her here, and there was just a feeling in my spirit, if that makes sense, that there was still reason to pray for her and to not stop.

"I couldn't understand why God would be prompting me to pray for Jane, unless there was maybe a chance that she was still out there, somewhere."

Morgan looked down at the coffee table and flexed his facial muscles, feeling a great deal of reproach that he, who once was a man of prayer, hadn't bothered to at least try praying for his little sister. At the same time, he was immensely touched and grateful that Cora had been, and looked up at her with strong emotion in his eyes.

"Thank you, Cora," he said softly.

She rested her arm on the back of the sofa and ran her fingers through his dark curls. "She's your sister and you love her," she simply said.

Morgan silently added that to his list of reasons for being in love with this woman.

"I also hired a private company to drag the river and so far, they've found nothing. They've expressed their difficulty in believing that they can anticipate finding a body for several reasons, one being the amount of debris and limbs, and boulders in the water in that immediate area, that would certainly hinder a body's being swept away. That entire part of the river is filled with fallen, rotted trees, and trash, and any number of obstacles.

"There have been no dam releases that would have affected the water level," he added with a tired stretch.

Cora smiled faintly at him, when he glanced her way and realized that extending his limbs in an effort to relieve his stiff muscles had made her have to find her comfort zone, again.

"Can't you be still?" he demanded, able to keep a straight face and a stern expression, until she burst into one of her soft giggles that always made him smile.

He rested his head against hers and thought about what he'd been telling her.

"And so on, and so forth," he said, stifling a little yawn.

Cora looked at him closely.

"So, long flight, long drive and only one pitiful cup of coffee," she observed. "Why do I feel like you're about to blame me for this?"

He laughed quietly.

"There are times when you're so perceptive, you're scary."

He reached for her hand and gave it a little caress.

"Let's talk about something else, Cora, and then I need to get to my hotel room and sleep like Rip Van Winkle."

"I'd invite you to crash in the guestroom, but I want my dad to continue to really like you," she kidded.

"Does your dad really like me?" Morgan asked, in a lazy, soothing voice.

"He does. He's actually kept up with your career. At least, that's what he told me when I was there last week. I wish you could have seen my face when he told me he had met you."

Morgan thought about that.

"Why was I the topic of your conversation, Cora?"

She drew in a breath and confessed.

"I asked him how I could fall hopelessly in love with a man that I had only known for three days. When I told him your name and he then began to tell me about your business achievements, I just sat there in shock. I couldn't believe that my parents knew your parents and regarded them as friends."

Morgan nodded, still thinking of what she had asked her father. "Did he have an answer for you?"

"He asked me if I was trying to discover if I really loved you, or if I was just questioning the logic of it.

"I told him that I was more in love with you every day, but I was completely at a loss for how something like this could happen to someone like me."

She glanced over at him. "I guess I have a little bit of a reputation for not paying attention to men or returning any interest they show in me. It's not something I'm known for. I've always felt honed in on what I wanted to do, and never had any interest at all in anything remotely related to romance."

"Thank God you made an exception in my case," Morgan said quietly, giving her hand a little squeeze.

He tried to gently raise himself up a little straighter in order to focus on what he wanted to say, and not simply stay cozy next to Cora and end up falling asleep.

"We don't have to work anything out tonight, but I want us to spend some time this weekend talking about any upcoming demands or opportunities our careers may present, and choices we may be asked to make.

"There may be some things that would cause us to be apart for a while, which is why I want you to keep revisiting what I said to you upstairs, and hide it in your heart for those times ahead."

"I guess I need to tell you about this tour thing," she said, so softly that it sounded as if she were only thinking out loud.

He waited, then finally prompted her.

"You've been asked to tour?"

She nodded. "It's not something that I necessarily want to do, but I probably need to beef up my bank account again. It's with an orchestra that I really do enjoy playing with, but it would be about three months, and I was hoping to begin working on my opus." She twisted a strand of her hair, and Morgan decided that her habit of doing that seemed stress related.

"What would be your instrument?" he asked softly, choosing to focus on her contribution to the tour, rather than on her not always being available to him, for a while.

"Mostly cello, but I would also have a featured original piano performance, the finale. If I go," she finished.

"When you say that it's not something you really want to do, is that more about your opus, or something else?"

She met his eyes. "If I'm being honest?"

"Yes. You and I are going to be honest."

She looked down at her hands. "I'm worried about your not being able to reach me, if you need me."

"What is it about that, that worries you, sweetheart?"

Cora bit her lip and struggled, then finally told him.

"I guess I'm afraid that if you need someone to talk to, or to bare your heart to, and you can't reach me, then some other woman will want to fill that need."

Her eyes were brimming with the threat of tears, but she valiantly tried to control them.

Morgan lifted his arm and let her move under it to press in close against him, then gave her shoulder a caress.

"Before you came along, I never bared my heart to anyone, Cora. Why would I suddenly just go to the next woman in line, if I couldn't reach you? Good grief, I'd hire a shrink before I did that."

He rested his eyes on her beautiful, sad face. "But it's not about you and I needing to reassure each other. Either we are committed to one another, or we aren't."

He watched her carefully, seeing her make the effort to accept what he was saying.

"Look at me."

She lifted her eyes to his.

"Perhaps you've never stopped to think about it, but you do realize, don't you, that I'm not a man who is going to be content to just sit and hold hands with you the rest of my life? You can't forever be my girlfriend."

She frowned, not understanding.

"I'm going to want more," he told her. "I very much intend to marry you, so if that's a place you think you can't go with me, say so now."

She drew in her breath, feeling her heart against her ribs, then whispered, "I dare you to ask me."

"Do you?" he replied, lightly. "Do you think I'm scared?"

"I guess we'll find out," she said, with the familiar hint of a playful challenge coming back into her eyes.

Morgan fixed his gaze on her for a long moment, before lifting himself up from the sofa.

Cora watched him move toward the door, where he had hung his leather jacket on a coat rack. When he returned, he knelt in front of her, with a breathtaking platinum ring, beautifully set with a single, colorless, excellent cut, two-carat diamond solitaire held carefully between his fingertips, and she immediately covered her mouth with her hands, forgetting all about controlling her tears.

"If you're sure that you love me," he said, in a hushed, gentle voice, "and if you have faith in my love for you... and if you're willing to persistently love me during times of separation and to live with the knowledge that your being absent from me will not weaken my trust in our pledge to each other... if you share my desire to build a life together, to walk together, to be passionate together, and fail or succeed together... to grow old together, then marry me, Cora Hartmann."

Morgan allowed a charming grin to steal across his handsome face. "I dare you to say yes."

He had never seen this woman look as beautiful as she looked now, with all the love she had for him lighting up her sweet, green eyes and gently sweeping over her.

She leaned forward to take his face between her hands.

"I love you with everything in me, that is even capable of love. I am completely yours and just as you say that I own you, you own me, Morgan Roberts. I gladly embrace everything you've asked of me, and I long to grow old with you. Yes."

Morgan kissed her left hand, before slipping the token of his pledge onto her finger, then raised himself up to return to her side and gather her close.

He took a moment to allow himself a decidedly indulgent kiss, before pulling back and sharing a knowing look with her.

"Well, enough of that," he muttered, causing her to blush, and smile down at her left hand.

"If I need to talk, and I can't reach you," he said, "then perhaps I'll try talking to God, since He'll be able to see you and maybe give you a message for me."

"I kinda thought you were mad at Him," Cora admitted.

"Well, I might have been, but He gave you to me, so He must not be mad at me. That'll be a good conversation starter for us, I think."

Chapter Ten

Gary Lenard looked around the busy dining room of Ingleside Fare, before letting the girl at the counter know that he'd just located the party he was to meet. He thanked her and made his way over to the table near the fireplace.

Morgan stood and took his hand in greeting, then rested a caress on Cora's shoulder.

"Cora, this is Gary Lenard, head of the investigative team I hired to look into Jane's speculated drowning.

"Gary, Cora Hartmann, my fiancée," he said, glancing down at her with a soft wink, as she smiled up at him, before offering her hand to the detective.

"A pleasure," the gray-haired man assured her, taking a seat, then pausing to study her more carefully.

"Are you a musician, Miss Hartmann?"

She traded another look with Morgan, before simply nodding in surprise.

"My wife has a set of Christmas recordings and I wonder if you might be the same Cora Hartmann listed on the credits for cello? She keeps playing this one song over and over. I love my wife, and I love the song, but Christmas is over. Nevertheless, she's still playing it."

"I suppose I am," she said apologetically.

"I'm sorry she's not with me, then," he said. "She's going to be really disappointed to have missed meeting you."

He glanced up as Sandra Birch approached their table and handed him a menu, then asked for his drink order and as he was making his choice, Morgan sat looking at his beautiful Cora with a hint of admiration in his eyes.

Gary Lenard focused his attention back to the couple he was sharing the table with.

"Miss Hartmann, I hope our subject matter today won't be upsetting to you in any way?"

She smiled at him, and shook her head. "No, I'm fairly familiar with the situation."

Morgan reached over and took her hand, cradling it gently in his own. "Cora has gone through this with me, since the very beginning, Gary. In fact, if you ever have difficulty reaching me and have something urgent to report, speaking with Cora is the same as speaking to me."

"I'll remember," he promised, reaching into his pocket and pulling out a small notepad. "Would you mind sharing your phone number with me, Miss Hartmann?"

She took the pen and wrote it down, then handed it back to him, as he thanked her.

"I was supposed to meet with Kyle Corbett before you, Morgan, but his daughter ran into a flagpole on the schoolyard, playing crack-the-whip, and got herself a busted lip. He said he was taking her to get a few stitches, and he'll get with me later. But he did email me his report."

He pulled it out of a folder he'd brought in with him and handed it to Morgan, who spread it out on the table so that Cora could also see it.

"Kyle is the head of the dive team who have been searching the river," he explained quietly, letting his eyes scan over the report, but not seeing anything unexpected.

After a moment, he glanced up at Gary and tapped the report with his index finger.

"So he's stating in his conclusion that it is unlikely, given the time frame stated by Michael Tewks and the location he claims is where Jane fell into the river, that a body would have continued to move out of that area and into any current."

Gary Lenard nodded in agreement, and reached over to pull the report around to flip through it. He indicated the list of factors supporting Kyle Corbett's position and pushed the report back over to Morgan.

"That particular area is stagnant for the most part, because of the build up of debris and everything else they found.

"Apparently, people have been dumping their broken down junk in that part of the river, for years. They found an old door off of a stove, some paint cans, an old hot water heater. It's a mess."

He waved his hand. "Just a lot of junk that created a sort of dam, maybe as far out as twenty feet. Kyle said that he was hired to search that part of the river before for a woman who claimed that a locket fell off her neck around there, so he was already familiar with it. But he went at it with fresh eyes, especially when the situation involved a potential drowning."

"But, bottom line, he doesn't see any indication that a drowning occurred?" Morgan asked, looking at him with alert brown eyes that returned to the report's conclusion.

"His professional opinion is no," Gary Lenard confirmed.

Morgan sat back in his chair and crossed his arms, studying his investigator closely, and waiting.

"I was told I could find a Debra Gregory who works here?" Gary asked, glancing around.

"She was at the counter when you came in," Cora offered softly, not seeing her now, but managing to catch Sandra's eye.

Sandra came over to their table, bringing Gary Lenard's iced tea to him, and deliberately not giving in to her usual habit of teasing the customers, since she knew what they were meeting about. She laid her hand affectionately on Cora's back and looked down at her with her unspoken question.

Cora introduced her to Gary Lenard and told her that he was working for Morgan in regard to his sister, Jane.

"Sandra, Mr. Lenard is hoping to be able to speak to Debra, if that's okay."

"I don't see why it wouldn't be," she replied. "I'll go see what's she's doing and send her out here."

"What is Debra Gregory's connection to Jane, Gary?" Morgan asked, while they were waiting.

"Apparently, the two had become friends. I mainly just want to determine if your sister confided anything to her that could shed some light on what might have been going on."

Morgan looked up past the detective, as the young mother who worked for Sandra approached their table with a blend of curiosity and nervousness.

"Hi, Debra." Cora stood up and gave her a light hug, since she had gotten to know Debra Gregory fairly well while living upstairs, and really liked her.

Seeing Cora there put the girl at ease and she sat down in the chair Cora invited her to take.

"Debra, I don't know if you ever met Morgan Roberts," Cora said gently. "Morgan is Jane's brother."

She looked startled at first, then seemed to be studying him. "Yes, I can see the resemblance," she said, taking the hand Morgan offered and returning his greeting.

Cora introduced her to Gary Lenard and let her know that Morgan had hired him to investigate Jane's disappearance.

A look of relief passed over Debra's face.

"I'm glad to hear that, Mr. Roberts."

"Morgan," he corrected quietly. "You were friends with my sister, Debra?"

"We didn't know each other very long but it was easy to talk to her, so we did talk a lot. She was funny, and she made me laugh," she said, with a sad smile.

Gary Lenard sat listening to their exchanges silently, before resting his eyes on the young woman's face and giving her a friendly smile.

"Debra, are you aware of the findings of the local sheriff's department, concerning your friend?"

She nodded. "I know what they claim happened," she admitted, "but they got that from Mike Tewks, so that should have told them right away, that it was a lie."

Morgan fixed his dark eyes, that were very much like his sister's, on her friend. "Were they really married, Debra?"

She nodded. "Unfortunately, according to Jane. I was pretty upset about it because I already knew what a loser Mike Tewks is, but right after she met him, the next thing I know, she told me that they got married. I was mad, and said some mean things that I wish now I hadn't said.

"Not that they weren't true, but all I did was upset her and I felt bad about that."

"Why do you say that Michael Tewks was lying about Jane drowning, Debra?" Gary Lenard asked.

"Well, first of all, whatever Mike says, you can pretty much believe the opposite," she informed him dryly. "They had been evicted out of Jane's little house, out there off of Route 4, and they were staying with some of Mike's drug buddies. But I heard that he told the sheriff that he and Jane had been living in a tent at the river, so right there, he just flat out lied.

"He did have a tent and he went out there sometimes, to make a drug deal or just get high, but he didn't live in it, and Jane never would go out there."

Morgan was looking at her intently.

"Debra, what is the period between the last time you saw Jane and the day she was said to have drowned?"

"I've thought about that," she answered. "There was a birthday party planned for Pastor Nichol's granddaughter and Jane was working on a portrait of her and her llama."

She looked up at Morgan with a grin. "The kid has a llama," she informed him. "All I ever had was a goldfish."

He returned her grin and waited.

"So that was in July, toward the end. She delivered the portrait to the party. That didn't go well, I heard."

"Did something happen at the party?"

She nodded and an anger settled in her eyes.

"I found out about it from Ben. That's my husband, and Mike Tewks had come in where Ben was playing pool and was bragging about it.

"Of course, Pastor Nichols could tell you more, but Ben said that Mike Tewks showed up at the birthday party and just showed out, demanding the money that Jane was paid for the portrait and ordering her to leave with him. He said Pastor Nichols asked Jane if she wanted him to call the sheriff, and she asked him not to."

Morgan had latched on to something Debra said in passing and now stopped her with a question.

"You said that Jane delivered the portrait, Debra?" He waited for her nod. "Do you know if she drove herself there, or if Tewks drove her and then came in to get the money?"

"Well, she didn't drive herself, because she slung a rod in that old Beetle of hers a good while before that, and left it on the side of the road.   It got hauled off.   Harley took her."

Confused looks were exchanged around the table, before Gary asked her who that was.

"Harley Fisher.   Mike and Jane were staying at his brother's house. Harley's not a druggie, like the rest of them are. He's older and he actually works. He's a decent sort and I guess he felt sorry for Jane. He's given her rides before, after her car broke down, and Mike was off on a drunk, somewhere."

"Was the day of the party the last time you saw Jane?" Morgan asked her.

"It was. She came by here to see what time I got off work, because she thought she might have to ask Ben and me to pick her up and give her a ride home. But she never did call, so I figured that Harley either waited around for her or came back to pick her up. That was the last Saturday in July, but I don't remember the date. Then, a couple of days later, I heard that Mike got picked up on a warrant and that Jane had drowned. But, like I said, she never would go out there to that tent."

Gary wrote down his name, and a strange expression came to rest on his face, as if a thought had occurred to him. He looked up from his notepad at Debra Gregory.

"You mentioned that Harley was a decent sort and that he felt sorry for Jane. Is this something Jane told you or is this something you've observed, on your own?"

"I guess a little of both. Ben said Harley had come by the pool hall after work one night, and they were just talking and then I guess Harley got a text. Then Ben said Harley called Mike and said, 'If I find out that you've ever laid a hand on Jane again, I'll go to jail, and you'll go to hell'. Ben said it might have been Jane who texted him but whoever it was, it seemed like they had just tipped Harley off that Mike had done something to her."

Cora looked over at Morgan, whose face had taken on a dark, angry look and laced her fingers into his. He took in a deep breath and gave her hand a little squeeze.

"Any idea how I could contact Harley, Debra?" Gary asked hopefully.

"I actually have his number because Ben called me from his house one night and said he was helping him put a set of head gaskets on his truck, and I put the number in my contacts."

She fished around in her pocket for her phone, then searched it until she found the number and held it up to Gary, who hurriedly jotted it down.

"He lives out past the co-op, on Fullerton," Debra thought to add. "It's a white house with a camper parked next to it and an old tire swing in the front yard."

Debra looked at Morgan with a sad face.

"I hope Jane's okay, Morgan. I've known all along that Mike Tewks was lying about her drowning, but I hope it's not to cover up something else that he's guilty of."

She was saying what they had already begun to suspect.

Morgan repeated his knock on the door frame of the house, and glanced around, satisfying himself that this place fit the description. He began to hear movement inside and after a moment, the door was opened slowly and a young man peered through the screen.

He had obviously been asleep and stood rubbing his eyes, and trying to focus on the tall stranger standing there.

"Can I help you?" he asked, pushing his blonde hair back out of his eyes and glancing around for the sweatshirt that he reached for to pull over his head.

"Are you Harley?" Morgan asked quietly.

"I am, unless you're sellin' something," he said with a little grin, telling Morgan what he wanted to know.

Harley Fisher made an effort to be more alert. "Was there something I could help you with?"

"I was told that you and my sister were friends. Jane."

Harley opened the screen door and stepped out onto the porch to see Morgan better. A closer inspection confirmed to him that he was indeed looking at Jane's brother.

"You look like her," he decided, then smiled. "But you're older, so I guess it's the other way around."

Morgan subconsciously returned his smile without realizing it. "I talked to Debra Gregory, today."

Harley let a thoughtful look come across his face, but made no comment.

"Harley, do you have any idea where my sister is? Is she's alive?" Morgan seemed to be quietly pleading.

"I see you're not buyin' that lie that ol' Tewks told the sheriff, are you?" Harley asked.

He shook his head.

"You're afraid that he's trying to cover something up."

Harley had seemed to become the one asking the questions, but Morgan turned it back on him.

"I know that you threatened to kill him if he ever laid a hand on Jane again."

Harley crossed his arms and looked around the yard, as he remembered what the man was talking about. "That wasn't a threat, that was a promise," he muttered, allowing a flash of old anger to revisit him.

"Morgan," he said to himself, looking over at him and remembering. "She said her brother's name was Morgan."

"Yes. Do you need to see some ID?"

He laughed shortly. "No, brother, I'm good."

"Debra made it sound as if Jane trusted you."

"She knew I had her back," he agreed. "And Tewks knew I'd put a bullet in his, if he messed with her again."

"Is it true that he got Jane messed up with meth, Harley?"

A scornful look washed across the young man's face. "I guess good ol' Sheriff Garvey Hibbard told you that. He don't know crap. Jane never messed with any of it. Ol' Garvey just writes down whatever anybody tells him, and calls it a report."

Morgan reached a hand to rub his neck, and glared down at the floor of the porch.

"Why would Jane have married that fool? He's not someone my sister would have ever gone out with, let alone married. None of this makes any sense."

"Well she ended up regrettin' it, pretty much right away, I can tell you that much," her protector declared.

Morgan was beginning to feel weary and emotional. He stood next to the young man, clenching his jaw and staring across the yard, into the field beyond the road.

"I have to find her," he whispered. "I don't believe she's dead, but she's not trying to reach me. Why isn't she calling me? Why isn't she telling me where to come and get her?"

He laid his fingers over his mouth and stood blinking back tears, and trying to make sense of all this.

"She told me once that you were her only family," Harley said, watching the big guy wipe his face and hang his head, and feeling sorry for him.

He nodded. "It was just us."

"Maybe it still is," Harley said, in a low voice.

Morgan drew his brows and turned to look at him.

"Is she alive?" he demanded, in a hoarse voice. "You don't have to tell me where she is, if you made promises, but is she alive? Do you know if she's okay?"

Harley moved forward toward the railing across the front of his porch and rested his hands on it, looking out and seeming to wrestle with his answer.

"The last time I saw her, she was safe," he finally offered. "Tewks had already been picked up. I guess he thought he'd killed her. He tried to, and then he made tracks to get out to that so-called hideout of his, out there on the river.

"By then, I guess he was so stinkin' drunk that he made up that story about her drownin' and threw some of her things around that he had taken from Carter's house. That's my kid brother," he added, looking down at a cut on his thumb and idly rubbing his finger over it, then turning to look around his porch to see if he'd left a cigarette lying around.

He turned back to look around again. "I gave her a ride back over there, because that's where they were livin', after she lost her house. She'd been out to Preacher Nichol's place to give that grandkid of his a painting. Then Tewks showed up, because he knew Jane was gonna get money for it, and he wanted it.

"Nichols wanted to call the law but Jane asked him not to. She was afraid Tewks would take it out on her, later. She gave him the money so he'd leave and I guess that's all he wanted, because he did leave.

"I took her back to Carter's and she told me that since she'd given him the money, she didn't expect any trouble and she wasn't worried. She seemed to want me to leave, so I did.

"I had to be up early, so I went on to bed, but sometime after that, she called me. I could tell she was hurt, so I jumped up and drove over there. Tewks had come in the house, three sheets to the wind and high, on top of that, and started slappin' her around and talkin' crazy.

"Carter wasn't anywhere around because, even if he is a little cuss, he wouldn't have just stood there and watched him do that to Jane. Tewks tried to shoot her but the gun was empty, so he hit her in the head with it and of course, she went down.

"She didn't move, she just stayed down and let him think he'd killed her. He pulled some of her things out of a drawer and took off to that tent of his.

"I guess he thought he had time to get out there and make everything look like he wanted and then go back and get her body, and drop it in the river. If he even thought at all.

"I never did find out how he managed to get picked up for that warrant, but it mighta just been a deputy patrollin' around there, because they all knew about his drug deals.

"Anyway, when they got him, he started runnin' off at the mouth about Jane bein' drowned, and actin' like he was cryin'. I guess he was pretty convincin' with his story, because those fools at the sheriff's office just took his word for it.

"I bet after he sobered up though, he started to panic." He seemed to enjoy that image and smiled.

"If you tell the law that a woman drowned, then maybe you shouldn't leave the body back at the place where you're livin', 'cause that ain't drownin'. Tewks ain't that bright."

Harley laughed quietly to himself and seemed to be done, then rested his elbows on the rail and turned to look back at Jane's brother.

"I came into the house and found her lyin' on the floor, right where he'd left her. Tewks had taken her phone before, but I beat it out of him one night and told him I'd kill him, if he took it again. I gave it back to her, and she had it on her that night. She was able to call me, but she was smart enough to stay down on the floor, in case he came back before I could get there.

"I got a wet rag out of the bathroom and some ice and tried to clean her up the best I could, so I'd be able to see how bad it was. He clocked her right upside the temple and it's a miracle he didn't kill her.

"I brought her back over here and kept a watch over her, even though I'm no doctor. If I was, this place would look a lot different." He laughed, as he said this.

Morgan folded his arms and shook his head, his mind racing with everything he'd just been told.

"Why didn't you tell the sheriff's office what Tewks did, Harley? Especially when you found out that he was claiming she drowned, and you knew she hadn't?"

The young man watched a bright red cardinal land on the end of the railing and begin hopping over to the corn he knew he'd find in a little pile there, then looked back out to the field with a little smile on his face.

"I'm just bidin' my time. I expect they picked him up on some little ticky tack misdemeanor. He'll be out, soon enough, and I'll be waitin' on him. I told him what would happen."

Morgan looked quickly over at him.

"Harley, Carter needs you, especially now. Don't do anything that will take you away from him. Tewks will come to his own end."

Harley shrugged, then nodded off to one side.

"Jane stayed right over there in that little camper, while she mended up and then she called a friend of hers from out of state and she came and took Jane away."

Morgan stood looking at it, overcome with gratitude for what this young man had done for his sister.

"Thank you for saving her," he said, clearing his throat and wiping his face impatiently. "Thank you, Harley."

"Nah," he said, brushing it off. "I treat my friends the way I want to be treated. Jane was my friend."

Morgan looked up at the sky and closed his eyes, breathing a silent prayer of thanks to God, the first one he had offered in years. He looked back at Harley, with the obvious question in his eyes and Harley looked regretful.

"If I knew, I'd tell you, Morgan, I surely would. I don't have a sister, but I got that sawed off runt of a kid brother and if he came up missin', I'd do just what you're doing right now and go lookin' for answers.

"Jane wouldn't tell me the woman's name who came and got her, because she was afraid that Tewks would someday find out and come lookin' for her. All I can tell you is that she was another hippie."

He laughed at what he'd just said.

"No disrespect to your sister, Morgan, but she was right out of Woodstock."

Morgan smiled and nodded.

"I think she was born that way."

organ lay on the sofa in his sock feet, with one arm resting across his forehead and his eyes closed, listening as Cora sat playing a nocturne on the piano. She hadn't told him, but Morgan somehow knew that it was her own.

He breathed in and out, slowly and deeply, letting the music wash over him and seeming to feel layers of care and tension slipping away from him.

Cora had first spent some time softly playing her cello, and this is what had caused Morgan to slip off his shoes and stretch himself out on the soft leather sofa to watch the flames dancing in the fireplace, completely taken captive by the beauty she called forth out of her instrument.

She thought he had fallen asleep and quietly rested her cello but as she was standing, Morgan asked her not to stop, although his eyes remained closed, as if he were murmuring softly in his dreams.

She smiled over at him and moved to sit at her piano, softly touching a few notes, allowing him to recognize the change, but keeping to her tranquil theme. Now, the nocturne that she had worked on a little at a time, over the years, and had only recently revived, began to move softly through the air and breathe on Morgan's tired spirit.

Cora played with a reverence, and soon forgot that she wasn't alone, so that introversion and shyness faded away and something remarkable began to come from her hands.

Morgan slowly opened his eyes, but remained still, not wanting to remind her that he was there, and witnessed what could only be described as greatness.

She seemed to be playing spontaneously, and Morgan couldn't stop himself from turning over quietly to watch her.

She was looking upward, as if reading some beautiful, invisible story and telling it through her instrument. She very slowly and softly brought the tale to its conclusion, as if gently closing a cherished book, and laying a loving hand to rest on it.

She lowered her head and looked down, feeling the music still echoing inside her as it floated away. After a moment, she looked up to see Morgan sitting and considering her in a way he never had.

"I'm torn," he said quietly.

Cora stood up and came over to him, lowering herself to sit beside him and wait.

"When you told me about the tour you've been invited to be part of, my first instinct was to encourage you to go. I've been asked to go down to South America on business and I've yet to agree, because I knew it would keep me tied up for several weeks and likely months. Knowing that you would be touring and busy would have helped me decide to go, but now, I'm not sure. What you just played, Cora, is that a part of the opus you're composing?"

"I've felt as if it could be," she replied, looking at him with soft eyes, wondering why he was asking.

He leaned back against the sofa to study the fireplace, and seemed to be in deep thought.

"If you were to complete your opus, what would happen after that?" he wondered.

She relaxed beside him and thought about it.

"Of course, I hadn't expected to complete what I would consider to be my opus magnum for many years. I'm considered to be quite young in my field, although I already have a fairly large catalog of original compositions."

Morgan nodded slightly. He had read this about her in an interview transcript.

"The opus I'm currently focusing on is not my first. I do feel that I'm very close to capturing it, but I hadn't thought that it would represent any sort of pinnacle of my achievements, as an opus magnum is meant to do. It could still be a part of it, I guess. Maybe as one of the movements.

"I had hoped to still be many years away from that target. Once you reach the peak, it's all downhill from there," she said, with a little laugh. "But when it's ready, I have to release it."

She paused and thought about his question. "As far as what would happen, I would have several choices, so in that regard, I'm very blessed. If I announce a completed opus, I would be invited to perform it on a tour circuit, I'm sure.

"I could return to solo concerts. I could take it to a recording studio, or I could simply publish it. Again, I'm a bit young to have gained what recognition I have, but much of that is because I've had tunnel vision, where my career has been concerned, and have pushed for it, to the exclusion of all else."

She smiled to herself, then looked at him revealingly.

"Take you, for example."

"Are you about to exclude me?" he asked, laughing quietly.

"I'm about to tell you that you are my first kiss."

Morgan seemed slightly startled, and looked over at her searchingly to determine if she was teasing him.

"I'm not sure I believe you," he said slowly. "The level of proficiency, not to mention the fervency you brought to our first kiss suggests that you are deceiving me."

She rippled out a little laugh. "Trust me, Morgan, that was all you! I was just responding."

"Oh my," he said lightly, returning his gaze to the fire and smiling faintly. "Is there no end to your talent?"

Cora snuggled against him and shared his interest in watching the hypnotic flames.

"You have yet to tell me what you're torn about," she reminded him quietly.

"I just wondered if touring would cause you to not get around to finishing your opus, but now that you've explained that it's not your first one, it doesn't seem to be as difficult a choice, I would think."

She lifted her left hand and touched her ring with a tender smile. "My first reluctance in deciding to tour had more to do with being separated from you, than anything else. You took that fear away from me.

"It's not as difficult now, but I just moved in, and I kind of hate to pack up all over again and take off." She gave a little sigh. "Andrew has left several messages, and I know he wants an answer, so I'm feeling the pressure to decide soon."

"And Andrew would be?"

"He's the conductor."

Morgan lifted his brows and smiled vaguely ahead, continuing to seem lost in thought, but still ready to tease her.

"He's of course portly and paunchy?"

Cora shrugged lightly.

"Some women find him attractive, I suppose."

She raised her hands to his arm, to wrap them around his hard bicep and rested her chin on his shoulder, looking at him with an exaggerated come-hither look. "But he's no pirate."

He dropped his gaze away from the fireplace and turned his head slightly to look down at her upturned face, his deep brown eyes thoroughly inspecting her.

"So I'm your first."

She nodded slowly.

After a long, charged moment, he regarded her with the hint of a smile hiding in his eyes and touched his bottom lip.

"Show me what you've learned."

His telephone put an end to discovery as Morgan recognized the special tone he'd assigned to his investigator, to ensure that he didn't simply ignore a call.

He sighed and leaned forward to pick up his phone from the coffee table.

"Hello, Gary."

"Hello, Morgan. I wish I had better news, but I can't get either Judge Walsh or Judge Reitzell to budge on your sister's phone records. They both sing the same song, that she's an adult and that she reached out to her friend of her own accord.

"The best I can do, at this point, is to try to find out if the number she had when she left is the same one you've always used to reach her. It may be, since we're not getting a recording about it no longer being in service.

"Debra Gregory thinks it's the same number but she also said that Harley would be the one to know. She warned me that Harley can be difficult to interview, but you seem to have gained his trust. Do you want to ask him about the number, or would you like me to give it a try?"

Morgan sat in silence, thinking it over. "I'm not sure I'd find him at home before I have to fly back, Gary. He works long hours and odd ones, on top of that.

"It's already getting late and I fly out in the morning."

He seemed to wrestle with it. "Let me work through it. I'll try to make it happen and if I just can't, I'll give you a call back. Thanks for trying, Gary, as far as the records. We knew that was a long shot."

He ended the call and sat staring down at his phone, trying to think about whether to drive out to Harley's house again tonight. He flexed the muscles around his mouth, mulling it over and Cora watched him with concern.

After a quiet moment, she risked a question. "I hope you believe me, Morgan, when I say I'm not just trying to keep you here longer, but is Monday some sort of urgent date that you absolutely must be back for?"

He blew out a tired breath. "It's not so much that, as it is the backlog of meetings and decisions that I've already tabled that are causing my inner office staff a bit of alarm."

He reached forward to lay his phone on the table and relaxed back against the sofa, taking Cora's hand and absently lifting it to kiss, as he continued to follow after his thoughts.

"I feel that I'm close to finding her, which is causing me to want to pass on the South America thing. Of course, they won't easily let that go, they'll just keep offering me more time to decide." He smiled dryly at that.

"My Chief Forester, Blake, is more than capable of dealing with the day to day operations but he balks at negotiations, and rightfully so. I wouldn't hand that off to anyone."

"Do you know any of Jane's women friends, Morgan?"

He thought about it. "I've met a couple of them, but names escape me."

He glanced over at her with a little grin. "I'm sure they were names I deliberately tried to forget, like Moon Dew, or Lotus Essence."

Cora looked up at him with wide eyes.

"Jane's friends were stewed in the same pot with her. Apparently, they're all one tie-dyed mess of irresponsibility. One of them follows you around, wanting to 'candle your ear', whatever that means, and the other makes it her business to read your aura and warn you of impending doom, unless you let her sprinkle crap all over you."

Cora laughed, in spite of her best efforts not to. "They sound kind of nice, though, Morgan."

He just shook his head. "If you believe that, then you and Jane would get along famously."

He closed his eyes, and tried to remember which of all his sister's crazy friends she talked about most. Cora sat looking at his handsome profile and wondering if he might end up staying another day.

She watched his brow draw and thought he might be remembering something.

"Raven."

He looked over at her. "Apparently the name Jane wasn't good enough, so they named her Raven."

"Because she's dark, like you?"

"Am I dark?" He seemed to enjoy teasing her.

"You're a pirate," she reminded him. "In fact, Sandra Birch calls you 'Tall, Dark and Handsome'. So yes, you are, but in a dreamy way."

"In a dreamy way." He laughed quietly. "I suppose I'll take that, over being portly and paunchy."

His smile faded, as he sat idly playing with her fingers and trying to decide how to move forward.

"I guess I should head back to the hotel, Cora, and give Blake a call. I need to determine how things are going there, and then either drive out to Harley's tonight, or first thing in the morning. I think, at this point, he'd tell me the number, if Jane was using a different one."

She looked confused.

"What is it?" He took in her frown and gave her hand a little squeeze.

"Are you going straight on to the airport, in the morning?"

"No, sweetheart. Did you really think I'd just take off, without seeing you again?"

She must have thought that, because she didn't smile as spontaneously as she normally would have.

"If I have to take a later flight, I will," he told her softly. "As much as I love my sister, and I do love her, you're going to be my wife. You've become my first priority. Yes, I very much want to know where she is, but I do know that she's alive and she's safe, even if she is with that bunch of freaks."

✳✳✳

Harley Fisher pulled his head out from under the hood of his old Dodge truck and watched Morgan Roberts bring his vehicle to a stop just behind it.

He motioned for his younger brother to stop bumping the starter and came around, wiping his hands on an old tee shirt.

"I figured you'd have headed back home, by now," Harley greeted. He looked around at his brother, who had hopped out of the cab of the truck and came around with a curious stare to see who Harley was talking to.

"This is Carter," Harley indicated with the rag.

"Hello, Carter," Morgan said, with a slight nod. "What's the issue with your truck, Harley?"

"I was hoping it was the starter, because I can get my hands on another one pretty easily, but I don't guess that's it. It's not firing, though."

Morgan came around and peered under the hood before glancing back at him. "Is this an eighty-nine?"

"It is," Harley confirmed. "It's been runnin' alright, but it won't fire at all, this mornin'. It's not fuel, though, I figured that much out."

"You might try replacing that ignition coil," Morgan said quietly. "It shouldn't run more than twenty dollars to find out, but I used to mess around with old trucks and even though everyone kept trying to make me believe that coils rarely fail, I've seen my share of them that have."

Harley leaned onto the top edge of the grill panel and looked thoughtfully at the motor. "I bet I got one in that old shed, Carter."

He turned his blonde head to look at his brother with a challenging grin. "Would you even know one, if it jumped off the shelf and bit you?"

Carter shot him a grimace and headed off to see what he could find and Harley looked back at Morgan with a smile.

"I'm making Carter stay close to home for a while, so he's a little mad at me. I can handle a little sulkin', though."

Morgan laughed at that, and watched Harley's kid brother disappear into an old shed in the backyard.

"Harley, I should have asked you this when I was here before, but do you know if Jane changed her phone number? I've been calling her for months and I'm still getting a recording that the voicemail is full, but I'm not getting a message that the number is no longer in service."

"Well, then it probably still is, but she ain't gonna be answering it. It's here." He dropped his voice. "She wanted me to take pictures of her with it, the night I found her on the floor. I figured she was out of her head, but she said it might help her someday if Tewks started trying to find her. So I did, and gave the phone back to her, but when she left here, she told me she was leaving it in the camper, under the kitchen sink."

Harley glanced around to make sure Carter was still in the shed. "She got one of them burner phones, now. She said she'd leave the number in the camper, but I never had a reason to call her, so I never even checked. I keep it locked up.

"Carter don't know nothing about that, so I don't want him to hear me talkin' about it. Carter's a good kid, but he thinks Tewks is a tough guy and he's got some kinda loyalty to him, although he really thought a lot of Jane, too."

He felt around in his overall pockets and fished out a key ring and flipped through it before isolating one.

"Try this one and see if it'll open. If she did remember to leave a number, it outta be right out in the open, there on the counter."

Morgan took it and looked over at the camper. "Thank you, Harley. I won't mess with anything in there, I'll just look for the phone, and for a number if she did write one down."

"Oh, give it a good look," he returned, with a little wave. "There ain't nothing in there that I care anything about."

Morgan smiled and headed over to where the little camper was parked, and went around to try the key.

It opened easily enough and he stepped up and inside, reaching to open the little kitchen curtains, when the light switch didn't seem to be working.

He did spot some paper on the counter and held it up to the window, feeling a little lump in his throat as he recognized his sister's handwriting. His heart beat faster, as he read not only what phone number she could be reached at but a request that if her brother ever came looking for her, for Harley to ask him if he remembered her friend who was a beekeeper. That was all it said, but Morgan knew it was her way of telling him where she was going.

He dug around under the sink, and found the phone, dead by now, but he could charge it.

He folded the paper and put it in his pocket, then closed the curtains and let himself out of the camper, locking it again and bringing the key back over to Harley, who was standing with his thumbs hooked in his overall pockets, staring impatiently at the shed in the backyard.

"I found it all, Harley," Morgan told him, handing him back the key. "Do you want me to copy the number for you?"

"Nah." He waved his arm. "I expect the best I thing I can do for your sister now, is to bow on outta this story and let you take it from here."

"I can't understand why she didn't just call me, though," Morgan said quietly, still trying figure that out.

"I do," Harley explained. "She said that she's a screw up and that you're a big, important guy.

"She thought it would be better if she just let her friends help her, and keep you out of it. I told her she was all day dumb, and that no brother worth a durn would feel like that, but she was pretty embarrassed at the way her life turned out.

"She said she was supposed to be a great artist and you would be ashamed of her, now."

Morgan looked as if Harley had just punched him in the gut, and drew in a sharp breath.

"I wouldn't-a said nothin', Morgan, but I don't want you to spend the rest of your life wonderin' about that. I know if you were to find her, she'd let all that go, and be happy to see you."

He swallowed and nodded, then looked up and gave Harley's shoulder a clasp. "You've been a big help, Harley, with all this. I can't thank you enough, but I'll find a way to try."

"Naw, don't worry about it," he replied lightly. "I guess I better go see what's keepin' Carter. He don't know an ignition coil from a bug light. I expect he's about ready to come out here with an extension cord, or somethin'."

He laughed at himself and tossed a wave to Morgan. "Take care of yourself!"

"You too, Harley."

Morgan watched him stride out toward the shed to find out what was keeping Carter, then got into his vehicle, to drive back out to the little cabin, and hopefully figure out where to go from here.

Chapter Twelve

Sheriff Garvey Hibbard sat back in his swivel chair, using the support of the armrests, and looked quietly at the two men who sat across from him, both with intent expressions, but the dark eyed man on the left with a simmering anger that suggested that he meant business.

The sheriff couldn't blame him. He had spoken to him before, and had watched the way he slowly rose from his chair and left his office with his head down and had felt sorry for him, but without any witnesses to refute what Michael Tewks had claimed, there was no reason to disbelieve his account of his wife drowning, especially since she hadn't been seen alive since.

Now he sat in possession of evidence that left him silent. He looked up to regard Morgan Roberts with cautious curiosity.

"You know for a fact that your sister is alive?"

"I do."

"Just because Harley Fisher told you?"

"I'd take Harley Fisher's word over that fool Tewks you're protecting, any day of the week!"

Morgan's eyes were smoldering. "Professional divers will testify in court that not only was no body found where Tewks staged it to look as if Jane had drowned, to cover up the murder he thought he had committed, but that it wouldn't have been possible for her body, or any one else's, to have moved beyond the place of entry into that water. It's nothing more than an underwater dump site.

"My sister is not only alive, but she was able to call a friend to come and get her to a safe location, and let me tell you something else, Sheriff Hibbard," Morgan added, waving away Gary Lenard's gesture for calm.

"Jane wasn't hooked on meth or anything else, and I resent like hell, the insinuation that she was just another crack head that didn't deserve to be searched for!"

The sheriff glanced over at the investigator, choosing to address him, rather than the furious man who seemed ready to come across his desk to get to him.

"Are you willing to provide us with a copy of your full report, Mr. Lenard?"

"I brought a copy for you," he said, pulling it from his briefcase and sliding it across the desk to him. "And this."

He glanced over at Morgan, then pulled Jane's phone out of his briefcase and turned it on.

"This is how Harley Fisher found her, lying there. She still had her phone, which is how she was able to call him for help. He took these pictures. The date and time stamps are all there."

The sheriff put on his glasses and swiped through the images, then slowly read through the investigator's report, while Morgan sat seething at the memory of the sheriff being so willing to let him walk out of this office thinking that his sister was dead, without anything more to substantiate it, than a drunk fool's made up story.

As if reading his mind, Sheriff Hibbard looked up at him with an expression of remorse.

"Of course, Mr. Roberts, I do acknowledge that this office owes you an apology for simply passing on to you what we were told, when you came here to file a missing person report on your sister. It was said to you more as an explanation of why we felt no report needed to be filed, but it's true that we believed what Tewks told us.

"No one else ever came forward with any other story, and until you showed up, no one else was looking for her. It seemed that she really was dead after all, and with no witnesses, all we had was his story to go on.

"I know that sounds like a lot of excuses and buck passing, and maybe it is, but the fact is, you went through a lot of unnecessary grief, and for that, I apologize."

Morgan continued to simply size him up wordlessly, while Gary Lenard made an attempt to do what they had come here to do, which was to confront Michael Tewks.

"I think Mr. Roberts would be more willing to accept what you're saying, Sheriff Hibbard, if we could be permitted to speak to your prisoner."

"I think he's earned that." Rather than refuse them, the sheriff actually seemed glad to facilitate the meeting, and stood to his feet, taking his set of keys out of his desk drawer.

"I'd be interested to hear this exchange, myself," he admitted. He reached for the door behind him, then paused to look back at the two men. "Only let me have my say first, and let's see his reaction. Then you can have him."

They both nodded, and he lead the way through the door and beyond a few cells until he halted in front of the one where Michael Tewks was still waiting to appear in court for his outstanding warrant.

He was lying on his bunk with one leg propped up in the air on a ledge, reading a racing magazine and oblivious of their presence until Sheriff Hibbard unlocked his cell door with an exaggerated loud jingling of his keys.

"Get up from there, Tewks," he instructed, nodding for Morgan and Gary to enter with him, and locking the cell door behind them.

"Who is this?" the thin, wild-eyed man demanded, standing to his feet and clutching the magazine in front of him, as if it were some sort of shield.

He looked at both of them and when he encountered Morgan Robert's dark, stormy face, he took a step back, realizing who he was.

"It was an accident!" he yelled. "Nobody can prove it wasn't! It was an accident!"

"You're talking about the drowning?" Sheriff Hibbard asked him calmly enough.

"That's right! You already know about that. I told you what happened!"

"You said your wife drowned," he returned quietly.

"She did!"

The sheriff stopped him by lifting his hand and explained that in conjunction with his warrant, he was also now being held for attempted murder.

He informed him of his rights, since he was in jail on an unrelated charge. By now, Michael Tewks was rambling on, unwilling or unable to stop talking.

"What are you talking about? She drowned! I told you!"

"If that's true, Tewks," Sheriff Hibbard replied, crossing his arms and taking a step toward him, "then whose body was that found lying on the floor at Carter Fisher's house?"

"You're just trying to trick me!" he yelled. "The body is in the river! Whatever you're trying to pull, it won't work!"

"I asked you a question," the sheriff reminded him, with quiet persistence. "If Jane's body is in the river, then whose body is this?"

He turned on the phone and showed him the pictures of a woman lying pale and still with blood on the side of her head.

Michael Tewks stepped backward and slumped down on the side of his bunk, his face as pale as the woman's in the photos. Finally he looked up, his eyes darting back and forth.

"That was an accident! I didn't mean to kill her, and I panicked, but it was an accident! I was gonna come back and get her and put her body in the river, then I got picked up before I could, but it was an accident!"

"That's not what she says," the sheriff contradicted.

Tewks put a hand over his heart and seemed to be having trouble breathing. He stared up at the sheriff in shock.

"She's dead! I know she's dead!"

"Apparently, she's not as dead as you think," Morgan Roberts said, in a low, menacing voice, stepping toward him, and causing Michael Tewks to push himself backward across the bunk to the wall behind him.

"Don't touch me," he begged, closing his eyes.

"The way you touched my sister? Is that how you mean?"

Gary laid his hand on Morgan's arm.

"We've got him," he said in a low, quiet voice. "Let's let the law take it from here."

Both the sheriff and Gary wondered for a moment, if Morgan Roberts was going to have to be restrained. Neither of them had ever seen that much anger in a man's face, but the cold discipline he finally employed left them just as surprised.

He did lean forward and mutter something to Michael Tewks that neither of them could hear, but Michael Tewks did, and crawled even further into the corner.

Morgan stood regarding him with disgust then turned to nod at Sheriff Hibbard, who quietly unlocked the door and allowed them to proceed him into the walkway, before he secured the cell door and shook it.

"You better lawyer up, Tewks," he advised dryly, before leading the men back through the door into his office.

✳✳✳

Morgan stood watching Cora organizing pages of musical scores and placing them in different folders. He leaned against a window in the studio, turning his attention to the dusting of snow that had begun. It seemed as if it might stick, this time.

"When do you leave?" he asked softly, continuing to stare vacantly out at the gathering collection of snow.

She looked up at him and tried to interpret his mood, before laying a stack of sheet music down and coming over to the window to join him.

She reached a hand to his face and he turned his attention away from the snow to focus his dark eyes on her sad ones.

"Not until Thursday," she answered quietly.

He turned away and Cora again touched his handsome face and coaxed him to look at her. When he did, she slid her arms around his waist and pulled him closer.

"Don't resist me, Morgan, please," she whispered, when he seemed unwilling to be embraced.

"So, what did you do?" he asked pointedly, not pushing her away, but not giving in to her. "Did you get bored when Gary and I were at the sheriff's office?

121

"Did you think, 'Oh, I know what I can do, I can call Andrew and tell him I'm going on tour with him,' and you were in such a hurry to do it that you couldn't even wait for me to drive back out here, to talk to me first?"

"But, Morgan..." she faltered. "Maybe I misunderstood, but you seemed fine with it, and you said you might go ahead to South America, if I went."

He moved away from the window. "I'll be leaving pretty soon, so if you don't mind, I'm going down to the kitchen to heat up a cup of coffee."

As he made his way down the stairs, she was stunned. She tried to think back on their conversation. She had believed that Morgan was fine with her touring. In fact, it had never seemed to Cora as if he had a problem with it, especially when she explained to him that the opus she was working on wasn't time sensitive.

She felt tears stinging her lashes as she came down the stairs to find him rinsing out the old coffee and preparing to brew a fresh pot.

"Would you like for me to do that, Morgan?" she asked.

He heard her voice shaking and froze, staring out the kitchen window, bewildered at why he was so upset with her. She was right, he had told her that he was okay with her touring. He didn't understand why he was so angry now.

He hadn't answered her, so she turned and walked out into the living room. He knew she was crying.

He left everything sitting in the sink, and came into the room, to find her kneeling in front of the fireplace, just staring into the flames with empty eyes.

Morgan lowered himself to the floor and gathered her close, quietly hushing her as she began crying in earnest.

"I'm sorry," he whispered. "Don't cry, sweetheart."

She didn't seem to be able to stop, but she clung to him tightly, as he stroked her hair and caressed her back.

"Come here," he said, raising himself up and reaching to lift her. She let him lead her over to the sofa, and sat trembling beside him, looking anywhere but at him.

"I guess I just thought that you'd tell me your decision first, before you called your conductor. I wasn't expecting to see you packing when I walked in. I'm really sorry."

"I don't have to go," she said feebly.

"Yes, you do. Because if I weren't in the picture, you'd be happy about going."

"But you are in the picture," she protested, raising her sweet eyes to his.

"Sweetheart, I don't want you to lose your identity and just merge into mine. Your music is who you are and I love that about you. I think my frustration stems from the loose way that you and I are leaving everything between us."

She bit her lip and wrinkled her brow in confusion.

"How do you mean?"

"There's no wedding date, there's no plan, there's just a ring. We're not actually aiming at anything, are we?"

She breathed a sigh, and shook her head. "I guess not."

"Is that how we're leaving it?" he asked quietly.

"I hope not, Morgan," she whispered.

"It doesn't feel real," he said, lifting his arm around her and drawing her closer. "It feels like a sweet moment we had, when we said some very loving things to each other, and sealed it with a ring and a kiss, but then it just sort of faded away, after that. Then again, maybe I'm just mentally exhausted and have no idea what I'm talking about."

He drew a little smile from her.

"I won't stay upset with you, Cora, for not waiting for me to get back before you decided. You had other people waiting on you, and you needed to make a decision. I get that."

"I feel that I made the wrong one, though," she sighed.

"I don't think you did. I think I'm just fixated on being with you and not handling another separation very well. Besides, when I called Blake to tell him I'd be another day or two coming back, I could hear the panic in his voice. I really need to get back up there, and take some of the load off of him."

"We haven't had a chance to talk about how things went with you and Harley, and also at the sheriff's office," Cora said.

"I had intended to sit down with you and tell you what I found out, but when I came upstairs looking for you and saw you packing your music, I guess I forgot about all that."

"Can you tell me now?" she asked, looking at his face and thinking about how much she loved him.

"Not with you looking at me like that," he replied, leaning in and spending a few moments giving her soft little kisses, hoping to undo some of the pain he had caused her.

"Can you tell me now?" she repeated with a smile, once he had brought her into a snug embrace again.

"No, because now, we're going to pick a wedding date."

She giggled softly at him, and he smiled.

"When is your tour over?" he asked.

"The end of March."

"So, the first week of April, then," he decided.

"Don't you have to check with your office, first?" she asked, looking up at him and touching his chin.

"Why? They're not the boss of me."

She smiled. "Maybe you'll still be in South America," she pointed out.

"I'm not going."

She looked up at him in surprise.

"Then why am I going on tour?"

"Honey, is that why you said you were going? Because you thought I was going to be out of the country?"

"Yes!" She was genuinely upset.

"Wait a minute," he cautioned. "The closest I ever came to saying I was going to South America, was that knowing you were touring would help me to decide."

Cora looked down and start rubbing her forehead, clearly frustrated, and Morgan caught her hand.

"Here are the facts," he said. "If I'm back up north, and you're here, we won't be together, anyway. All we'll be doing is what we did before, having videos calls whenever we can. We can still do that, if you're touring, can't we?"

"I guess." She didn't sound too enthusiastic about it.

"Then, unless you're particularly inspired to write your opus, you might as well be touring. Maybe it'll make the time pass more quickly."

"Then you might as well go to South America."

"Oh, good grief," Morgan grumbled. "Let's just knock each other in the head and put ourselves out of our misery."

He was glad he could make her laugh.

"Regardless of the tour, you and I have a wedding date. The first week in April, and we can tighten up the actual day of week soon, since both of us are comfortable here, and too lazy to get up off the sofa and go look for a calendar."

"The first week in April," she agreed, then looked up at him curiously. "Where?"

"Wherever you say, love. Besides touring, you also have to plan a wedding. Just keep it small, that's all I ask."

"I can keep it really small. I don't want a wedding, I just want a marriage."

"Women usually recant on that, the minute they see a dress they fall in love with."

She raised herself up to put her lips next to his ear. "I really, really, really just want a marriage."

"Don't say that, or I'll marry you right here," he threatened with a little smile.

"You say that like it's a bad thing," she laughed. "All that does is make me want to say it again."

"Well, we didn't get a license and your dad's not here, so no luck. But soon."

"I guess." She gave him a little pout, then rested her head against his shoulder.

"So you went to Harley's house and then..."

"And then, I found my sister."

Cora sat up straight and stared at him. "How?"

"She left a note in that little camper I told you she'd been staying in. She told Harley that if I came looking for her to tell me that she was with her friend who was a beekeeper."

"Would that be Moon Dew, or Lotus Essence?" she asked.

"Neither. That would be Amanda."

Cora frowned. "What kind of hippie name is Amanda?"

"It's not, thank God. Jane finally did something that made sense, and called a woman that we've known for years. She's a beekeeper in Ohio. Amanda is an outdoors kind of woman, I guess, and she's refreshingly normal, compared to any of Jane's other friends, or even Jane, herself.

"But it was Lily, another friend of Jane's, who came to get her and take her up to Ohio, and Lily is a bonafide hippie, as Harley would tell you. She's also nuts, but in a nice way."

"Is this why you're not going to South America?" she asked, looking at him with soft eyes that were drawing him in.

"It is," he admitted, leaning in and kissing her. "And if you want to hear the rest of it, stop messing with me."

She closed her eyes, and made him laugh.

He made a stack of pillows against the arm of the sofa and rested his head on them, inviting Cora to join him. She snuggled close and he reached for the blanket on the back of the sofa and pulled it over them.

"The rest of it," he said, "is that Harley turns out to be one of the finest people I've ever met in my life, and I'm going to make it my business to do something nice for him, when I get back home, to let him know how much I appreciate the way he took care of Jane."

He realized that he shouldn't have laid down because his eyes immediately became heavy, so he had to concentrate to be able to continue.

He told her how Harley had taken the photos of Jane and had hidden her away in the camper until she was healed up. He said that it was because of Harley that Michael Tewks would now be tried for attempted murder.

Cora tried asking a few questions but Morgan stopped answering because he had fallen asleep, and she soon drifted off, herself.

Chapter Thirteen

Morgan waved away the heartfelt apologies of the employee at the airport's car rental counter, who was flustered that his car hadn't already been made ready for him. She hurriedly got her superior on the phone and informed him that Mr. Morgan Roberts was being kept waiting, and the man immediately came out of his office to see what the problem was, and to add his effusive regrets to those of his employee.

Morgan simply pulled his attention away from the newspaper he was reading and quietly informed the both of them that he was in no hurry. He was shown to a private seating area, which he did appreciate, and was assured that they were working as quickly as they could to accommodate him.

He simply nodded and returned to the review of Cora's performance in the paper, smiling to himself when the reviewer spent quite a bit of time and effort noting her brilliance as both a composer and performer.

The photo of her in her beautiful gown was breathtaking and he touched it with a gentle finger, and a tender look on his face. He almost regretted finding the article, because it only served to intensify his longing for her, but he knew that she longed for him as well, since she had taken the time to text him both before and after her performance to tell him how much she was looking forward to April and how much she loved him.

Morgan raised his eyes when he heard his name, then folded his paper and stood to follow the car rental employee. She had someone bring his luggage to the car that was waiting for him at the front curb and watched him drive away with great relief that he had not been angry.

He tried to put his thoughts of Cora to one side long enough to think ahead in anticipation of finally being able to see his sister, at long last.

When he called the number of her new phone, he assumed he would have to leave her a message, but she surprised him by answering immediately.

"Well, it's about time," he had said gently, and she responded by bursting into tears. Morgan had spent much of the call quietly comforting her and telling her that he wasn't angry with her and that he loved her, and when he asked her if he could fly out to see her at Amanda's place, she joyfully let him know that she would be waiting for him.

He hadn't seen his kid sister in so long, and hearing her voice and knowing that she was safe was like a tonic to him. He hadn't seen Amanda Hester in even longer. The last time he could remember, she must have been just out of college.

Her beekeeping had begun as a school project but she soon realized that she was naturally gifted in hive maintenance and management and had become more and more in demand for her pollination services to the local farmers.

At one time, Morgan kidded her about her bees, but she had to be admired for what was obviously more of a science than simply a hobby, as he had assumed it was.

He was greatly relieved when he found the note in Harley's camper from Jane, saying that she was with her friend who was a beekeeper. Jane knew that Morgan would immediately know how to find her.

After Cora left for her tour, Morgan had met with the party from the small South American country who desired his help and had let them know that he had pressing family issues that had to be addressed, but that he would be available in an advisory capacity at regular intervals, for such time as he could manage it. Of course, the men were disappointed but still grateful to have him offer his insight.

He immediately packed his bags and flew to Ohio to see Jane, and to determine her condition.

When he pulled his car onto the farm's road, and then into the drive, true to her word, Jane came bounding out of the house and ran straight to him, almost knocking him down with her enthusiasm.

Morgan held onto her tightly, with tears crowding his eyes, then pulled back to look down at her.

"You stinker," he muttered, smiling down at his sister's beautiful dark eyes and ruffling her dark curls that were like his.

She looked up at him with wet cheeks.

"I hope you can forgive me, Morgan."

"Well, I can't," he said lightly. "That's why I stopped everything, and got on a plane, and rented a vehicle, and drove all the way out here, just to tell you that I can't forgive you."

His beautiful, expressive eyes were laughing and she buried her face in his chest and clung to him for dear life.

"I thought you were dead," he said hoarsely, his voice packed with emotion. "I thought I'd lost you, Janie."

She looked up at him with fresh tears. "I'm so sorry!"

He studied her closely, shaking his head.

"Jane, you're such a brat," he breathed.

"I know," she admitted. "But I'm trying to grow up, even if I've left it a bit late."

She caught his hand to lead him into the farmhouse.

"Don't be mad that Amanda didn't call about me coming. I told her I would. She's out with her bees, but she knows you were headed here. We have a room all ready for you. I have so much to tell you, Morgan!"

"Well, I have a few things to tell you, as well," he replied. "But we'll start with you."

He followed his sister into the home of their friend, and she immediately led him into the kitchen to have him sit, while she made a fresh pot of coffee for him.

Morgan watched her flitting around the kitchen with an overwhelming sense of gratitude, and again thanked God for restoring Jane to him. He had gone from such heartrending grief to the greatest joy he could imagine, all within the space of a few short months.

Of course, the memory of all that brought Cora to him. His face softened as he thought about the way she had walked through his pain with him and helped him cry his tears and search for answers.

He remembered the night he sat with her in front of Ingleside Fare, and told her what he'd learned from the sheriff, and how she lifted her beautiful, tear-filled eyes to his, and rested in his arms, just being with him, and listening to him.

He was filled with a strong desire to feel her touch and look into those eyes and it caused a deep sigh to be heard by his sister, from across the room.

She came over to sit beside him, while the coffee was brewing and fastened him with a shrewd look, seeming to be trying to read him. "You're different," she observed.

"In what way?" he smiled, watching her narrow her eyes to view him closely.

"You're in love," she finally said, and Morgan wrinkled his brow, wondering how she could possibly have known that.

"I am," he freely admitted. "In fact, I'm getting married."

She lowered her eyes and a little frown settled on her face.

"Some socialite?" she finally asked, trying to sound as if she were teasing.

"Hardly," Morgan replied, becoming aware of a passing resentment that began to surface.

"I'm not here, Jane, to submit my personal life for your approval," he informed her in a gentle but firm tone. "There are many things that need to be discussed, but my role will primarily be to listen."

"In other words, you want me to explain myself."

"Unless you feel that you are perfectly justified in every one of your actions and decisions and that, as your only living relative, I have no right to an explanation."

She shook her head. "No, I know I made a mess of things and all you ever tried to do was help me, Morgan. I'm not trying to come off as suddenly having an attitude, I'm really not. But I know that's how it sounded, and I'm sorry."

He reached a hand over and laid it on hers. "We're good."

She gave him a little grin and settled back against the kitchen chair to continue looking at the brother she loved.

"One more comment, and then I'll drop it?"

"It depends." He lifted one brow and waited.

"I just want to say that you must love her a lot. Because I can see that you miss her."

"I'm lost without her," he confessed faintly.

"Then why didn't you bring her with you, Morgan?" she wondered, puzzled. "It would have been okay."

"She's on tour," he replied, causing his sister to stare.

"What kind of tour?"

"She's a classically trained musician and composer, and she's currently touring with an orchestra."

"You love classical music," Jane observed.

"I do."

"Where did you meet her?"

She was more than a little curious, since Morgan had never seemed interested in anything but his career.

"That's a long story," he said with an odd little grin. "And I'll be happy to tell it to you, but first things first. I'm here to find out about you, Janie."

He gave her hand a little squeeze. "Jane, why did you marry Michael Tewks?"

She blinked, a little surprised that this was his first question. She had expected him to grill her about losing the house he'd bought for her.

"I guess we just got caught up in the moment." She watched him look away with a slight eye roll.

"We were with some of my friends at a tribal gathering and a shaman performed a ceremony to unite us. The wedding was actually lovely, but the bliss didn't last."

She breathed out a sigh, and Morgan sat back and crossed his arms, fixing his naive sister with a hard stare.

"A shaman."

She nodded.

"The bliss."

She frowned and nodded again.

Morgan continued to gaze at his sister, wondering how she had made as many trips around the sun as she'd managed, so far.

"So, of course, you both went down to the county clerk of court's office and obtained your marriage license, before you headed on over to your tribal gathering."

"No, we just threw everything into the Bug and met up with everyone at the camp."

Morgan blew out a breath of relief. "Well, thank God for that," he muttered, causing his sister to look at him oddly.

He rested his eyes on her pretty face and relented, reaching out a finger and tapping her on the nose.

"Honey, you're not married, then."

She was more bewildered than ever. "I was there, Morgan, I know if we were married or not."

"Jane, if you didn't obtain a marriage license, you weren't married. I don't care how much smudging and handfasting and drum poundings went on. That's not how it works in the real world, Sis."

She managed to look both doubtful and relieved, simply regarding him with her childlike brown eyes, and telling herself that Morgan would always tell her the truth.

"Darrin is going to check into it for me."

"Darrin, as in Amanda's brother?"

She nodded. "He's an attorney."

"I knew he was aiming for that target, but I hadn't kept up with how it turned out," Morgan said. "But, Janie, there's hardly a need for an attorney. It's not even up for debate. You and Tewks were never married."

"Then why did Darrin tell me that he'd help me?"

Morgan smiled to himself, deciding that Darrin Hester was pulling a fast one over on his sister. He had always carried a torch for Jane and Morgan suspected he was using this an excuse to interact with her.

Jane looked at his smile and wondered what it meant, but he waved all that aside.

"Tell me about the house, Jane."

She lowered her eyes and focused on her hands.

"Morgan, I'm really sorry about losing the house. I know saying I'm sorry doesn't make up for it, but I'm sorrier than I can even say."

He immediately thought of the day his beautiful Cora walked right into him and wouldn't back down, when he demanded to know what she was doing there. A tender smile rested around his mouth. He wouldn't have Cora, if the house hadn't come up for auction.

"I'm not upset," he assured her, causing her to look up at him quickly in disbelief.

"Everything happens for a reason," he continued. "I only want to know what the circumstances were, that caused you to have to take out a second mortgage. I can only assume that losing the house involved Tewks."

She nodded. "I took out the second mortgage before I met him. I wanted to start a studio and art store downtown. But I met him a little while later and after he moved in, money just seemed to get tighter and tighter, and then we started missing payments."

"Sweetie, why didn't you just call me for the money, if you wanted to start a business?"

She shrugged. "I guess I was starting to feel like a nobody. I was afraid you'd think I only called you when I wanted money. So I tried to do it on my own. I think I could have managed it, if I hadn't gotten married."

He flashed her a look and she corrected herself. "If he hadn't moved into the house, I mean."

"Why didn't you at least take Ned Frazier's calls to see if he could help you work something out?"

"Michael took my phone. He had it for a long time."

Harley had told him that, he remembered. He just shook his head again.

"When did things begin to get violent with Tewks, Jane?"

She folded her arms and looked out toward the window in the back door, and the daylight reflected in her eyes.

"I guess not long after he moved in. It was mostly just yelling and threatening until we got evicted. Then it got worse."

"I'm sorry that I waited so long to come looking for you, Jane," Morgan said softly, with a sadness in his eyes.

"I could have called you, Morgan, at any time. Even if I had to borrow someone's phone, I could have gotten in touch with you, so that's on me. You had to have known that."

"I did know that, which only confused me more. You and I would occasionally have trouble getting in touch, but sooner or later, we'd manage to talk. I'd gotten so involved with a land dispute that by the time I realized how long it had been since we talked, and you still weren't responding, I grabbed a flight and took off to see what was going on. That's when I found out that you were gone.

"Tewks had told the sheriff that you had drowned, and when I first heard it I was devastated, but after I had time to work through it, I knew something was wrong with his story.

"I hired an investigator and a dive team to help me figure things out. Your friend Debra, at the restaurant, was very helpful in pointing us in the right direction and Harley was invaluable. I owe that young man a huge debt."

Jane smiled at the mention of her protector and friend. "Harley always looked out for me. He has the spirit of an eagle."

Morgan couldn't resist giving his sister another eye roll, and laughed quietly.

"You're a mess, Janie," he informed her.

"But you love me, anyway."

"I suppose so."

They both looked up as the back door opened suddenly and Amanda Hester came in, pulling loose straw from her auburn hair and removing her coat.

She turned to recognize Morgan with a friendly grin. Her face was tanned, even in winter, from her time outdoors and she looked down at her damp jeans in apology.

"Excuse my welcoming you from a distance," she laughed, as Morgan stood to greet her. "I've been packing straw around the hives and mucking around in what was pretty snow, but now it's just gray slush. I'm a mess!"

She pulled off her gloves. "How are you, Morgan?"

"I'm very well, Amanda. How are you and the bees?"

"So far, so good," she laughed. "I've been having a time the past few days keeping them warm, but I reduced some of the entrances to keep the drafts out and that should help."

She moved over to a nearby stool and lifted herself up onto it to remove her wet socks.

"I don't normally end up with my feet wet, but I misjudged the depth of what I thought was just a puddle."

She drew in a deep breath. "I may never be warm again."

With that, she hopped off the stool and headed toward the hallway. "But I'm gonna try. Excuse me just a moment, please, while I thaw out in a hot shower and do what I can to be a little more presentable."

They watched her leave, and Morgan sat back down and gave his sister a questioning look.

"It's not that I'm not glad that Amanda was able to take you in, Jane, but what made you think of calling her? And, again, not to put too fine a point on it, why didn't you simply call me to come get you?"

She folded her arms on the table and laid her head down, to rest her chin on them. "I thought if I could get far away from there, I could maybe start over, and I remembered how nice this farm is and how sweet Amanda always was to me.

"I didn't see how I could fit into your life up north, Morgan. You're so busy and even though you work in timber, you spend most of your time in skyscrapers and board meetings and things like that. I wouldn't even know what to do with myself. I just thought that coming to the country might be a better solution.

"And by then, I was already too ashamed to call you anyway. I was too big of a screw up."

Morgan remembered Harley telling him this, and a sense of remorse settled on him, as he realized that his little sister had felt left behind in his wake. He lifted his eyes and she saw the sorrow in them and wished immediately that she chosen her words more carefully.

"Jane, when Mom and Dad left us, I didn't stop to think how you would have been affected. I deliberately buried myself in my work and you were left on your own. I'm so sorry."

She felt tears crowding her eyes and hopped up to come around behind his chair and wrap her arms around him.

"I've always been so proud of you, Morgan. Don't ever feel that you failed me. I've always known that you were just a phone call away. You can't take the blame for my bad choices."

He reached up to clasp her arms and she dropped a kiss on his cheek, before reaching to pull her chair closer to his and settle back down.

"You were going to tell me where you met your fiancée," she reminded him.

Chapter Fourteen

Amanda Hester had been mortified when she had rushed into the back door only to have Morgan Roberts, of all people, witness the wet, muddy state she was in. Of course, she'd known he was coming but she thought she'd have time to get out to the hives and come back.

That hadn't been the case, and after she caught her reflection in the bathroom mirror, she stared at her flushed cheeks and messy hair and continued to feel embarrassed about her filthy condition.

Morgan and Jane were her old friends, so she realized that she was making a big deal out of nothing, but when he had looked up at her with a slight reaction, she had wanted to sink through the floor.

Now she stood, to "thaw out" in her shower, and washed the remaining straw and filth out of her long hair, then hopped out to bend over and work a hair dryer through it, causing the natural curl to return, as her auburn locks began to lightly move, drying in the current.

She climbed into a more respectable pair of jeans and a sweatshirt, then inspected her face for the need to apply any makeup, but decided that she was who she was, and after what Morgan had just witnessed, it couldn't be any worse.

She drew in a deep breath, her blue eyes critically looking for any dirt she might have missed, before she cleaned up the bathroom and headed back out to begin planning dinner.

When she silently padded back into the kitchen, she heard Morgan telling his sister about the woman he'd found at Jane's little house, who had bought it and had fixed it up to live in.

Morgan glanced up, startled at Amanda's transformation and she looked down at herself with a self-conscious little laugh.

"Can you imagine, if I worked with pigs, instead of just bees, Morgan?"

She began taking some ingredients out of the refrigerator to begin their evening meal, and he smiled at her question.

"I have to admit, you clean up well, Amanda."

Jane turned around to give her friend a wide-eyed stare.

"Can you believe this, Amanda? Morgan went out to my old house looking for me, and found a woman there that he's now engaged to!"

Amanda was glad she had her back to them, since it gave her a moment to recover. She glanced back at them now with a little grin.

"I suppose I have to believe it, since it sounds like one of those things people say you can't make up."

"She's a musician," Jane added, "and she's touring with an orchestra now. My family was always into classical music and Mom and Dad took us to a lot of concerts, when we were growing up. I think that's how she cracked Morgan's hard shell, since no other woman ever has."

Jane looked over at her brother, with a question in her dark eyes. "You never told me her name."

"Cora Hartmann," he supplied, enjoying the sound of it.

Amanda drew in a breath. Cora Hartmann was a beauty. She had read the article in the paper about her, but she had also seen her when she and Darrin went to a Christmas concert in Cincinnati, a couple of years ago.

"Cora Hartmann is a lovely woman," she admitted lightly. "And very gifted. Darrin and I saw her in concert."

Morgan looked up quickly. "Then you've had an honor I've not yet had, although I can claim a personal performance recently that had me spellbound."

He caught Jane's brows lifting and laughed at her.

"Her piano and cello are at the little cabin now, and I was finally able to convince her to play for me. She's writing an opus and she let me hear a nocturne that's likely to be a part of it."

"Oh, it's a cabin now?" Jane latched onto that, and Morgan pulled out his phone to show her the changes.

Jane drew in her breath and placed a hand over her heart as she saw how the little ugly duckling of a house had become a beautiful swan.

She thought of something and frowned up at her brother. "I'm afraid I left a lot of junk in the attic."

"First of all, it wasn't junk, Janie. It was some of your finest work. In fact, Cora and I claimed what we call twin paintings, and we each have one."

"You mean the view from the porch," she grinned.

"It's very lovely." He reached over and tweaked her nose with a little wink. "Cora carefully wrapped the rest of your art, piece by piece, and we placed it in a climate-controlled storage facility, so it's much safer there than in the attic."

"That was a lot of trouble," she said woefully, before changing her expression to all smiles. "But I'm glad you did it. Thank you."

She leaned over and smacked him on the cheek.

Amanda watched them with a little smile, relieved that Jane had managed to land on her feet. Amanda sat down with her, shortly after Lily brought her and her duffle bag to her front door, and made Jane tell her the whole, incredible story.

It could have ended so differently, and she knew that Morgan would have been inconsolable if his fairy of a sister had ended up dead, as she was rumored to have been.

She wasn't sure what Jane's long-term plans were, but she was no trouble, and wasn't in the way, and it was nice to actually have someone else around, since her evenings could get lonely, even though her days were long and tiresome.

She finished dressing the chicken for the roasting pan and slid it into the oven, then stood washing her hands at the sink, looking at across the fields that were a dark gray now that the sun had set.

Morgan watched her, wondering if she might be having second thoughts about having Jane there, and possibly hoping that he'd come to urge her to come home with him.

He purposed in his heart to do that very thing, the next time he and Jane were alone, before he returned to the airport to fly back home, the next day.

"I told Darrin you would be here, so he's joining us for dinner," she said, continuing to peer out the window at her old dog who was dragging something into the backyard.

She shook her head with a sigh. "Hang on. Bentley seems to have been pillaging from across the road, again."

She headed out the backdoor, and Jane read Morgan's mind with a little laugh.

"Yep, it's the same Bentley. He'll outlive us all."

He just shook his head with a grin.

"So, Darrin's dropping by," he ventured, watching her face carefully for any tell-tale expression.

She folded her arms and gave him a deadpan look.

"Oh, stop it."

"I'm just saying it'll be good to see him again."

Morgan laughed at her pursed lips and little fist.

"It's not like that," she insisted.

"I don't see why not," he teased. "It always was like that."

Jane hopped up and surprised him by getting him into a headlock and threatening to decapitate him.

He gently foiled her plan by releasing her grip with little effort, reminding her who was the bigger and stronger one.

"I missed you, you little pest," he said softly, raking a hand through her unruly curls.

He made her let him stand, so that he could go retrieve his bag from the car and let her show him to his room, so that he could hopefully manage to speak with Cora before dinner.

✳✳✳

Cora stood shuffling her music into order and then tapping the sheets onto the table top, making a neat stack, before slipping it all inside her leather portfolio case.

She looked up as Andrew Holland paused to watch her.

"Tonight was some of your finest work, Cora," he complimented lightly.

"Thank you, Andrew," she replied wearily. "I do wish I could play my last number just after intermission though, rather than at the end of the program. I'm always so tired by then, that all I want to do is just get through it, so I can leave."

He frowned and moved closer to inspect her. "That's hardly the attitude I expect from my solo artist."

"Well, it's the one you're going to get," she sighed, lifting a hand to the side of her neck and then down, to grasp her right trapezius muscle to begin slowly kneading it.

He reached over to do that for her, but she walked away, and began gathering the rest of her things.

The conductor noticed the way she put distance between them. He wasn't used to being rebuffed by the female members of the touring orchestra. In his early forties, with his dark hair beginning to gray around the temples and his lean good looks, he never seemed to lack the attention of not only the women in the orchestra, but of fans, as well.

Cora Hartmann, however, had always managed to not only seem oblivious to his charm, but coolly detached in a way that implied only the most basic tolerance, and that for the sake of the tour.

Andrew Holland had not only noticed Cora's indifferent manner, he had also seen the engagement ring on her left hand, and immediately decided that it would not suit his purposes at all for his star performer to get married.

Having Cora Hartmann as his featured soloist guaranteed sold out performances, and the last thing he needed was for her to make a husband her priority over her music.

"So, Cora," he ventured, aimlessly pacing around the room, "I see congratulations are in order."

She looked up at him with a puzzled frown, until he nodded toward her ring. She smiled down at it, and glanced back up with a much brighter countenance.

"Thank you."

"When is the big day?" he asked, nonchalantly.

"The first week in April."

He frowned and looked up with surprise. "Immediately following the tour?"

"Yes, the very next thing, in fact."

"How are you able to plan something as big as a wedding, and still keep up with the tour?" he wondered, in an effort to gather information.

"It won't be a big wedding," she replied. "Just something small and intimate. That's all we want."

"And who is the lucky groom, if that's not privileged information?"

She touched a finger to her ring, with a softness resting on her face. "Morgan Roberts."

He repeated the name, as if trying to place it. "It sounds vaguely familiar. Is he a fellow musician, or perhaps a patron of the arts?"

"He may be a patron, but that's not how he's known. He's a timber baron up in the northwest."

Andrew raised his brows. He did know of him. Morgan Roberts was interviewed on various newscasts, from time to time, sought out for his knowledge of environmental practices, his occasionally testifying before government committees, and his many acquisitions.

He couldn't imagine how Cora had made his acquaintance, but he determined that she would not become one of Morgan Robert's acquisitions.

"I do think it's very much to our advantage to save the piano portion of your performance for the end of the program, Cora. If it were to be moved to occur just after intermission, then what's to stop people from suddenly feeling the need to leave early, once you've played?"

She raised her eyes to regard him with disapproval.

"I agreed to join this tour as a soloist, but not as a workhorse. I need to either be allowed to take breaks during those times when my presence is not absolutely vital to the concert, or I may have to cut the tour short. I'm beginning to feel used as a celebrity trap, and I don't like it.

"I should not have to be on stage for the entire program, and the fact that I seem to be expected to be, suggests that I am appearing solely to guarantee attendance.

"If that's the case, then I have a life, and I might as well get on with living it."

Andrew drew in his breath and hurried to smooth things over with Cora.

"I did notice your seeming to have some soreness around your shoulders, Cora, so perhaps you're right. I expect I get so caught up in the way this particular orchestra melds so seamlessly together, that I'm reluctant to do without any one member, but at the same time, I can't have you becoming so tired and worn out, that you feel leaving the tour is necessary."

She folded her arms and seemed to be trying to discern his sudden change of heart, when he had been so insistent on her remaining visible to the audience for the entire concert.

He pulled a copy of the program from his own portfolio and looked down at it, moving closer to her and offering it for her to view, as well.

"I believe that this will work. We already have an overture before your cello solo, prior to intermission. You can slip out before the overture begins and come back when it's time for your solo. Just make sure that your instrument is dialed in, before you return to it."

He continued poring over the program, seeming to stand even closer, but Cora was so ready to be granted a reasonable break that she hadn't noticed, but kept scanning the sheet for another possibility.

"Of course, we can have a concerto grosso just before your final piano performance. You can simply walk onstage after that, to the recognition and applause of the audience."

He turned to look at her.

"In fact, that might be rather special, I would think."

She didn't return his gaze, but continued focusing on the two sections he had pointed out to her and nodded.

"That sounds reasonable, Andrew," she agreed. "Let's try that then, and see how it works."

"Absolutely! And you're no workhorse or celebrity trap, Cora. I'm very sorry to have made you feel that way."

He gave her a smile and a slight nod, then made his way out of the room, leaving Cora equally surprised and bewildered.

Andrew Holland never gave in that easily, so she had already prepared herself to leave the tour, since she knew she couldn't keep up with the demands he was placing on her.

She stared after him thoughtfully, before slipping her perfectly tailored floor-length cashmere overcoat over her lovely evening gown, gathering her belongings and leaving to meet the driver that the hotel had sent to pick her up.

She allowed him to open the rear door in order for her to be seated, then he waited until she had lifted her long garments inside the car, before closing the door and coming around to drive her to her accommodations.

She pulled her phone out of her bag, and was dismayed to see that Morgan had tried to reach her. She hurriedly sent a text to him, asking if he would try again in a half hour.

"I'm so sorry, Morgan. My phone was turned off, and I've only just now found that I missed your call. I should be at the hotel and in my room within a half hour. I hope you will please try again. I love you so much, and I desperately miss you. All I want in this world, outside of being in your arms, is to at least hear your voice. No, that's not true. I also long, with all my heart, for the first week in April."

Morgan heard the text come in and his dark, stoic demeanor instantly changed to quiet joy.

The others around the dinner table noticed it and Jane gave her brother a little nudge with her foot, but other than a lifting of her brows and a little grin, she resisted the urge to tease him. He gave her a soft wink, then hurried to send Cora a brief reply, assuring her that he would certainly try again.

"I'm sorry, I don't mean to be rude," he apologized to Amanda and her brother. "I did need to reply, but I'm not the sort to stare at my phone during dinner, I can assure you."

Amanda looked down at her plate with a little smile and Morgan noticed her uneasiness. He hurried to compliment the meal, and tease her about not putting honey in everything.

She laughed at that and admitted that she knew enough recipes with honey to write a cook book with that theme.

He smiled and checked the time, then allowed himself to relax, looking over at Darrin Hester with a mischievous air.

"So, Darrin... I'm sure you've worked long and hard to determine the validity of Jane's marriage. Have you been able to find a loophole that would work to her advantage?"

Darrin caught the humorous sarcasm in Morgan's question and returned his look with a wry grin, while Jane gazed up at him hopefully.

"Why yes, I have, Morgan," he returned cheerfully, causing the man to rest a hand over his mouth and shake with silent laughter, while Jane clapped her fingers together in excitement.

"It turns out that Jane's wedding was only ceremonial in context but lacked the conditions required to make it legally binding. She is, therefore, married to no one."

"You don't say," Morgan commented, with amusement hovering in his eyes.

"Oh, it's true!" Darrin assured him, having a hard time to keep from laughing, himself.

He had known that Morgan would see through his offer to help Jane, but the fact that he was playing along wasn't a surprise. Darrin had always pegged Morgan Roberts to be a stand-up kind of guy.

Suddenly, Jane took on a look of dismay. "But that means none of the others were married, either!"

"I would say not," Darrin agreed, raising his eyes to Morgan's with laughter still threatening.

"Oh, that's so sad," Jane breathed. "Not for me, though, because there was no bliss. But for the others, that is just too sad to think about."

"If you'll please excuse me," Morgan said, rising as much to keep from laughing out loud at his sister, as to go to his room to call Cora, "I need to take care of something. Amanda, dinner was amazing. Thank you so much."

He shot Darrin another dangerously comical look, before smiling his way to his room, to talk to the woman he loved.

Chapter Fifteen

Jane balanced on a log while she chattered away to her brother, who stood watching her with affection and amusement. He listened not so much to what she was telling him, although it was certainly entertaining, but more to the childlike, whimsical lilt in her voice that he'd feared he might never hear again.

"Honey, the bark on that log is peeling off. You need to be careful, or you'll end up sitting in the mud."

She halted in her riveting tale of a gathering that she and Lily had gone to and how they had taken part in a cleansing ritual that was so invigorating, although she was allergic to whatever was in the tea they brewed for her, and her face was splotchy for over a week.

Now, she gave Morgan an eye roll. "Mud is one of the best things you can sit in! Mud baths have spiritual properties and its composition is completely organic. A cleansing mud bath is an ancient ritual that rejuvenates your spirit and soothes away the stress that you may not even know you have."

"Trust me, when I have stress, I'm well aware of it," Morgan laughed quietly. "In any event, I don't think the mud used in spas is what's on the ground, here. It smells as if Bentley might have contributed to its organic composition."

Jane stopped walking up and down the length of the log and gave her brother a little giggle. She pretended that she couldn't get down by herself and held her arms out to Morgan, who caught her and swung her away from the mud, so that she could plant her feet on solid ground.

She folded her arms and gave her brother an affected sad face, along with what he called her puppy eyes.

"Why do you have to go back, today?"

"I have a lot to tend to."

"But you just got here yesterday."

"I've been gone from my office a great deal the past few months, Janie, and I need to get back up there and take some of the load off my head of operations, and fulfill my promise to a country that's trying to implement some preservation methods."

She gave him a expressionless gape. "I don't even know what language you're speaking."

He grinned at her and ruffled her dark hair. "I've experienced that same sort of confusion myself, over the years."

Jane's attention was drawn past him to Amanda, who had gone out of the back door and could now been seen from where she and Morgan were standing, as she made her way out to check on her hives.

"Amanda's pretty, don't you think?"

"Yes," he conceded. "And so are you." He bopped her harmlessly on her head.

"Sisters don't count."

"Since I'm in love with Cora, and plan to marry her soon, neither does Amanda, or any other woman," Morgan informed his kid sister, gently chiding her, by the way he rested his eyes on hers and examined her.

"What's she like?" Jane demanded, turning her attention back to him and letting him catch her hand to lead her into the house, in order to finish his packing.

"She's very beautiful, of course, so let's go ahead and establish that," he said with a little smile.

He opened the door for her and followed her over to sit for a few minutes, before he had to leave her.

"She's gentle."

"How do you mean, gentle?" Jane wondered, idly wrapping her arms around a pillow and gazing up at him.

"I don't mean weak, or that's she's a sissy, if that's what you're thinking," he replied. "I mean she's meek, even though she has strength. The day I met her, I was angry and about as rude as I could be, but she just stood there unafraid, and calmly watched me with her beautiful, green eyes."

"Green eyes are actually rare," Jane observed.

"Hers certainly are," Morgan said softly.

"She felt sorry for the situation I was faced with, but she had no intention of just rolling over and giving up the house she bought, and she wasn't about to let me bully her."

He saw that Jane was feeling badly about how upset he'd been, and he gave her a soft wink.

"Cora's an amazing, talented musician and composer, and music just seems to flow out of her."

He stopped and contemplated Jane. "She's a Christian."

Jane looked as if she didn't know why he threw that in.

"Okay," she finally said slowly.

"Jane, Mom and Dad were Christians, and they raised us to be. As a little girl, you seemed to be very devoted to your beliefs, but the day came, when you were still just a girl, that you began seeking everywhere else for whatever it was you seemed to need. What was that about, honey?"

He wasn't criticizing her, because he was certainly not the model of a Christian man, himself, but he had always felt that Jane abandoned her faith for a reason, rather than she had just become bored and more interested in other practices.

She shrugged. "I was just exploring all my options."

"Do you believe that all those other things you follow after are a means to enter Heaven, Janie?" Morgan drew his brows and frowned.

She let out a loud, exaggerated sigh. "Oh, I don't know, Morgan. This is getting too deep."

She stopped and gave him a coy look.

"Tell me the most fascinating thing about Cora Hartmann, that will really tell me who she is."

"I can actually do that," he replied lightly. "Although this fascinating thing was a year or so before Cora came into this world." He smiled at her curious face.

"You knew Cora's mother."

Jane widened her eyes in amazement.

"How is that even possible?"

"Because when you were just a little thing, Cora's mother and father came to our house to visit. They had become friends with Mom and Dad. And you..." he reached over to touch the tip of her nose lightly, "for whatever reason, were fascinated, to use your word, with Cora's mother, and you wouldn't keep your little hands off of her, the entire time they were there."

"She had a light inside her," Jane whispered to herself.

Morgan heard her, but he didn't understand.

Jane looked up at him, with a peaceful expression in her eyes. "Does Cora have a light inside her, Morgan?"

He gave her a tender smile. "She does."

"Maybe I'll get to see it, then," she breathed.

"At our wedding, Janie."

She seemed to be thinking hard about something, but lifted her eyes to his.

"So, first week in April?"

"Absolutely."

She appeared to be processing. "Maybe I'll make it."

He held up a fist and a mock look of fierceness.

"If I have to come looking for you again, Miss Priss, you'd better know that whatever weird astrological alignment you're currently chasing after, it won't actually get you into Heaven. That'll be useful information, for when I get my hands on you."

She grabbed his fist in both hands and held onto it, then rested her cheek on it.

"I love you, Morgan."

"Well, I love you too, pipsqueak," he returned, giving her a quiet, searching look. She seemed to be troubled.

"Are you okay, Janie?"

"I'm amazing," she claimed, with a big grin.

"Wait!" She hurriedly changed her expression to one of theatrical fatigue and malaise.

"No, I'm not! You'd better stay here, Morgan, and just keep an eye on me. I think my chakras are all clogged up."

He laughed indulgently and dropped a little kiss on her brow. "Nice try, squirt. But I know nothing of chakras, so you're on your own."

She hopped up when he began to make his way to the guestroom to gather his things together, and landed on the bed with a bounce.

"I'm very relieved to know that I can still call myself Jane Roberts," she let her brother know. "Tewks is not a pleasing name, to me. It never flowed."

"I'm glad to hear that," Morgan declared, grabbing his phone charger and tablet and slipping them into his carry on. "Plus, as you pointed out, there was no bliss."

"Bliss is vital to achieve happiness. If there's no bliss, then all you have is someone living in the house with you, who leaves dirty socks everywhere and beer cans on every horizontal service. But when there's bliss, you don't mind, as much. I told you Darrin would help me," she reminded him, a bit smugly.

"Oh, I'm sure he was awake all night, until he could figure out a way to rescue you out of that marriage," her brother murmured, deliberately not looking at her, in order to not hurt her feelings by laughing at her.

He stopped to consider her thoughtfully. "Jane, you turned thirty on your last birthday."

"It's an important milestone," she assured him, with wide, serious brown eyes.

"Oh, it is," he agreed. "I'll be reaching forty in a couple of years, and I hear that one is pretty important as well."

"Yes, but forty makes men unbalanced," Jane let him know, with the same expert tone of a trained psychologist.

"Does it?" he laughed. "I'll try to watch out for that."

He glanced around, satisfying himself that he had everything together, then sat down beside her on the bed, and gave her an intent look.

"Don't say sad stuff," his little sister implored, with a rush of emotion coming into her pretty face.

She pressed her lips together tightly and Morgan slipped an arm around her, to pull her close.

After a moment of rocking back and forth, she raised her somber face and regarded Morgan with such a sorrowful look, that it stung him.

"What's wrong, little one?" he asked, his own eyes beginning to mist over.

"Goodbyes are hard."

He thought about that. "We've said goodbye plenty of times, and I expect we'll say plenty of them in the future. Why is this one hurting you so much?"

She stared down at her hands, and simply shook her head.

Morgan waited, trying to think of anything he could say to bring a smile to her face, but he could see that their time of laughing and teasing had come to an end. He reached a hand to pull her hair back and rested his head against hers.

"What can I do, JR?" he whispered.

She smiled and looked up at him. "Remember, we had a long talk about you reducing me down to the alphabet?"

He grinned at that. "I remember your getting mad at me and using the alphabet to skillfully cuss me out, right in front of Mom and Dad. That's what I remember."

She giggled, in spite of her sadness. "Remember when mom figured out what KMA stood for, and sent me to my room, right when it was time for Bob Ross to come on TV?"

"Oh, that had to be the worst for you," he laughed. "That was the equivalent of making a kid miss Christmas."

"I showed her! I stayed in my room the rest of the night, and painted my own happy landscape and it was awesome!"

She looked up in the general direction of Heaven. "Joke's on you, Mom!"

They both laughed, but Jane couldn't seem to hold it together, and began to cry, in spite of her determination not to.

Morgan wrapped her up protectively and kissed the top of her head, staring vacantly down at the floor and feeling powerless to help her. Whatever it was, he knew her well enough to know that she wasn't ready to talk about it.

"Well, Jane Roberts, will you be escorting me out to my car, so that you can give me all your last minute wisdom?"

She twisted her lips into a pout. "I guess so."

He stood and slung his carry on over his shoulder, and grabbed the handle of his small, wheeled suitcase, keeping a hand free to take hold of Jane's.

She walked out to the rental car and stood hugging herself while he tossed everything into the backseat, then stepped into his hug, giving him a tight squeeze.

"Thank you, Morgan, for coming to look for me. And for coming here to see me."

He pulled back and looked down at her steadily. "You don't have to thank me for that, Janie. You're my family, and I'm yours. So, there's love."

"There is," she agreed.

"Please thank Amanda for her hospitality, Jane, and tell Darrin how very much I appreciate all the work and trouble he invested, in order to help you."

He kept a straight face, in spite of the look of incredulity she gave him.

"I know, right? That was so totally amazing of him to do all that for me!"

"You've got some good friends here, sweetie. I hope you stay put for a while." Morgan brushed her long bangs back out of her eyes. "Amanda said that you are a breath of fresh air and that you can stay as long as you want."

"Well..." She smiled down at the ground and shrugged. "Maybe. I do have a couple of things I want to do with some friends in March, but I guess I could come back here, after that."

Morgan sighed and looked away, feeling troubled.

"Sis, please do come back here, after that. Either call me to come get you and I'll drop everything to make it happen, or do come back here, but please always let me know where you are, and that you're okay."

"I'll write you," she promised.

"Do people still do that?"

"I do. I write beautiful letters and infuse them with essential oils and add some art on the back. People love my letters, just so you know!"

He looked down at her fondly. "Why haven't I ever gotten one of those letters, Janie?"

"You will! I promise. I love you, MR."

He laughed and gave her one last hug.

"I love you too, JR."

She knew she couldn't stand there and watch her brother drive away, and he seemed to know it as well, so he smiled as she danced her way back to the porch and blew him a kiss, before heading inside.

He couldn't understand why he cried most of the way to the airport.

Chapter Sixteen

Cora lifted the weight of her hair off her neck and looked around for something to hold it up, so that it didn't fall forward every time she bent her head down to read her music.

She spotted a pencil and pushed it up and then back down through her twisted hair, stopping to remember when she'd done that in her cabin's studio and had forgotten about it, until Morgan surprised her with a video call and immediately reacted.

It had been a couple of days since she'd spoken to Morgan but she knew that he was just getting back after spending a little time with Jane, and Cora certainly understood how traveling seemed to throw everything off course.

She glanced down at her phone, always hoping to find a text from him that she might have missed, but there was nothing that she hadn't already responded to.

After a long, unsatisfied moment, she told herself that no rule had been established since the invention of the smart phone that prohibited a woman from being the first one to text. She realized that he was probably in a meeting, but she couldn't stop herself from texting a heart to him.

Before she could lay her phone back down, it dinged and she checked her texts to find that he had sent her two hearts.

She grinned and sent him three, and he volleyed with four. When she sent him five hearts, he sent back a trophy, a smiling emoji and a clock. Cora knew that was his way of telling her that she'd won, for now. She sent him a lipstick kiss mark, just to mess with him, in case he was getting these texts in front of a table full of board members, and he sent back heart eyes and TTYL. She laid her phone back down with a lift to her spirit, excited for the "talk to you later" abbreviation that he added.

She had trouble getting back into the proper mindset to prepare for tonight's performance, because Morgan was not one to simply pass through her mind, and then move on. Morgan Roberts moved *in*.

She glanced at the clock and decided that she'd earned a break and closed her eyes to envision him. She could never think of Morgan without the little daydream of seeing him coming through the trees to her, that Jane's painting always inspired, whenever she'd stare at it.

Cora had taken a photo of the painting before she left for the tour and looked at it first thing in the morning and last, at night. It was a connection between them.

She jumped when her phone rang, thinking it was too good to be true for it to be Morgan, and it was. She rolled her pretty eyes and debated whether or not to answer it, but then finally decided that Andrew Holland would show up at her door, if she didn't.

"Yes, Andrew?"

"Cora, are you planning to be present for sound check, or not? If you are, you're welcome to ride with me. I'll be leaving in an hour, if that's not rushing you?"

She scowled, then breathed a sigh. "Actually, Andrew, I'm going to stay here until shortly before concert time. My cello is already there, and I don't anticipate any major tuning issues. I keep it pretty much dialed in."

He frowned with displeasure. "How are you arriving?"

"I'll send for a car. Don't worry, I'll allow plenty of time."

The conductor continued to be vexed by his star performer's streak of independence and was unsuccessful at covering up his impatience.

"Please check in with me the moment you arrive."

He hung up abruptly, but Cora wasted no time worrying about his disappointment. She knew it would be a long night, once she arrived at the hall, and the likelihood of her getting to speak with Morgan would be very slim, after midnight.

If there was any chance of hearing from him before she left, she would just stay in her room, as long as she could.

She pulled her music back over to look through it and make sure that everything was in the correct order listed in the program, then laid it down with a restless sigh.

She had about three hours before she had to be at the hall, and surely Morgan's meeting wouldn't last that long. If that's what he was doing, she amended. He might simply just be swamped, due to all the time he'd been gone.

He'd sent her a selfie he'd taken of Jane and him the day he arrived in Ohio to see her, and Cora looked at it again, smiling at how very much Jane resembled her brother.

Morgan had once told her that the both of them favored his father, Evan, and that his mother had complained that she did all the work and grew the babies, and neither of them even had the decency to look like her.

In fact, as Morgan had observed, sifting Cora's golden locks through his fingers and appreciating her fair, flawless complexion, it was a shame that his mother had never met her, since she actually resembled Candace Roberts far more than her own children. He seemed pleased to have made that discovery.

Cora studied Jane intently, and could almost hear her voice, and her laugh, but as she looked closer, she saw an expression in Jane's eyes that made her sad. She looked lost somehow, even held in her brother's safe arms, and with a smile on her beautiful face.

Surely Morgan was aware of it, being as close to Jane as he was, Cora decided. She felt a pang of regret that she had never met Jane, and hoped that she would somehow be able to attend their wedding in April.

Her eyes were of course drawn to Morgan's handsome face and to the smile of joy that came from having his sister safely by his side, after fearing the worst.

She couldn't help indulging in a quiet laugh, thinking about Morgan calling her while he was there, and telling her that Jane had never been married after all, since a shaman officiated at their campfire wedding, but that their attorney friend made it seem as if he was working fearlessly and putting in long hours to help her break out of her prison of a marriage.

When Morgan told her about it, he'd had to get up off the bed, and make sure the door was closed, so that they wouldn't hear him laughing. He found it incredibly funny, and she got to see him lay back against the pillows on his bed and laugh until tears began to form.

She kissed her fingertip and touched his face, before putting her phone away and considering if a nice hot shower might help her relax before the concert, then deciding that she didn't want to risk a video call that would prove far more embarrassing than being caught with a pencil stuck in her hair.

As she thought of the pencil, she hurried to pull it out, in case he did call, and let her hair fall back down.

She was glad she had decided to hold off on taking a shower, and her pulse began racing when a special ringtone told her that Morgan was calling.

She answered right away, and his eyes lit up when he could see her beautiful face.

"There's my sweetheart," he murmured, giving her a look that made her feel as if he had just kissed her.

"I love you," she breathed.

He gave her a lazy grin. "I love you, as well. Especially when you're texting me hearts and kisses while I'm in the middle of meeting with South American government officials."

"Oh, I'm sorry," she began, but he gave her a soft wink and slightly shook his head.

"Don't you ever be sorry for letting me know that you love me, Cora."

She lifted a hand to her face, feeling a slight rush of color, and he took a moment to just trade a long look with her.

"So, March is upon us," he finally said lightly. "Four more weeks of touring, then?"

She nodded and grimaced. "I'm so over it."

"Would you be so over it, if I wasn't part of the picture?"

"You're the entire picture, Morgan. I just want to check out of this hotel and grab a plane back home, so badly."

"Do you miss the little cabin?" he asked, ignoring his office phone by simply reaching a hand to silence it.

"I miss the sofa," she laughed and he happily agreed.

"There's not another sofa like that one, in all the world. Wherever you and I set up housekeeping, we must have it."

She had such a longing in her face, that it struck him and he whispered her name to comfort her.

"We can do this," he assured her. "We're well over the halfway mark, so we'll just stay focused, sweetheart, and before you know it, I'll be flying down to meet you at the cabin. I'll be the one on the sofa."

She laughed at that, and he glanced down with a wash of annoyance, as his secretary apparently felt the need to persist in her efforts to continue calling him.

"That sounds as if it may be important," Cora observed. "I should let you go, Morgan. I just wanted to see your face and hear your voice before I leave for the hall."

"One of these days, you'll be seeing my face more than you'd like, especially when you find dirty socks strewn about and beer cans on every horizontal surface. But it'll be fine, because in our case, there'll be bliss."

She wrinkled her brow and he laughed.

"Just something my crazy Janie said. Since I'm decidedly anti-clutter and I'm not a beer drinker, I expect our bliss will be all the more pleasurable."

She continued to look confused but gave him a sweet smile, and he sighed with an aching to hold her.

He hadn't denied that his phone ringing was likely an important matter, so Cora reluctantly told him that she'd let him get back to business and prepare to head for the hall.

They each shared a soft "I love you" before the call was reluctantly ended and each sat alone, dealing with the emotions that these brief interactions always seemed to stir.

When Andrew Holland spied Cora entering the stage, he held up a hand to signal his concertmaster.

"Can you leave that, until after you make certain that Cora's cello is ready? I see she's just arrived."

Richard Ackerman glanced over and immediately made his way to meet her at her instrument, as Andrew watched her speak to a few musicians and slowly move toward her chair.

Richard busied himself with hearing Cora test her tuning and then examined her bow, providing a backup to lay next to it. When he was done, he moved on to fulfill his other duties as concertmaster and Cora gave another listen to the resonance of her strings, not noticing Andrew slowly coming to stand next to her and observe.

"Were you able to get a nap?" he inquired.

She looked up at him, and then returned her focus to her cello. "I didn't feel the need for one."

"Well, you've mentioned how tired you are, so I just assumed that you bought yourself a few extra hours to catch up on your rest. I also assume that you're ready?"

She flashed him an annoyed expression. "Is that my track record, Andrew, that I'm not likely to be ready?"

He smiled tightly without replying, then strolled over to stand behind his elevated podium, moving his eyes over the entire orchestra, waiting for them to look at him and get quiet.

"It's almost concert time," he informed them. "I want you all to focus on unity, precision and an emotional connection with the music. In position, at the ready. All eyes on me."

The concert was underway and for one hour until the intermission, the audience was enchanted with very pleasing layers of musical complexity and skill.

When Cora Hartmann was featured at her cello, she held them spellbound. She was relieved when Andrew didn't single her out to stand during the applause, as she felt this sort of thing chipped away at the unanimity and cohesion of the orchestra as a whole, although she had come to expect his insistence that she do so after her final performance at the end of each concert.

Now, she slipped away for the twenty minute intermission to steal a few moments alone and stretch her toned arms, and rub the back of her neck.

She saw Andrew enter the green room and rather than remain standing, she decided to sit in a winged back chair, in order to discourage him from offering to assist her in relieving her sore muscles, as he had tried to do on occasion.

Instead, he moved casually around the room, conversing with different musicians and patrons, before glancing down at his watch and mentioning the need to prepare to take the stage again. He watched Cora rise from her chair in order to leave.

"Am I sensing a disconnect between you and your instrument tonight, Cora?"

She frowned and fixed him with an unreadable look. "How could I possibly know what you're sensing, Andrew?"

"You may interpret my question as a rhetorical one, then, since I believe the answer is evident."

"It may be that the disconnect is between my music and your interpretation of it," she returned coolly. "Thankfully, there are only a few weeks more for you to have to endure it."

She quietly moved out of the room and joined the others on their way back to the stage area, leaving him with narrowed eyes and a frown of his own.

For the second half of the evening's concert, Cora moved from her cello to the piano and played with the orchestra until time for the concerto grosso. She then slipped away for a moment to do some deep breathing and prepare herself for her featured piano performance, at the end of the concert.

She leisurely paced around the green room, thinking about playing the piano for Morgan at the cabin, and about how completely engrossed he had been with the nocturne she had written. She smiled to herself, as she realized that music was another way the two of them found to connect, which made her love him, all the more.

Cora was careful to remain aware of what was happening onstage and soon made her way to stand in the wings, to enter at the conclusion of the concerto grosso.

As she did, there was an excited burst of applause from the audience and she graciously acknowledged them with a smile and a slight bow, before seating herself at her instrument.

Although this was her solo performance of one of her original compositions, parts had been scored for the orchestra to lend support.

Cora began alone, entering the song with a reverent touch, before gradually building on her masterful performance. The string section was the first to begin embellishing her composition, and other sections began to quietly enter.

As she played, Cora found herself once again at the cabin and could almost feel Morgan's dark, compelling eyes on her. This sensation began to cause Cora to deviate from the score and, without realizing it, she began to deliver a completely spontaneous work of art.

The orchestra members had never heard anything like it, and the audience was held captive by greatness. Cora's eyes were closed and, in that moment, she played for Morgan, alone.

Members of the audience began to display emotional responses as tears gathered, hands were lifted to cheeks, or laid on hearts. Something unexplainably beautiful unfolded.

Finally, Cora began to slowly come back to herself, and realized that she had departed from the score. She very deliberately and professionally simply created an impulsive, natural arrangement that seamlessly connected with the last pages of the score. This was done in such a way as to become once again recognized by the orchestra, who were then able to enter again into the composition and softly arrive with her at its conclusion. Cora slowly opened her eyes, lifted her head and gave all of them a beautiful smile.

The concert hall erupted into a standing ovation, and as Andrew held out a hand toward her, she stood, meekly acknowledging their appreciation, then gesturing to the rest of the orchestra, who rose in recognition of their audience.

It was some time before the freedom to leave the stage and congregate in the green room, and then be able to return to their hotel rooms finally came. Cora graciously thanked the stage crew member who safely secured her cello and assured her that he would personally deliver it to the orchestra's specially designed transport van.

She retrieved her long cloak and slipped it over her evening gown, then reached for her portfolio and belongings.

"Since we're all returning to the same hotel, Cora, please ride with me," Andrew said, stopping to look at her curiously. "I'd like an opportunity to speak with you, and I'm sure when we reach the hotel, you'll wish to retire immediately."

She started to decline, as she always would, but decided that it was a short distance to the hotel and if she agreed to ride with Andrew, he could simply say whatever it was he felt he needed to say, and Cora could put this long evening behind her.

She thanked the driver who had opened the door to the limousine for her before slipping in, already recognizing how good it felt to sit, and realizing how tired she was.

Andrew joined her and then looked at her soberly.

"First of all, you threw the rest of us a curve tonight."

She made no reply. He was the one had who expressed a desire to talk, and she felt no compulsion at all to add to the conversation.

"I'm not saying that it wasn't beautiful. In fact, I've never heard you play the piano as completely uninhibited and powerfully as you played it tonight."

He continued to fix her with a pointed look. "It would have been nice if the conductor and the rest of the orchestra had been given the scores, as that last number is obviously not from a chart that any of us had in our possessions."

He stopped and seemed to be waiting for something.

"Is there something you wish me to say, Andrew?"

She leveled her green eyes at him and remained completely impassive, causing him to become even more frustrated.

Just when she expected him to attempt to take her to task for veering from the program, he surprised her with his next statement.

"Have you no more regard for the time and effort you have invested in becoming not only a musical virtuoso, but one of the most compelling composers in decades, than to simply be willing to fade into oblivion by becoming a simple housewife, or a social accessory on some man's arm?"

"Some *man* is named Morgan Roberts, and I hardly think you need to concern yourself with my life choices, Andrew. I did agree to this tour, but not to answering to you or anybody else for the rest of my decisions or how I live my life."

The rest of their ride was made in silence, since Andrew Holland saw that he would only provoke Cora by continuing to try to reason with her.

The limousine driver delivered them smoothly to their hotel and Andrew let himself out, then stood waiting for Cora to join him.

She did slide out of the vehicle, but rather than allowing him to escort her in, she smiled at a waiting doorman who quickly attended to her and saw her to the elevator.

Andrew had been recognized and hailed by some patrons in the lounge, much to Cora's relief. She returned to her room, solidly locking her door and hurriedly checking her phone, just in case Morgan had tried to call her.

He hadn't, since he knew she was in concert and that it would likely be after midnight before she was back, so she just reminded herself that she had already known that would be the case, and climbed wearily into a hot shower, then dragged herself into bed.

organ Roberts rested his fingertips together and gave Blake Jenkins an amused smile. His Chief Forester wondered if he'd misheard his boss and looked up from his notes with a cautious expression and waited to see if Morgan would repeat what he'd just said.

"I hope your hesitation is only due to your not being sure that you heard correctly, and not to your reluctance to accept." Morgan continued to examine him.

"I'm not sure I did hear correctly," Blake admitted. "You didn't just offer me a promotion, did you?"

"If you accept the position of Timber Operations Manager, then yes, that would be a promotion. The work would be at a higher level, which I'm sure you can manage, and of course would include a raise and various perks."

Blake began to smile with uncertainty. "Do you have someone in mind to take on Chief Forester?"

"Hiring a Chief Forester would fall within the scope of your duties as TOM," Morgan informed him. "Of course, I would want to meet whomever you select, since this would be your first hire, but I don't intend to breathe down your neck."

Blake's expression began to morph from confusion to gladness. "Thank you, Morgan. I won't disappoint you."

"No, I realize that, which is why I left the position empty after Crawford retired and gave you time to work as a CF, first. But I can see that you're more than ready."

He leaned forward to rest his forearms on his desk. "I need to be honest with you, though, Blake, and tell you that if the need arises for this company to have boots on the ground in South America, I don't intend for them to be my boots.

"I have something coming up in my near future which makes it vital that I remain in the states.

"Would you be okay with being the one to travel back and forth, should it become necessary?"

Blake assumed that Morgan was referring to something that involved his younger sister, since he'd been made aware of her missing status, during the time that Morgan was away for so long, and quickly nodded.

"Absolutely, Morgan, I'm fine with that."

He grinned at him with relief, and settled back in his chair.

"Good to know. Well, in anticipation of your accepting, I've already notified personnel to expect you to come in to sign papers that should already be prepared for you. You've got a full day ahead of you.

"Besides satisfying the demands of our Mrs. Chapman who, I hear, cracks a pretty loud whip in that department, you also need to notify her of your intention to set up interviews for the CF position."

Blake rose from his seat and reached over to shake hands with his boss. "Thank you, Morgan, for having faith in me."

"You've never given me a reason not to," he returned, standing to his feet and clasping his former Chief Forester's hand. "I'm confident you'll do a good job."

He watched the happy man leave his office and settled back down in his chair with relief. After a moment, he opened his laptop and browsed to a bookmark of a reviewer who was following Cora's tour, and noted that the man had already managed to upload it to his blog.

He tapped on his trackpad for the full review and slowly began to smile.

Cora Hartmann, as lovely and polished as ever, elegantly seated herself at the grand piano tonight and turned in what could only be described as the performance of a lifetime, during the concert's finale.

It was while interviewing members of the traveling orchestra, that this reviewer learned that the hauntingly beautiful music emanating from the gifted hands of Miss Hartmann was a departure from the score she began playing and was, in fact, a risky foray into unexpected brilliance.

Its plaintive notes evoked a sense of longing, yet at the same time, there was a hopefulness in its entirety as she brought this improvisation softly back to merge seamlessly with the original score which, I am told was also a composition by Miss Hartmann who, at her young age, has already achieved well deserved recognition as one of the most important composers in many years, certainly in my existence.

If you have not yet been fortunate to witness such a breathtaking performance by Cora Hartmann, you may have left it a bit late, as the remaining two weeks of this tour have since been sold out."

Morgan rested his eyes lovingly on the photo of Cora seated at her instrument, with her eyes closed and a softness on her face that drew his heart to her. The Dupioni Silk dark plum evening gown was exquisite and seemed to have been tailored to fit her to perfection, especially in the second photo, which was of Cora, after she had risen to acknowledge the standing ovation she received.

Morgan again chided himself for not having secured tickets to see Cora in concert, but the orchestra wasn't playing anywhere near him, and he had been gone too much, as it was. He again wondered why they were not traveling to his state, especially since the city he lived in was famous for hosting some of the most prolific operas and concerts ever performed.

He comforted himself with the reminder that he had experienced what no reviewer or ticket holder ever would, as the memory of Cora playing for him alone, in the privacy of the little cabin washed over him. He had to agree with this reviewer. She was lovely, polished and brilliant.

Two weeks remaining in the tour, the reviewer had said. This caused Morgan to answer his secretary's call with so much cheerfulness that she wrinkled her forehead and wondered if she had pressed the wrong button.

"Cora, I realize that you've had your fill of receptions and hosted dinners, but this patron is as responsible for our being able to tour as several of our patrons, put together.

"He's particularly eager to meet you, and it would be very hard for me to explain your absence. I can't very well make up some two hour malady, since you'll be onstage tonight."

Cora had learned a long time ago that simply wishing Andrew Holland away was ineffective, and if she put words to her wishes, it usually caused more conflict than she was willing to put up with.

She waved a hand in his general direction with a sigh. "Fine. I'll appear, meet your patron, and then I'm returning back here before tonight's concert."

"There are only two weeks remaining," her conductor pointed out. "I can't understand why you're not enjoying this tour. You always have, in the past, and I've been allowing concession after concession for you, in order to make things easier. You seemed determined to remain displeased."

She drew in a deep breath. As much as Andrew annoyed her, Cora knew he was right. She could at least manage some level of appreciation. She had no patience for divas, and no wish to be compared to one, so she nodded and relented.

"I know, I'm sorry. I'll work on being more available for the rest of the tour, Andrew. It won't be easy, since I'm trying to plan a wedding at the same time, so if I'm more irritable or tired lately, I'm sure it's stress."

Her mention of her wedding served to strengthen her conductor's determination that there would be no wedding, but he hid his irritation and flashed her a conciliatory smile.

"That's all I ask. We're to be at the reception at four."

"Why couldn't it have been held here, in one of this hotel's banquet rooms?" she wondered, with a touch of annoyance.

"I'm sure it could have, and I agree it would have been much more convenient, but this particular venue is the finest in the city, and I would imagine that our host simply wanted us to be treated with the best."

"I'm sure that's very thoughtful of him, but most gestures like that end up being public relations fodder, so I wouldn't be surprised if that were the case."

She laid a hand on her door's handle and prepared to step into her room, since their conversation was happening out in the wide hallway.

"Alright, Andrew, I'll be there at four, then my intention is to leave soon after and to return here, so please don't be surprised when I make my apologies to the host."

He set his chin, but made no reply, accepting her conditions for now.

Cora let herself into her hotel room, relieved with being done with yet another of Andrew Holland's efforts to persuade her to do something she had absolutely no wish to do.

Of course, her first thought, the minute she was ever alone, was to reach out to Morgan, but he'd told her that he was in a series of meetings with his staff today. Even though he'd not seemed to mind her little emoticons during his last meeting, she decided not to push her luck.

She checked her phone and saw that her father had called and smiled to herself. He checked on his only child at regular intervals, regardless of the fact that she was no longer a child.

He answered her call almost immediately.

"Cora, my sweet girl!"

"Hi, Dad," she returned, with a smile lighting up her face.

"You know me, honey, I can't let more than two days go by without checking on you. I expect that'll never change."

"I do know you," she laughed. "I'm fine, Dad, but just a little tired. I'm pretty sure stress is a big factor, and of course, Andrew is a big pain, but I knew that before I signed on, so at the end of the day, it's my fault."

He laughed with her. "Speaking of the tour, Cora, are you sure the reviewer doesn't have a secret crush on you? He was so flowery today, that I've begun to wonder about him."

She shook her head and brushed a strand of hair out of her eyes, before wandering over to the large window of her hotel room to look out over the city.

"I've never met him, that I know of, Dad, but if there has to be a reviewer following this tour, I'm glad it's him. So far, that is," she added. "He's very generous."

"He's more than generous, he's absolutely effusive," her father declared. "But I don't disagree with any of his statements, so I'll just assume that he recognizes talent and beauty and simply writes what he sees."

He paused, remembering this morning's review. "I don't suppose there's a chance in this world, that last night's finale was recorded, Cora?"

"Usually no. There's a chance, since Andrew has been wanting to release a live recording project. I wouldn't know if he's using this tour or not, and I honestly wouldn't do it, myself. If he is, he wouldn't tell us though, in case it might affect our performance. He would just have his guys mix in with the house audio people. That would be a mistake. I think it would sound terrible, but you never know. Maybe, Dad."

"I hope so," Paul Hartmann said. "It sounds as if you had a very special moment last night, and I'd love to hear it."

"Andrew would be even less pleased with the fact that I improvised and changed the arrangement, if he knew that Morgan had inspired it," Cora confessed.

"I expect he would," he agreed. "How are things with you and Morgan, honey? Are you both still hearing wedding bells?"

"You'd better believe it!" she replied, with her happiness so evident that her father, who would normally be concerned about the rapid nature of their relationship, was glad for her.

"Dad, you're being wonderful about Morgan," Cora told him, letting her eyes travel over the river she could view from her room, and idly watching a tugboat pushing a barge.

"That's partly due to the fact that he's not Warren Abernathy," he replied, making his daughter gush out a quick bit of laughter. "No, I believe you have a good man in Morgan Roberts. He comes from fine stock.

"Of course, I saw him and his sister Jane at their parents' funeral service, but I didn't approach him to remind him of our acquaintance. Other than that, I've not seen him since he was a young lad. But I do appreciate the fact that he can't be found in any gossip columns' crosshairs. I don't doubt that he loves you as much as I can see you love him."

"And I love *you*," she said warmly, feeling so grateful for her father's understanding and support.

"You just want me to show up in April to marry the two of you," he teased. "But I will, because I love you, too."

Cora tarried on the call for a while longer, cherishing the way her father always made time for her and listened to whatever it was she wanted to talk about. He was like a safe harbor for her, and she treasured him.

They finally ended their visit, with Cora promising to find out about a possible recording and get it to him, if she could.

She made her way over to her closet to choose something to wear for the tonight's performance, along with something a bit more casual for the reception, then sat cross-legged on the bed to look over her notes for the wedding that Sandra Birch was excited to host at Ingleside Fare.

She was surprised when a text arrived confirming the car that would be picking her up, and noted that she needed to hurry and get dressed and head to the lobby, in order to get to the reception.

When she arrived, she saw that the host had engaged a professional coat check service. She willingly allowed the attendant to take her coat and her personal belongings, before moving across the floor, first approaching Andrew Holland.

"Excuse me, Andrew," she began, when he glanced up at her while speaking to a woman who had him engaged, and was hanging onto his every word.

She smiled apologetically at the woman who obviously recognized her, then continued.

"I'm sorry to interrupt, but I spoke with my father earlier, and he wants to know if any recording was made of last night's concert? I'm sure that's not something you'd ordinarily tell us, but it's simply for my father to know, not anyone else."

He folded his arms and viewed her curiously. "I confess that I've tried to have our concerts recorded but I doubt that anything captured so far, will be useful to us. Our venues' engineers typically mix for a live audience, which I don't believe will translate well into a high quality recording.

"I suppose that might be something I could furnish him with, if he's not concerned with the professionalism. Does he want the entire concert, or is he mainly interested in the finale?"

"I'm sure the finale is all he's asking about," she replied. "Thank you, Andrew, I appreciate it. I'll let him know that I may be able to send him something."

She flashed another quick smile to the woman, who was obviously relieved that she would have the handsome conductor to herself again, and began to make her way slowly around the room, having difficulty in avoiding requests for photos and autographs, as she did.

A congenial, elderly man smiled in delight and held out his hand, hoping she would take it.

"Hello," Cora said, accepting his handshake.

"Oh, hello! We've not met, Miss Hartmann, but I'm following the tour and reviewing it for my blog. I'm Thomas Delcourt. It's an honor to meet you."

"No, it's my honor," she corrected. "I don't mean to imply that your reviews are biased in any way, but at the same time, I want to thank you for your generosity. I'm afraid I can't always guarantee a solid performance, especially during those times that I'm particularly stressed or not feeling well. I hope, on those occasions, that you'll have mercy on me."

He laughed and gave her hand a little pat before releasing it. "I promise to take all of that into consideration."

They exchanged a few more pleasantries, before the patron hosting the event realized that Cora Hartmann had arrived and claimed her to introduce his wife to her.

Andrew strolled idly around the room before approaching the coat check area to retrieve a business card for the woman he'd been talking to earlier. The attendant glanced up at the conductor with a friendly smile and he asked if he could remove something from his coat pocket.

As he waited, he heard Cora's phone, and recognized the ringtone she had assigned to Morgan Roberts, since it grated on him every time he heard it.

"Oh dear, would you mind? I hear Cora's phone and that's a friend of ours calling. I'll take it, please."

The attendant certainly recognized Andrew Holland as being Cora Hartmann's conductor and handed him her phone without question.

"Hello," he greeted the caller pleasantly.

Morgan drew his brows and frowned. He knew he had dialed correctly, since he simply tapped Cora's number from their last call.

"Please ask Cora to come to her phone," he simply said.

Andrew pulled his cards out of his coat pocket and handed it back to the attendant with a smile.

"I'm afraid Cora's completely tied up, just now. We're at a reception, and since she is something of a celebrity, she is in much demand, at the moment."

"To whom am I speaking?" Morgan asked shortly.

"I'm Andrew, Cora's conductor and very good friend," he replied airily. "May I pass some sort of message on to Cora?"

"What you may do," Morgan replied, in a low, impatient tone, "is explain to me, Cora's fiancé, why you believe that being her conductor entitles you to answer her phone."

"Her fiancé!" Andrew feigned surprise. "That's news to me, and trust me, I'm the first one who would know."

"Just answer the question."

"I don't see the problem," Andrew returned nonchalantly. "She knows she's perfectly welcome to answer mine. Now that she's agreed to stay on with the tour through the end of May, I suppose she's a bit more relaxed about that sort of thing."

Morgan was silent for a moment, causing Andrew to smirk with satisfaction.

"Hang on, though, she appears to be looking at me," Andrew lied, holding the phone up in a way that allowed Morgan to hear the loud, ambient room noise.

"Oh, darling!" he lightly called to no one, since Cora was well across the room. "Cora, sweetheart, you have a call! He says he's your fiancé. Have you just been toying with me, then?"

Andrew held the phone back up to his ear to inform Morgan Roberts that Cora would try to get back to him, but he had obviously hung up, causing Andrew to hand the phone back to the attendant with an overabundance of smug charm.

Chapter Eighteen

Sandra Birch paused, then tried another knock. After a moment, Cora opened the door of the cabin and gave her a sad, hollow smile, then stepped back so that she could come in.

Sandra turned around after entering the living room, and gave Cora a tender, knowing look. She held up a small crock of soup and nodded toward what she could see was the kitchen beyond the freestanding fireplace.

"I know you're getting ready to tell me that you're not hungry, sweetie, but just show me where to put this, in case you change your mind, later on."

Cora simply led the way into the kitchen and opened the fridge door. "I guess there's room in here," she said, in a small, feeble voice.

Sandra looked inside the nearly empty refrigerator with a shake of her head. "Well, I guess there is. Don't you eat solid food anymore, honey?"

Cora tried to smile at her question, but tears began to rush down her cheeks.

"Oh, baby girl!" Sandra closed the fridge door and wrapped her up in a big hug, reaching a hand to lift strands of hair over her shoulder.

"It's okay. Or it will be. I know you don't believe that, but it has to be. We don't stay in these places of hurt the rest of our lives, thank God. But while we're in them, they feel as if they'll last forever."

She patted Cora's back comfortingly. "But they don't."

Cora stood looking down at the floor and nodded, unable to do much more than that.

"Come on back in here, Cora, and let's sit."

Sandra settled down on the sofa and Cora took a rocker next to it and stared at nothing.

"Honey, if I ask you some questions, will you please try to know that I'm not just being a nosey old woman, but that I'm genuinely trying to understand your situation?"

She took the tissue Sandra pulled from the dispenser on the coffee table and nodded.

"Am I right that you haven't spoken to Morgan at all, since returning from the tour?"

Cora tried to speak and had to stop to clear her throat.

"The last time I talked to Morgan, was about two weeks before the end of the tour. Everything was fine." Her voice began to shake with emotion. "I just don't understand."

"So when you two spoke, there no disagreement about anything or something that might have been misunderstood?"

"The last thing we said to each other was 'I love you' and then nothing, after that," she whispered, continuing to blink back tears and dab at her face with the tissue.

"Do you think something might have happened with his sister?" Sandra knew that he had recently been to see her.

Cora shook her head. "That wouldn't make him ignore all my calls. He'd share that with me, because we had already gone through his fears about Jane, together."

She lifted her beautiful, sorrowful eyes to her friend. "That wouldn't make him let our wedding day come and go and never even say a word, knowing that I was here, waiting."

She burst into fresh sobbing and Sandra came over to her and put an arm around her.

"Oh, sweetie, I'm so sorry. I can't tell you how sorry I am that you're hurting like this. I wish I could just come up with some reasonable explanation, but I can't seem to.

"I did wonder if something might have happened to him, but I think we would have heard it on the news or something."

Cora shook her head. "No, I checked his social media. He's very involved with current things right now, so he's fine."

After a moment, she looked off past her piano, toward the window, seeming to be thinking.

"Maybe he and Amanda began to get close, and he's decided he has feelings for her," she speculated, in a dull voice.

"Who is that, Cora? Is that the woman that his sister is living with?"

She nodded, still staring at the trees outside the window.

"Has he known her a long time?"

"For a lot of years. I guess he and Amanda and her brother Darrin and Jane are all good friends, and Jane picked Amanda to run to, when she needed a safe place."

"You've never met her," Sandra decided.

"No. I did look her up on the Internet, once. She's a beekeeper in Ohio and she wasn't that hard to find. She's very pretty," Cora added sadly.

Sandra frowned at that.

"Cora Hartmann, she can't possibly be any prettier than you are! Besides, Morgan Roberts sees beautiful women all the time, and he certainly knew what Amanda looked like when he fell in love with you. I hardly think the fact that she's pretty would be enough to turn his head."

"Maybe not, but their families go way back, and they consider themselves to be longtime friends. She's helping with Jane. Sometimes friendship can turn into something deeper."

Sandra shook her head.

"I'm sorry, I can't accept that. Not just because I don't want to, but even though I'm angry with Morgan Roberts right now, I can't accept that he would simply decide he cares for Amanda or any other woman, and just leave you hanging, without even the decency to talk to you about it. I'm a pretty good judge of character, Cora, and I do believe that Morgan is fundamentally a decent man."

Cora had run out of things to say. She desperately wanted to believe Sandra but she was so weary from crying for days and not sleeping and not eating, that all she could do now was just sit and stare. Finally, she offered in a faint voice, "My dad was here until this morning."

"Was he? Oh, I would have loved to have met him," Sandra said. "He came to check on his girl, then."

Cora tried to smile at that. "He wanted to be with me. He left here angry, though. I could tell."

"Well, I expect so! I wouldn't be surprised if he gave Morgan Roberts an ear full," Sandra declared strongly.

"I asked him not to," Cora admitted. "I think if I can just have a little more time, I'll be okay. I just need..."

She couldn't finish, so Sandra finished for her.

"You need to cry, and scream, and yell and all of that, but at the end of it, you need to pray, darlin', and ask God to give you some peace. And then you need to wash your face, put on some makeup, stop by the restaurant every now and then, and get some sort of routine going.

"You came here to write your opus, Cora, and don't you let Morgan Roberts or anybody else stop you from doing it. You're still the strong, determined woman who bought this house, insisted on paying for the renovations yourself, and stood your ground when your presence here was challenged.

"Okay, so you don't know what happened. You may never know, so go ahead and accept that. But don't ghost around this cabin from now on, sparking rumors that these woods are haunted. You get your life back, Cora. It belongs to you and to no one else!"

Cora drew in a deep breath and made a swipe across her face with the back of her hand.

"You're right," she admitted. She thought a minute then looked over at Sandra cautiously.

"Does everybody at Ingleside know, then?"

"All they know is that you were wiped out after that tour and you're too exhausted to try to fit a wedding in, or anything else right now. And that's all they need to know."

"Thank you, Sandra." She breathed out a sigh of relief, then got up when her friend stood to prepare to leave.

"Well, it's none of their business," she said simply.

She gave Cora a searching look. "I put a bag of cornbread muffins in beside the soup, Cora. Go get a hot shower and heat all that up, and eat something. Trust me. It's good."

"Oh, I already know that," she said with a faint smile.

She followed her to the door and gave her a hug, then stood watching Sandra back her truck around and gave her a last little wave.

She continued to stand there, looking out at the trees where the dogwood and redbuds had already bloomed and heard a cardinal somewhere practicing his repertoire of love songs.

Sandra was right. She need to do what she had come here to do. Cora closed the door and headed to her bathroom to take the hot shower she had suggested, and to try to eat something.

Paul Hartmann was a man of gentle disposition and rare patience but he had driven away from his daughter's cabin with the fire of indignation burning inside him.

Cora was all he had in this world, and as long as Morgan Roberts had been a source of joy to her, he was willing to let his qualms regarding the impulsiveness of their relationship stay in the background, but he would never have been so understanding if he'd known how things would turn out.

Not even when Cora lost her sweet mother, had she shown the complete devastation and heartbreak that she had been unable to hide from him. He had spent the past two days holding her while she cried to such an extent that he feared she was becoming ill. The only time she slept was due to simply passing out with fatigue on the sofa.

He had kept a careful watch over her, and covered her with blankets, brought her coffee, tried to tempt her with his efforts at cooking, but she could do little more than stay curled up in a fetal position, either crying softly or staring vacantly.

His heart was crushed, but not so badly that he didn't relish the idea of confronting Morgan Roberts and demanding an explanation for his behavior.

He had a drive of several hours, so he plugged the flash drive Cora gave him into his car's stereo system to listen to the finale of the concert that Thomas Delcourt had been speaking of, when he lavished so much praise on his daughter.

Paul's first reaction was one of absolute astonishment. He had never heard anything like this come from his Cora. She had told him that Morgan Roberts had inspired it and he could hear the depth and passion of her love for him to such a degree that he was now also able to feel the sting of her pain and the agonizing level of her grief.

She had bared her heart on that stage. If Morgan Roberts had read the review, he must have sensed what that kind of performance was actually about. Surely he had to have known she had him in her heart as she performed!

Then how, in the name of all things sacred, could he have suddenly cut her out of his own heart?

Professor Hartmann tried to will himself to stop dwelling on it and not let it rob him of his peace, but as soon as he steered his vehicle into his driveway, he pulled the flash drive out of the stereo port, and took it into the house with him.

He sat down at his desk and grabbed a sheet of stationary, firmly scrawling a reproachful note to Morgan Roberts.

How, young man, can you have drifted so far away from the influence of your fine parents, that you could call my daughter's gentle heart to come to yours and then, once you owned it, toss it back to her in the completely destroyed condition that it is in, now?

How can you hear what is on this recording, the finale that the reviewer was so enchanted with, that Cora told me the very next day was because of you, and somehow convince yourself that within twenty-four hours, she was not worth your love?

How could you have let the wedding day that the two of you were planning, come and go with not so much as a text, even if you couldn't bring yourself to show up at her door as a real man would have done?

I wonder, since you are so obviously capable of such heinous behavior, if it gives you some sort of morbid pleasure to know that my daughter still, up until the time that the ceremony was to have begun, kept hope alive that something, somehow, would bring you to her. Yes, she would have married you that very moment, even after the way you treated her.

And still, she loves you, against her better judgment. May God help me to forgive you, Morgan, and not have bitterness against you become an obstacle to my continuing to live out my faith.

Cora's father hastily found a padded envelope in his desk drawer and searched the Internet for the mailing address for Morgan Robert's office.

He picked up a red marker and wrote in large letters:
For Morgan Roberts only, Personal. Not to be opened by staff!

He put the letter and the flash drive into the envelope, sealed it and resolutely walked quickly down the sidewalk in his neighborhood to the nearest mail drop box, deliberately not second-guessing himself, intentionally waving away any thoughts of calming down, and slamming the lid loudly, for emphasis.

Cora was somehow able to manage to sleep, if only out of weariness. It was just breaking dawn when she opened her eyes and, of course, as always, her first thought was of Morgan. This was partly due to the painting that hung directly across from the foot of her bed.

She had purposely chosen that place for it as a way of connecting with him immediately every morning, and welcoming him into her thoughts and into her day but now, as she slowly focused on it, fresh tears stung her eyes. She grabbed the hem of the top sheet and wiped them away impatiently.

She was not going to do this again, all day long, she told herself firmly. She was going to get up, take a walk outdoors, then come back, find something to put on that made her feel pretty and be brave enough to walk into Ingleside Fare for breakfast, as if she still lived upstairs.

She realized that she could simply get rid of Jane's art, but she wasn't quite ready to do that. Besides, she told herself that if she could become able to see it as nothing more than a nice painting of her property, then that would be a much more convincing display of her having healed, than simply hiding it out of sight.

She pulled herself out of bed and climbed into a pair of old jeans and a thin sweatshirt, then clipped a holster with a small handgun to her waistband, in case she saw a snake outside.

Of course, summer was still several weeks away, but it was beginning to get quite warm during the day, and Cora had a strong dislike of snakes and at least felt braver if she had some sort of weapon.

She walked out onto the porch and breathed in something that smelled like honeysuckle, although she would have thought it was too early in the year for that. She drew in another deep breath of it and actually smiled at the way it made her feel.

"Thank you, God," she whispered, glancing up in His general direction before stepping off the porch and strolling down the driveway to be able to cross the stream.

She began walking along the still visible trail, used before the driveway had been poured, and turned when she reached the road, to look back toward the cabin. It was completely hidden from view now, until she ventured back, retracing her steps and watching it become slowly visible through the flowering trees.

She was glad she had taken before pictures, because the little cabin was no longer just an ugly white shack in the woods.

Cora stood looking at it now, seeing it as her refuge. She hugged herself and breathed out a quiet prayer.

Somehow, she knew in that moment that she didn't have to wait for healing to come, or to be able to laugh again, or to remember touches and glances and whispers, without pain. Her pain was trying to tell her something. She would make friends with it and listen carefully to what it was saying.

It was time to write her opus magnum.

Chapter Nineteen

Morgan's secretary had a stack of mail ready to bring into his office. She always brought anything that seemed to be of a personal nature straight to him, which he had insisted on, when she was interviewed for the position of personal assistant for the head of Morgan Roberts, Corp.

Of course, she had no way of knowing if he actually read through them or simply threw them away. She didn't know, for instance, that back in April, when an interesting padded envelope arrived with a warning in red that it was meant for Morgan Roberts only, that he had simply stared down at it, then shoved it into his desk drawer, deciding that he wasn't ready to either be bawled out by Cora's father or to have him try to smooth things over. He was still angry and, even now, the envelope remained hidden away in his desk.

As she made her way into his office after knocking, she placed the mail in front of him.

"There's a call holding for you, Mr. Roberts. She gave her name as Amanda Hester?"

Morgan looked up with a startled expression.

"Ring her through, please, Marcy."

She stepped out and immediately rang his phone. Morgan grabbed up the receiver, concern already in his eyes.

"Amanda? What's up?"

"Maybe nothing, Morgan. I may just be overreacting. The thing is, Jane never came back after she went to be with her friends in March. Do you remember her saying anything to you about that?"

"She did say there were a couple of things that she wanted to do in March, but that she'd more than likely come back to your place after that."

"Well... I mean I certainly don't know Jane as well as you do, but it seems that by now, I should have heard something, or you should have. But you haven't, I'm gathering?"

"No, but I knew she'd be out in the wilds, somewhere. When that happens, she can go for quite a long time with no phone signal, or even a way to charge her phone, if her group is really roughing it."

He sat trying to think, looking down at his calendar and surprised to see that it was already mid-summer. That seemed unreal to him, for some reason.

"Do you think she's probably alright, then, Morgan?" Amanda broke into his thoughts with her question.

"I just don't know," he admitted. "I'll try calling her, of course, and I may have the number for her friend Lily somewhere, maybe at home. I can try her as well. If one of us hears from Jane, we'll call the other, though."

"Sure, okay."

"Thank you, Amanda."

She could tell that he wanted to get off the phone and she reluctantly ended the call.

Morgan sat trying to think what his sister might possibly be up to, or where she might be. He hoped that at the very worst, she was still hanging out with her weird friends. At least, she'd be safe, even if he was using the term loosely.

He absently raked through his mail, then picked up a blue envelope and a slow smile began to light his face.

He reached for his letter opener and slit it open, then pulled out a letter that smelled of eucalyptus. True to her word, Jane had written him.

He grinned, thinking to himself that at least she hadn't made it smell like patchouli.

He pushed back from his desk and made his way over to his couch, to stack up a couple of pillows on one end and stretch out, in order to relax and to be able to take the time to read what she had obviously put a lot of effort into.

"Let's see what you've gotten yourself into, Janie," he murmured softly.

Dear Morgan,

I told you that I'd write to you, but you doubted me. 'Oh ye, of little faith!' (I think that's how that goes).

I'm writing you from northern Alabama! It looks like Tennessee here! Have you ever been to Tennessee? That's one of my favorite places. Well, not Nashville. They can have that. But I love the east part, especially where it runs into North Carolina. Have you ever been there?

But that's not where I am, so I don't know why I'm even talking about Tennessee or North Carolina. Northern Alabama is also very nice. You'd love it if you'd ever get out of your office and just see the country, and maybe even the world.

You should, you know. You should pull off that tie and fluff your hair out and buy some sandals and just go for it. Someday, maybe you and I can go camping and I'll show you how to look for edible herbs. Did you know that many herbs can cure you of hundreds of diseases?

Morgan laughed quietly as his enthusiastic sister's gift for prattling on about nothing, but at the moment, it was the most beautiful prattling he'd ever read.

Lily got stung by a carpenter wasp and I made a poultice out of crushed up yarrow and put on it and the next morning she was perfectly fine! I could make some up and send it to you, if you want to keep it on hand.

After we leave here, we'll probably drive through Tennessee (be still, my heart!) and on up into West Virginia. I can't think of West Virginia without thinking of John Denver. This makes me very sad. John Denver had the spirit of an eagle, I think.

We have a new member in our group. His name is Trapper Dan. I guess he must trap stuff? I haven't asked him but I should, because sometimes when I can't sleep, I think it must be because I'm lying awake trying to guess why he has that name, and if I knew, I could probably go to sleep. Maybe I'll ask him in the morning. (Don't worry, Brother... I don't plan on marrying Trapper Dan.) He's too old, anyway. He looks kind of like Santa, if Santa had a red beard. He's big, like Santa, too. He showed up riding a motorcycle and asked if we minded if he bunked out with us for the night, but he's been here four days, now.

He brews some interesting teas. I haven't tried them, but they don't seem to hurt him, so maybe. We'll see. I do like trying new things.

I keep thinking about our last time to talk. You were worried about me, and I felt bad about it later. Remember, you asked me why I started looking for God in other places and left my belief? I never really did leave my belief, Morgan. It's just that I was too young to know the difference between Christ and Christians and when one of the guys at the church's youth camp kind of creeped me out and was... well, let's just say inappropriate with me, I guess I just didn't really trust the whole church thing after that.

I should have stopped to realize that Mom and Dad were Christians and they were just lovely, so I guess I was just a dumb kid and sort of lumped everyone into the same bag. Then, I just never talked about it.

I can see your handsome face right now, Morgan, and you are frowning at this letter and maybe even scowling. That's one of the reasons people call you a pirate, ha ha! But don't scowl on my behalf. I do really know that Jesus and people who say they know Him are two different things. Anyway, I'm not saying that I'm a good person, because I do wrong things and I would know if I was good. But I do still believe in Jesus. I hope that helps. I hope I'm saying it right. I'm not very deep.

I'm so sorry I missed your wedding! I'm crying now, writing this because I said I would try, but I'm at the mercy of whoever has a vehicle and I just couldn't make it work out. Please tell your beautiful Cora with the gentle heart and lovely face that I do very much want to meet her and get to know her as my sister.

And please thank her again, for being so loving and careful with my paintings. That shows she has grace and she is merciful. I love her already.

Don't worry about me, Morgan, if you don't hear from me for a while. I'm fine, especially since there's no Michael Tewks trying to kill me. (What was his deal, anyway? You don't just kill people, sheesh!)

I love you. Oh, hey, don't forget to check the back. I love you more than all the stars up in the heavens. (Or something like that.) It's a song. You remember? And there's like a trumpet or something in it? Longer! That's the name. I guess that song's for couples, though. But you get what I'm saying. Anyway, I love you, Morgan.

Always, your Janie

Morgan held the letter to his chest for a moment, reeling with all the different emotions Jane had released in him. He was so angry to think that some man at church camp had dared to put his hands on Jane. He hadn't failed to recognize the way Jane had simply glossed over it in her letter, as if it hadn't really been that big of a deal, but he knew that was Jane's way.

Of course, she had certainly never said a word to their parents, but he felt deep regret that she hadn't come to him. The two of them had always been close.

The last youth camp he could remember Jane going to was when she was around nine or ten. He would have probably been a senior in high school and that might have been why she hadn't sought him out. He was on the football team and involved in all sorts of things, and she probably felt that he had grown up and left her behind. The thought gripped his heart so that he could actually feel its pain and laid a hand over his chest.

He made himself sit up, then stood to move over and look out of his wall of windows, down at the city below. Jane didn't know that he and Cora hadn't been married. She felt badly for missing a wedding that never happened.

He still had her letter in his hand and looked down at what she had written. *"Please tell your beautiful Cora with the gentle heart and lovely face that I do very much want to meet her and get to know her as my sister. And please thank her again, for being so loving and careful with my paintings. That shows she has grace and she is merciful. I love her already."*

Morgan looked back out at the skyline and furiously blinked back hot tears. He somehow knew that what Jane said about Cora was true but then, if it was, how could that same woman have bailed on their wedding and chosen to remain with the tour when she hadn't even told him that an extension was a possibility?

Why had she not told her conductor that she was getting married and why had she allowed Andrew Holland to call her darling, and sweetheart, and imply that she had been toying with him, by hiding a fiancé?

Surely she would have made him stop, but he'd heard her make no reply or voice any protest, at all.

He laid his head against the glass pane and reached a hand to wipe the corners of his eyes and take a deep breath. He had allowed himself to become so busy, that he thought he had moved on, but it was obvious that he was nowhere near over Cora Hartmann. He would just have to try harder.

Morgan looked down at the letter again, and remembered that Jane had told him to check the back of it.

He turned it over and a soft smile came to cover up his tears. She had beautifully drawn a picture of the two of them, as children, perhaps taken from a photo she must have been keeping all these years, since they were instantly both so recognizable.

She had drawn them sitting in the palm of a large hand that could only have belonged to God. In the background, instead of mountains or a large setting sun, or some other image indicative of a horizon, there was simply a large heart that encircled the entire image with a cross piercing it.

He wiped away more tears, but these were happy ones. Jane was telling him, in her own childlike way, that she really hadn't abandoned the God of her youth.

"Thank you, God," Morgan whispered softly.

He returned to his desk and opened the drawer to slip Jane's letter into it for safekeeping. He was slightly startled to see the envelope still lying inside from Cora's father and almost reached for it but regardless of what was inside, he couldn't manage any more strong emotions just now. He slid the drawer closed and picked up the phone to call Amanda back.

She answered right away and he let her know that he'd found a letter in the mail from Jane. He flipped the envelope over and saw a postmark of less than a week, so he told Amanda that with the plans Jane had shared about heading north and eventually going to West Virginia, it looked as if it would be a while before she contacted either of them.

He told her that Jane's friend Lily was with her, which was a relief to Amanda.

Although Lily was as much a hippie as any one of them, she was an older woman and had a maternal side to her that was comforting, in some way.

Each promised to let the other know if Jane made any other contact and Morgan hung up, with a great relief replacing his earlier concern. Now, if he could only do something about the pain he thought he was done with, until he read about the woman with the gentle heart and lovely face, he might be okay.

"Help me, Lord," he whispered out loud. If nothing else, this persistent pain had caused him to begin to pray again, little by little, and God was always faithful to comfort him.

Jane sat staring into the setting sun. Her friend Lily came over and settled herself down cross-legged onto the hard, rocky ground, before looking over at her with a grin.

"I'm sure that's bad for your eyes, Raven."

Jane smiled serenely. "Did you know that an eagle can tell when it's time to die and when that time comes, he flies to the highest place and turns and stares into the sun?"

"I've heard that," Lily admitted. "But when I told my teacher, Mr. Bennington that, he looked down his glasses at me and said, 'Miss Pope, eagles typically do not have the cognitive capacity to understand their own mortality or engage in deliberate actions related to their impending death'. I wanted to throw that word 'typically' back in his face, but I let it go."

Lily lifted her chin and employed an impressive highbrow accent as she quoted the man, then laughed at the memory.

"How could he know?" Jane demanded. "He'd have to be an eagle to know if that's true. Besides," she added, "if you don't believe it, then of course it's not true. You have to believe."

"Okay," her friend conceded. "I believe that staring into the sun is bad for your eyes and might end up giving you a headache, or even make you go blind."

Jane giggled at that, and reached over to give her friend a light bop on the shoulder.

"Sometimes you sound like my brother. He always has a funny comeback when I'm trying to explain something to him."

"Did you get that letter mailed to him that you were working on?" Lily wondered.

"I did, finally! I had so many distractions when I was writing it but I promised him, so I had to make it happen. When we stopped at that last gas station, they said I could put it in their mailbox and raise the flag.

"I don't think he's had time to get it yet, but as soon as he does, he won't be worried about me. I was supposed to go back to Amanda's after March, but I told him we had plans, so I think he'll probably just be relieved, now. So, all good."

Lily looked over at her thoughtfully.

"He really loves you, doesn't he, Jane?"

"Almost like a father would, instead of just a brother," she admitted. "We had a wonderful dad, but Morgan has always been like a dad for me, too. Now that he's married to his beautiful musician, I know he'll be happy, and that's what I want most. I used to think he and Amanda might end up together, but I saw love lights in his eyes when he told me about Cora. She's the one. She'll make him happy."

She raked a hand through her dark curls and looked back out at the dimming sun with a faded, weak smile.

"She's gonna take good care of him."

Chapter Twenty

Fayette County in West Virginia was one of the most staggeringly beautiful places Jane Roberts had ever seen. She felt a sense of loss that she had no paints or canvas with her so that she could capture it, but all that had been left behind in the attic of her old house.

She hugged herself and stared out over the great gorge with wide, expressive eyes that seemed to be memorizing every detail to hide in her heart.

It had taken their group several days to make the trip from northern Alabama, because they were never in a hurry and took the time to appreciate beauty, which was found more and more, the further they traveled toward their destination.

They had made camp and even though it was summer, a chill seemed to be settling over Jane's slim frame. She pulled a shawl out of her canvas bag and brought it around her shoulders, not yet ready to join the others at their campfire.

Lily had made some coffee on the fire and came over with a cup for her friend, who looked up with a grateful smile and reached for it.

"Your name is who you are, Lily," she said, grinning up at her brightly, before raising the metal cup to her lips.

Lily gave a little laugh and lowered herself to sit. "You mean I'm pale and soft, and wilt if I don't drink enough?"

Jane rolled her eyes. "The soft part, yes. But you're more like an Asiatic lily. You're resilient and you adapt to your environment, and you bring unexpected color wherever you go. Your mother must have known this is who you were meant to be, when she named you."

Lily felt surprised by the sting of tears. Jane, or Raven, as they all called her, was known for her spontaneous praise of others, but her words now were especially sweet.

"It's a good thing I adapt to my environment," Lily kidded, "since our environment seems to change every day."

Jane smiled over at her with eyes that reflected excitement. "That's the beauty of life, though, Lily!"

"I guess you're right."

They both sat looking out over the majestically beautiful, but intimidating gorge, when Jane reached a hand to clasp Lily's arm, then pointed ahead.

"Eagles," she whispered.

Lily joined her in watching the graceful birds as they appeared to simply float across the ravine, seeming to gradually descend to the river below. She looked over at the captivated expression on her young friend's face.

"You're especially fascinated by eagles, aren't you?"

She simply nodded, seeming to hold her breath as she continued to watch them glide effortlessly through the air.

"Why do you think that is?" Lily prodded, when Jane lapsed into a long silence.

She lowered her eyes, apparently registering a reaction to Lily's question.

"I was rescued by an eagle once," she ventured, almost too quietly to be heard.

"How, honey?" Lily finally asked, when Jane seemed to be done, and rested her chin on one palm.

"There were eagles where I grew up, when I was a little girl" she began softly. "I would see them, but I never really paid a lot of attention, because there were also blue herons and white pelicans and tundra swans. So, the eagles were just mixed in with all of those."

She sat her cup down on the ground and wrapped her arms around her knees, never taking her eyes off the ballet in front of her, as the eagles gracefully crisscrossed over each other in perfect motion.

"I used to go to church with Morgan and my parents, when I was a little girl. Every summer, there was youth camp, and my best friend, Carly Rhodes and I always went together.

"It was for both boys and girls, but the girls' cabins were on one side of the field where there was volley ball and baseball and stuff, and the boys' were on the other. We always had fun there." She seemed to be reliving it.

"When I was nine, though, Carly couldn't go with me, because she had mumps, or measles. One of those things kids always get; I can't remember. I didn't want to go without her, but I knew I couldn't play with her if I stayed home, so at the last minute, I went ahead."

She looked over at Lily with tears puddling in her eyes and the saddest, most apologetic smile on her pretty face that Lily could imagine ever seeing and she reached a hand to stop her.

"Oh, Raven, I think I've made you go to a dark place. I'm so sorry. You don't have to tell me."

Jane pressed her lips together and gestured with a wave that she wanted to forge ahead, and Lily waited with a bleak sense of foreboding.

"We all ate together, the boys and the girls. All the counselors for both were there. They had their own table.

"So, we always stayed behind after lunch, Carly and I, and cleaned up the mess hall. We didn't have to, it wasn't for a punishment, or anything like that. We just liked doing it.

"That year, I was asked by one of the boys' counselors if I wanted to do that, and I just figured he'd also asked one of the other girls to help me.

"But it turned out that I was the only one. He came back into the kitchen area after everyone else had left and said he'd help me. He did start out clearing tables and bagging up trash and stuff, so even though I'd felt uneasy, I finally relaxed and just kept washing off the counters and sweeping up."

Lily joined her in staring straight ahead. She knew from her own experience where this story was going, and even though she wanted to stop Jane, she also knew that sometimes, just finally telling someone else could help with healing.

"I took the broom back into the long, narrow room off to the side, where the freezer was kept and shelves of cleaning solutions and things like that.

"When I did, he followed me in and closed the door. I knew I was just a little girl, and that he was a big, tall grown up, and that even if I screamed, no one would hear me.

"I just remember there was a window at the end of the room, which is where I found myself, after I had kept backing away from him. I didn't want to look at him, so I just turned and kept staring out the window."

There was a steady, silent flow of tears raining down Jane's cheeks, but she seemed unaware of them. Lily rested an arm around her shoulders and again asked her quietly if she wouldn't rather leave the rest of it unspoken. It was if Jane hadn't heard.

"While I was staring out the window, an eagle came and landed on the limb of a nearby tree and seemed to be watching me. He seemed to be telling me to keep looking at him. Then he began swooping toward the window, back and forth, without a sound, just moving through the air, as if he were floating. I kept my eyes on him.

"Somehow, I was alone with just the eagle. I wasn't even in my body, I don't think, because I couldn't feel anything. After a while, I realized that I really was alone. I didn't even know when the man left. All I knew is that I was standing there, staring out the window, and my clothes were all messed up."

She gave Lily a faint smile. "The eagle seemed to know I was in trouble, and he came to keep me from being afraid or realizing what was happening to me."

She pursed her lips into a sorrowful expression, before glancing over at Lily.

"Whenever I discover someone who seems noble to me, I always think that person has the spirit of an eagle."

Lily was dealing with her own tears now, and gave Jane a tight squeeze. They sat together as the gorge grew steadily darker and watched the noble eagles in silence.

A quiet melody began to reach out to them from the guitar of one of their friends and the two women smiled at each other and rose to join the others at their campfire.

The guitar player had been given the name Whisper, because of his quiet, calm nature, as well as his soft strumming of his guitar late in the evening.

As they gathered around him, he began softly singing a familiar folk song from the 60s. Soon, they were all joining him and gently swaying back and forth.

Trapper Dan had set a pot on the fire to begin brewing one of his famous teas. Jane watched him with interest. She'd once had an allergic reaction to a tea she drinked, but she had learned that it was brewed with chamomile and this certainly wasn't that. It smelled wonderful.

He glanced over at her with a little smile.

"Are you partaking with us tonight, Raven, or will you be abstaining?"

"I might try a little," she breathed, watching him with a sense of wonder. "How many kinds of tea do you brew?"

"I'm open to pretty much anything," he laughed, causing a similar reaction from other members of the group who had tried his brews. "When it's ready, you can drink from the silver cup."

Jane opened her eyes wide and looked over at Lily with a pleased expression. "I didn't know we had a silver cup!"

"Trapper must have brought it with him," she supposed.

"I did, indeed," he confirmed. "I always choose someone special to have the honor of drinking from it, and tonight, if you choose to imbibe, you may have that honor, Raven."

She gave an exaggerated little shiver and silently clapped her fingers together.

When the tea was ready, true to his word, Trapper Dan poured some into an ornately beautiful silver cup. He offered some honey with it, and Jane nodded, remembering that some flower and herb teas could taste bitter.

He mixed it in and gave her the cup and then began filling other cups that were now being held out to him.

Jane tried her first cautious sip, and was relieved to not only taste the honey in it, but to still be able to smell the exotic fragrance that had attracted her in the first place.

Music continued to flow around the fire, as the mellow notes of a pan flute and the steady rhythm of a tipper against a bodhran drum added to richness of sound. Blankets were shared with partners and the heady smell of tonight's tea infused the air around them.

After a while, Jane rose to her feet, removing her shoes, and began slowly dancing around in a circle. It wasn't unusual for Jane to dance and she did so beautifully, but Lily felt an abnormally strange sense of anxiety, although nothing seemed obviously wrong.

Her friends smiled at her fluid movements, which seemed to become more and more choreographed. They had no way of knowing that Jane was now dancing with a tall, mysterious man who had suddenly appeared before her and was smiling down at her, leading her further and further away from them.

He seemed to be speaking to her without using words, and she was helpless to resist him.

Lily stood to her feet, with an expression of alarm on her face. She looked around at the others who had also been drinking the same tea, and they seemed to be oblivious to anything now, other than their own pleasures.

Lily hadn't taken any tea herself, but she picked up the silver cup that Jane had been drinking from, and stroked the insides of it with her fingertip, then touched it to her tongue.

Her heart almost stopped as she realized that Trapper Dan had brewed his tea with Angel Trumpet flowers.

She quickly looked up to see where Jane had gone.

"Raven?"

Lily saw her in the darkness and took a hesitant step toward her, stricken with panic as the beautiful woman danced closer and closer to the edge of the steep gorge.

"Jane?" She moved nearer and tried to coax her.

"Honey? Come back, now. Jane, sweetheart, look at me. Look, it's me, Lily. Come back, baby."

Jane turned and flashed her a brilliant smile. "I love you, Lily! I love all of you! I love Morgan and I love Jesus!"

"Jane!" Lily was sobbing now. "If you love me, come back. Come back to Lily!"

Jane turned back to look ahead and stopped dancing. The mysterious man was gone, but in his place, a large, beautifully noble eagle hovered in the air, beckoning her.

Lily came closer, afraid to startle Jane, but hoping to reach her in time to grasp her clothes and pull her back to safety.

"Come back, baby," she begged, with tears raining down.

"Don't cry, Lily."

Jane had turned once more to look at her with beautiful, dark eyes and a sweet, gentle smile, speaking to her in a soft, faraway voice, as if trying to soothe her.

"It's okay. My eagle has come for me. I'm going to be safe, now. I have to fly with my eagle. I have to go away."

Lily's scream pierced the dark night, as beautiful Jane silently leaped to her death.

She fell to her knees, wailing in anguish, then angrily forced herself to get up. She spun around glaring, shrieking at the group of inebriated, high, selfish people who seemed absolutely unaware of anything happening around them.

Lily ran to the old beat up van, and dug around in her bags until she found an old ham radio that she had learned to always have with her. On their drive, she had programmed in a set of emergency frequencies and now began to clumsily and frantically try every one of them until someone responded.

It took a while, but she was finally able to make them understand what had just happened. She told them the exit they had taken and where they camped and that Jane Roberts had fallen off the top of the gorge's edge.

That was all she could do. Now, she simply crumpled to the ground in inexpressible grief and rocked silently back and forth on her knees, crushed. Her beautiful friend was gone.

Chapter Twenty-One

When Morgan Robert's secretary came into his office without knocking and quietly told him that Lily Pope was on the phone, he froze and gazed up at her in consternation. He had several businessmen with him in a private meeting.

"Gentlemen," Marcy murmured, gesturing toward the door. "Please."

They looked at each other, then silently rose and followed her out, as Morgan stared down at the telephone, unwilling to lift the receiver.

His hands shook as he finally grasped it and tried to speak.

"Lily, please don't say it," he begged, dropping his head and beginning to tremble.

"I'm so sorry!" She heard the anguish in his voice and started to weep. "I don't want to say it, Morgan."

"Where are you?" he asked.

"I'm headed to Amanda Hester's house, but I've pulled over to call you, first. She knows I'm coming, but I asked her to let me tell you."

"What happened?" he demanded in a hoarse, ragged voice.

"She fell, Morgan..."

"No, stop! I can't hear it." He laid his head down on his desk and cried like a child.

Lily simply held onto her phone and cried with him.

After a while, Morgan tried to gather himself, and took a few deep breaths.

"You said you were heading to Amanda's house. Is that where they'll be taking her, Ohio?"

"Yes. We were in the New River Gorge area and I told the park officials who the next of kin is, and they know you.

"They contacted the funeral home near Amanda's town and asked them to cooperate with them for transfer. That was early this morning. It may have already happened, or at least be underway. I suppose the funeral home will need some sort of assurance of either coverage or payment, but they agreed to handle things there before continuing transport to where you intend to lay Jane to rest."

"Lily, can you stay there, once you arrive? Can you wait for me to get on a plane and get out there?"

"I will," she promised. "I should be at Amanda's house in about a half hour, Morgan, and I'll wait there. Please call me, for anything, or for nothing."

He quietly thanked her then buzzed for his secretary, who let herself in and stood wordlessly waiting for his instructions. She wrote them down then returned to her desk to have the corporate jet ready for Morgan when he arrived at the airport.

She made him agree to have a car take him to his house and then out to his plane. After he left, she contacted the funeral home in Ohio to advise them that their invoice would be paid in full, then called Blake Jenkin's office to let him know about Morgan's sister.

Morgan moved automatically through his house, throwing things into luggage without stopping to think of what he might need. He had no idea what was waiting for him when he arrived, but he could deal with all that later.

He reached for his phone to call Cora, then drew his hand back with alarm. Why had he done that? It was as if he forgot, for a moment, that she couldn't share this with him.

This caused him to rub his eyes roughly with the balls of his hands and let out a loud, angry oath, before picking up a piece of sculpture to send it flying into the wall and shattering.

He was fuming. This was all wrong! She was supposed to love him! She told him that she loved him! He needed her now, but where was she? Off somewhere with Andrew Holland?

Morgan glared around the room, not caring what his housekeeper would think when she found the broken sculpture and the damage to his wall.

He hurriedly grabbed the rest of what he could think of and headed out the door, where his driver stood waiting.

As he sat back during his flight to Ohio, Morgan closed his eyes and rubbed his temples, feeling an overwhelming sense of grief and loss. He was suddenly mourning the passing of the two women he loved, with all his heart.

He had been angry with Cora for so long but today, as he realized that he was completely unable to function without her, he began to move from anger to bereavement.

When he'd thought he'd lost his sweet Janie before, it was Cora's gentleness and what Jane called her mercy that allowed him to deal with it. It was her soft touch and her expressions of empathy and compassion and love that made him believe he could cope. Now, it was as if his pain was compounded to a degree that he felt he just couldn't shoulder.

Tears began to force their way through his lashes and onto his face, and he held a hand over his eyes as if to keep them in, before he gave way to quiet weeping.

After a while, he made himself get up and go splash some cold water in his face, then stared bleakly at his image, empty.

Lily had arrived and told Darrin and Amanda that Morgan was to be there soon. Darrin proposed to pick him up from the airport but Lily told him that Morgan's secretary had arranged for a driver. There was nothing to do but wait.

Amanda and Darrin held off questioning Lily, deciding that Morgan would do so himself, so they paced around, looking up at the clock and at each other, their faces lined with sadness.

Lily finally slipped outside to sit on the porch and be alone with her painful thoughts.

She wished, a thousand times over, that she had picked up on what Jane was trying to tell her, as she spoke about eagles knowing when it was their time to die. She heard her now, wistfully talking about it, and staring into the sun in a way that seemed to indicate Jane's premonition.

When she told Lily that Morgan's beautiful Cora would take care of him, she missed what she now understood, that Jane was reassuring herself that he would be comforted and cared for.

When the park officials had arrived at their campsite to oversee the rappel team's efforts to recover Jane's body, Lily pushed aside every accusation she knew she would face for being a traitor, and deliberately told the park officials what Trapper Dan had given Jane. She didn't care. He had killed her sweet friend and she was angry.

The National Park Service Rangers were called in to investigate and made an arrest. Lily had given them her contact information then began her long drive to Ohio, after advising the others that she would send someone to get them.

Now she sat slowly rocking and brushing away tears, looking up as she saw Morgan's car arriving.

She stopped rocking but stayed seated. Amanda and Darrin stepped out and hurried down the steps to greet him, but Lily waited where she was, not sure she could face Morgan, now that he was here and able to look her in the eyes. She didn't know how angry he would be, but she told herself that she deserved it. She was supposed to look out for Jane.

When Morgan took his bags from his driver and said something to him about his return, he allowed Darrin to take them and lifted his eyes to see Lily, sitting and waiting.

He stepped up onto the porch and stood reaching his hand out to her and resting his dark, sad eyes on her.

She looked up at his hand with uncertainty, then took it and allowed him to pull her to stand. Morgan surprised her by wrapping his arms around her and giving her a compassionate hug. He knew that of all her friends, Jane loved Lily the most, and that Lily's heart was broken.

She was overwhelmed by his kindness and shook slightly with a new wave of emotion, as he simply patted her back and comforted her, before asking her if she would come inside and sit with him for a while.

Amanda had brewed a pot of coffee and brought it over to the kitchen table, then poured it for the both of them. Lily thanked her quietly, and cradled the warm cup between her trembling hands.

Morgan gently questioned Lily, needing to know the details of his sister's death, but trying to balance that with being considerate of what this woman had seen, that she could never unsee, for the rest of her life.

At times, she would stop and quietly ask him if he was sure he wanted to know the specifics and he would touch her hand and assure that he needed closure.

When she talked to him about the two of them watching the eagles fly, he could see that she was keeping something back, and he gently took her hand and looked at her with a question in his eyes. Lily was so uncomfortable that Morgan realized it was too personal for her to share in front of others.

"That's alright, Lily," he said softly. "We can talk about that later, then."

She looked up at him with watery eyes that seemed to thank him.

She finally told him about Jane's drinking the tea that Trapper Dan had brewed with Angel Trumpet and that this caused Jane to begin to hallucinate.

She told him that she had reported what he had done and that the Rangers had arrested him, but for Lily, it was too little, too late, so she felt embarrassed to even tell Morgan that.

She broke down with quiet sobbing, seeming to relive her failure to save her friend from going over the edge of the gorge, although she had begged and pleaded with everything inside her.

Now, she looked up at the ceiling and drew in a shaky breath and whispered, "I'm so sorry, Morgan! I'm so, so sorry!"

Morgan moved his chair closer to her and put his arm around her, quietly hushing her.

"It's okay, Lily," he whispered. "You did everything you could. Jane was a free spirit and no one could completely contain her. But you tried, and I love you for that."

He looked up at Amanda and Darrin and asked if Lily would be staying with them, and Amanda was quick to assure him that she had a room ready for her and that his things had already been taken to the guestroom he had used before.

He nodded and suggested to Lily that she might benefit from an early evening and hopefully be able to get some sleep.

He watched her go, then stood wearily to his feet and asked Amanda and Darrin if they would please forgive him for also retiring early. He was suddenly drained.

Morgan managed to sleep somehow, but opened his eyes long before daylight and lay thinking about the letter Jane had written him.

He felt that he understood more clearly than ever now what people meant when they spoke of reading between the lines, or remarking that hindsight is twenty-twenty.

He felt a single tear roll from the corner of one eye, over his temple to the pillow beneath his head, as he realized that Jane's letter had been her goodbye. Somehow, she knew.

Lily had told him how, just a few evenings before her death, Jane had been sitting alone, staring into the sun, and when Lily joined her, she explained how eagles knew when it was their time to die, and that they would fly to the highest place and turn and gaze into the sun.

She'd also told him that Jane seemed happy and at peace when she said she had seen love lights in Morgan's eyes when he told her about Cora, and that she was somehow relieved as she confided to Lily that Cora would take care of Morgan.

Of course, he felt a sharp stab in his heart when she said these things to him, but simply stared down at the table and made no reply. None of them knew that Morgan and Cora had not married, and he certainly didn't wish to discuss it with any of them. Instead, he had continued to patiently let Lily attempt to share what she could.

He knew, though, that she was guarding a secret that she was unwilling to talk about in the presence of Amanda and Darrin. He decided he'd ask Lily to ride with him to meet with the funeral home director and perhaps she would tell him then.

He began to feel restless, not being one to lie in bed, once he was awake. He breathed out a sigh, remembering that this was also true of Cora, who had confessed to being an early riser.

He waved a hand impatiently through the air, telling himself that this was simply the way it was going to be. One thing or another would invariably cause him to remember these little details about the woman he had planned to spend his life with, and he might as well just let the memories come and go, since fighting against them made them all the more poignant.

He slipped out to the front porch and eased into the rocker, smiling faintly as old Bentley hesitantly approached him, lowering his head and looking up at him shyly.

"Get on over here, old man," Morgan said quietly.

Bentley's tail began to whip back and forth with what little excitement the old dog could manage and Morgan absently rubbed behind his ears, and let his eyes take in the beginnings of first light.

After a moment, the screen door opened and Amanda looked out with a smile.

"I thought you were up," she greeted.

"I hope I didn't wake you," Morgan said apologetically.

She shook her head. "No, Darrin left right after you turned in and I called it a night, also, so I guess with that bit of extra sleep, I was up early. Maybe I should make a habit of going to bed a lot earlier than I do."

She gestured toward the kitchen. "I have some coffee almost made, Morgan, whenever you feel like a cup."

"Thank you, Amanda," he smiled. "I think I'll just sit out here with this old boy for a bit longer, but I'll be in shortly."

She turned to go, and he stopped her.

"I hope you don't mind, Amanda, but I'd like to ask Lily to go with me today to meet with the funeral home director."

She looked puzzled. "Why would I mind?"

"Well, I know that you and Darrin are a lot like family, and I didn't want either of you to feel slighted."

She shook her head. "No, I don't mind. In fact, Lily probably needs as much closure as any of us, if not more, in some ways. I think it would be good for her."

He looked relieved and simply smiled as she headed back to the kitchen to check on the coffee.

Lily had actually been awake since around two in the morning. She had tossed and turned and punched her pillow but sleep had deserted her, so she had finally gotten out of bed and gone outside, having done the same thing Morgan was doing now. Bentley had approached her and she had gladly welcomed his company. Bentley was having an enjoyable day, so far.

Lily had slipped back inside and taken a shower while she was sure she wouldn't be keeping anyone else from being able to take one, and had stripped the bed sheets and folded them neatly, setting them to one side, and leaving the room in otherwise pristine condition, before quietly taking her things out to her van.

She had climbed inside her van to listen to her ham radio and check her phone for messages, and saw Morgan when he'd come out to sit.

Now, he looked up, clearly startled to see Lily get out of her van and walk toward him with an embarrassed smile.

"I hope my moving around this morning didn't wake everyone up," she said with a little grin.

"This is the first hint I've had of your being awake," he returned, with a soft smile.

He indicated the chair beside him with a little pat and Lily sank down next to him.

"I wonder, Lily, if you would mind riding with me today? I need to meet with the funeral director to make arrangements to have Jane transported back home."

She looked both touched and surprised. "I guess I would have expected Amanda and her brother to want to go with you."

"I'd rather it just be the two of us, if that's okay. I feel that you and I left some things unsaid last night and, correct me if I'm wrong, but I felt that you were uncomfortable because of Amanda and Darrin being there."

She nodded. "If I'm being honest though, Morgan, I'd be uncomfortable, regardless. But some things are meant to be shared no matter how painful they might be."

"And this will painful?" he asked softly, studying the rough flooring of the farmhouse porch.

"I'm afraid so."

"Well..." he finally said, looking up to see the sun reaching its fingers through the trees, "if I'm ever to let go of pain, I suppose I must embrace it, first."

Lily drew her brows, as his words seemed to resonate within her, then glanced over at him with a sad smile.

"There's a lot of truth packed in that, Morgan. You and Jane were more alike than you may realize."

Chapter Twenty-Two

Paul Hartmann wrestled with telling his daughter about the death of Jane Roberts, but he knew that she would want to know. He had heard mention of it on a morning news show that he habitually watched after his devotion time, and searched online for the obituary and funeral announcement.

Now, as he prepared to dress for today's lectures, he stopped and looked steadily at his phone, knowing what he had to do and deciding to just get on with it.

Cora wasn't surprised to see that her dad was calling, even at this early hour, and settled onto the side of her bed to answer.

"Cora, sweet girl." He began with his customary greeting.

She smiled softly. "Good morning, Dad."

"Honey, I'm afraid I have some bad news. I'm so sorry to start your day off with it, but I knew you'd be upset to learn that I had kept it from you. I didn't want that."

She put a hand to her throat and gasped slightly.

"Is it Morgan?" she whispered, her eyes wide with fear.

"No, sweetheart, and I should have realized that would be your first thought. But it is Jane, I'm afraid."

"Is she dead?" She waited in agony.

"Yes, honey. She is."

Tears instantly sprang forth from her eyes. "But she was doing so well, I thought, Dad."

"Well, honey, there was a tragic accident, and Jane fell off the top of a steep gorge..."

He stopped himself and waited, hearing the pitiful moan that came out of his daughter, followed by soft, labored weeping.

"I'm so sorry, Cora."

"No." She tried to control her tears. "No, Dad, I would have wanted to know. Thank you."

"Of course, you know how sensational some of these talk shows try to be for ratings, so they're very cleverly not calling it a suicide, but in the suggestive way that they have for being able to claim that they didn't say something."

"Do you think it was, Dad?" she asked quietly.

"No, honey, sadly I think the other scenario is more likely, that she had ingested something that caused her to be reckless."

Cora closed her eyes tightly and gripped her stomach, sick with the realization of what Morgan must be feeling.

"Do you want me to text you a link to the obituary, Cora?"

She pulled herself out of her thoughts to realize what her father had just asked and quickly replied that she did.

He paused a quiet moment, knowing his daughter well.

"You're thinking of going to the funeral?"

She took a moment to answer.

"I realize that I won't be welcomed and that I'm not wanted," she finally said slowly, "but if I go, it will be for me. I feel a connection with Jane, for so many reasons. I may, Dad, but if I do, I'll let you know that."

She hung up the phone and waited for his text to come through, then studied the details of the location and time of the service, which would take place the following day.

Cora tried to get quiet and pray about going and had begun to learn to obey the subtle checks in her spirit when something was ill-advised.

She was willing to recognize them now, but nothing was apparent. Instead, she was filled with a longing to attend Jane's service, or at least pay her respects and leave which would probably be more likely, she realized.

She booked a flight to the city where Jane's service would be held and where she knew Morgan lived.

The ticket agent recognized her and made sure she had first class accommodations. Cora thanked her quietly, then began to prepare for her trip.

She lived almost an hour from the airport, so she decided to drive herself in the new car she had replaced her old Jeep with. She would just leave it and it would be there when she returned which she felt certain would be almost immediately.

In fact, she wondered if she should have gone ahead and booked a round trip ticket, but she didn't want to complicate things now. She'd deal with that later.

At any point, Cora could have simply turned her car around during her hour long drive and changed her mind about going, but she was oddly compelled, and had stopped wrestling with her decision.

She arrived in northern Washington and checked into her hotel room, having been stopped several times during her trip by people recognizing her and asking for photos and autographs.

Cora was surprised by the number of fans of classical music that she would have supposed to be more likely to prefer soft rock or jazz, but she was grateful and touched by their appreciation of her.

The hotel's concierge escorted her to her room and she thankfully sank into the nearest chair and removed her shoes, before even taking note of her room's amenities. Cora had spent so much of her time in hotel rooms that they had all begun looking the same, but she could see that special touches had been made to welcome her.

She looked out her large window and watched the sea birds flying by, on their way to investigate the various fishing boats that seemed to be plentiful in Puget Sound.

She had been in this city plenty of times over the years, but it seemed to have a completely different feel now, and she knew that was because at least one of its residents was not a stranger to her, or at least, she hadn't believed him to be. Now, she was no longer sure.

Cora checked the clock and factored in her father's time zone, realizing that he was unlikely to answer his phone, but left him a voicemail letting him know that she had arrived in Washington and where she was staying. She promised to call again when she returned to her cabin.

The funeral was scheduled to begin at ten the following morning. Cora wondered about the possibility of being able to ask for a private viewing and then simply leave before Morgan or anyone else arrived.

She had been able to do this sort of thing before, when her main desire had been not to draw attention to herself and cause any sort of unpleasant distraction from the family's focus on their loved one's service.

She lifted her room's telephone and was immediately connected with the front desk's manager, who greeted her warmly and asked how he could be of service.

"I have what might be an unusual request, and please don't hesitate to let me know if this is not possible, but I'm here to attend a funeral..."

Cora waited and softly acknowledged the manager's expression of regret.

"Thank you so much. I wonder, please, if you could have someone contact the funeral home and ask if I might be allowed to either have a private viewing or attend at a time when others have not arrived? I don't wish for my presence to distract from the service in any way."

"Oh, it's not unusual at all, Miss Hartmann," he assured her. "If I may please just have the name of the funeral home and of the deceased, I'll certainly see if I can make this happen."

He raised his brows slightly when Cora told him that the service was for Jane Roberts, easily recognizing that she was the sister of Morgan Roberts who was certainly a well-known man, especially in this part of the United States.

"I'll call you right away, Miss Hartmann," he promised and Cora hung up, hoping that he would be able to help.

She suddenly had begun to feel that she should have perhaps either stayed home or had asked for permission to attend through Morgan's office, but she had done neither and it was a bit too late to change any of that now. She would try to do what she could to pay her respects undetected, but if she couldn't manage that, she would just have to deal with the fallout as graciously as she could.

The manager called her room within minutes and was glad to assure Cora that visitation was at ten and that if she could arrive at nine-thirty, the director would be happy to allow her to have a private viewing. He offered to have a car ready to drive her and she accepted gratefully.

Cora thanked him again and hung up with a feeling of relief washing over her. There was a time when she would have hoped for a chance to see Morgan, but she seemed to instinctively know that he wasn't hoping for a chance to see her.

She would just pay a silent tribute to the woman who had managed somehow to change her life and then quietly take herself away.

She reached for her carry on bag and slipped her hand inside to remove a small velvet box. Tears instantly splashed down her cheeks as she lifted the lid to take one last look at her beautiful engagement ring.

She had no wish to hurt Morgan, but she felt that even though etiquette allowed her to keep the ring, owing to the fact that their engagement was never officially called off and to the fact that Morgan simply never appeared on their wedding day, God would be pleased if she would be gracious to him and return the very costly ring.

She had prepared a larger gift box to place it in, with the intention of asking the funeral director to personally give it to Morgan Roberts, letting him assume that it was a memorial of some sort. Now, she crossed over to the desk and used some of the hotel's stationary to pen a note to him.

She stopped and rested her head on her folded arms, trying to get quiet and pray about what to write. Something began to come to her and she slowly penned it, then folded the note and placed it inside the larger box, along with the smaller one. She secured it with the hotel's sealing wax and stamp.

She set it to one side, then turned and looked thoughtfully back toward her carry on, remembering something else she'd brought with her.

She retrieved another small velvet box and opened it to reveal a stunning platinum artist's easel and paintbrush, on a beautiful chain. The colors on the easel were small precious gemstones.

Cora had intended to give this necklace to Jane at their wedding and looking at it now, a lump began to form in her throat and more tears rose to the surface.

She hoped it would not be resented if she could leave this with Jane, somehow. Perhaps she'd be able to do it without anyone seeing her or knowing who had left it.

Cora carefully unpacked her dress and hung it, then retired to the shower in order to try to relax, even though she doubted that she would sleep at all that night.

✳✳✳

Morgan stood reading the program for his sister's service with a numb sort of quietness in his manner. He glanced up at the funeral home director who hurried into the office with a look of apology.

"I'm so sorry to have kept you waiting, Mr. Roberts," he offered. "I was just saying goodbye to someone. In fact, she came to pay her respects to your sister before the general public began to arrive."

Morgan looked sharply at him. "Not a reporter?"

"Oh, no, certainly not! We would never allow such a thing," he was quick to reassure him. "No, this was a very lovely woman who didn't want to draw attention to herself because of her celebrity status. She merely wanted to pay tribute and leave. She was very discreet and quiet about it."

Morgan continued to look at the man with realization slowly settling on him.

"Was it Cora Hartmann?" he asked in a tight voice.

"Why, yes! I thought that if she knew your sister, you surely must also know her, so I gave permission when her hotel's concierge called on her behalf to request the viewing."

"You say she has gone?"

"Well, I would think so, by now. I did invite her to linger as long as she'd like, but she seemed mindful of the time."

214

Morgan frowned and held up a hand to the director, then hurried into the chapel where Jane was lying in state.

He looked around then saw a fleeting glimpse of long, golden hair as Cora passed out of the chapel and through the entrance's double glass doors to a waiting car.

He slowly moved toward the entrance and stared in disbelief, his heart threatening to stop altogether. He seemed to have trouble breathing.

He turned back to reenter the chapel and stopped to look at the guestbook, seeing her beautiful signature and the date.

After a long moment, he took in a deep breath and looked back through the chapel doors at Jane's beautiful casket and approached it with yet another sting of tears. He knew it would be a long time before they dried up, if ever, so he allowed them.

He wiped his eyes and looked down at Jane's folded hands then fingered the breathtaking necklace that Cora had placed between her fingers with obvious care. She had once texted Morgan a picture of the artist necklace after she had found it, excited to give it to Jane on their wedding day.

Morgan instinctively tucked the necklace beneath Jane's hand, in order to keep it from being seen or possibly taken by anyone else, but ensuring that it remained with Jane, as Cora had intended that it should.

He stepped back and put a hand over his mouth and pressed hard to stop a painful moan from escaping.

He looked around as he became aware that guests were beginning to arrive for the visitation and took himself back into the funeral director's office to collect himself.

"Mr. Roberts, I hope I haven't upset you by allowing Miss Hartmann to have a private viewing," he said hesitantly.

"No. No, that's fine."

"She did leave something else. I've put it in our safe to give you after the service, so that you don't have to carry it around during the entire service, unless you'd like it now?"

Morgan shook his head. Whatever it was, he couldn't handle any extra emotion just now.

"No thank you. I'll collect it when I return after the interment, if that's acceptable."

"Oh, absolutely!"

Morgan thanked him and then very reluctantly and mechanically made his way back into the chapel to attempt to be gracious in receiving the sympathies and good wishes of others.

Amanda and Darrin had come to the funeral home in Ohio to pay their respects and say their last goodbyes before Jane's body was returned home. Lily had a private goodbye the morning she had gone to the funeral home with Morgan to arrange for transport.

Now, it was primarily just Morgan and his associates and colleagues and a few older people who had known his parents and remembered Jane from her childhood days in Washington.

Morgan allowed fleeting moments of wishing he had Cora's gentle hand resting on his arm, but kept resolving to will her away somehow, if he could manage it.

He was grateful for the weather's cooperation and for the fact that the interment setting was beautiful and peaceful. He accepted a last few expressions of condolence from friends, before getting into the funeral home's limousine and returning to take care of any remaining business before leaving for home.

The director remembered to open his safe and remove the gift box waiting inside for him and also assured Morgan that any live plants and suitable arrangements would be given to nursing home residents in the area.

Morgan thanked him and wearily returned to his home, letting himself in the door with a feeling of emptiness that was overwhelming. He put everything down on a table and sank into an easy chair before looking over and noticing the gift box.

He remembered that the director had told him that Cora left it and reached over for it, noting the wax seal with a bit of surprise. He opened it and removed her note with shaking hands, since it was the first contact with her in a long time.

Dear Morgan,

I ask you to please not see this as any sort of cruelty on my part, especially since today is the day of Jane's funeral. I realize that the timing is so very bad, even now as I'm penning this note to you, and I am so sorry.

I don't know if I'll ever understand why our wedding never happened or why you couldn't tell me that you weren't able to marry me, after all. It doesn't seem like you, somehow.

But this is not a day to make accusations or to ask for explanations. This is the day for me to say that I will always be very grateful to you and to Jane for adding a dimension to my life that God is using in a way I could never have suspected.

There has been a great deal of pain, but somehow, pain is not the enemy I had always supposed it to be. I don't know if you've ever read the poem by Robert Browning Hamilton that ends with the words:

I walked a mile with Sorrow;
And ne'er a word said she;
But, oh! The things I learned from her,
When Sorrow walked with me.

If those words could ever become music, then I long to be able to capture them, somehow. Perhaps, someday.

Thank you for the sweet gift of your beautiful ring. It was worn with much joy and love. Thank you for once believing me to be worthy of it.

I pray for your heart to be healed in the wake of the tragic loss of your beautiful Jane. I saw the innocent, childlike sweetness on her face, that could not be diminished, even at the hands of those whose postmortem endeavors seek to create peaceful expressions of repose.

I should have asked your permission to come. I apologize for not doing that. I can't explain the connection between Jane and myself except to say that we are, somehow, truly linked.

May all of God's blessings find you, Morgan.

Cora

Morgan lifted the familiar velvet box and slowly opened it, with a quick intake of breath and a pang of emotion. He was glad he was alone now, so that he didn't have to put on a brave front or cover up tears.

He leaned forward, resting his elbows on his knees and tried desperately to understand what Cora meant by saying that she couldn't understand why their wedding had never happened or why he couldn't tell her that he wasn't able to marry her.

He sat up straight and pressed his fingers against his throbbing temples, trying to make some sort of sense out of what she'd written.

He looked carefully at the hotel stationary and grabbed his coat, rushing out to his vehicle and weaving his way through the city traffic to get to her and demand an explanation.

He threw his keys to the valet and hurried past the doorman to the front desk. The hotel manager recognized him and lifted his brows in surprise.

"Why, Mr. Roberts! I'm sorry, were we meant to have accommodations arranged for you?"

"Miss Hartmann! I must see her! Please, call her room and tell her I'm here."

The manager's face fell with regret.

"I'm sorry, Mr. Roberts, but Miss Hartmann left shortly after returning from the funeral home. We're so sorry for your loss," he added, greatly distressed by the man's agitation.

"She's gone?" He stepped back and simply stared at him.

"Why, yes. She was able to get a flight. I would expect she's probably on her way back home, by now."

He watched the man bow his head, then slowly walk out.

Chapter Twenty-Three

Sandra Birch wandered over to Cora's table with a pot of fresh coffee.

"Of course, I don't think you actually need any more coffee," she chided with a little grin, "but you look as though you might, so I don't want to risk it."

She topped Cora's cup off with a soft wink, and she looked up at her with a grateful smile.

"You must be in a good mood," Cora teased, and the woman laughed.

"Tell that to Walt over there. Apparently, he thinks I'm Ma Barker, today!"

The gentleman farmer heard her, as Sandra had intended for him to, and shook with silent laughter, before lifting his own cup of coffee up and shaking his head.

"Well," Sandra began, pulling out a chair and settling down as she usually did whenever she could steal a break, "how's that opus coming along?"

Cora frowned.

"Don't tell me you haven't even started it!" Sandra crossed her arms and gave her a pointed look. "Honey, that was one of my instructions for you. Take a walk, put on make up, come back to the restaurant and write your opus!"

"I've managed three of those," Cora reasoned with a little grin. "So it's not like there's been no progress, at all."

"Well," Sandra conceded, deciding to cut her some slack. "At least I'm getting to see your pretty face back in here, again. It's good for business," she added, laughing at Cora's comical expression.

"I just bet!" she said dryly.

"It is! I don't know what kind of musical stunt you pulled, during one of those concerts of yours near the end of your tour, but total strangers have been poking around this place, hoping to get a glimpse of you."

Cora looked startled at that. "Are you serious?"

"I am!" she insisted. "Of course, I may have bragged on you a little on my social media page, which I know should just be used for advertising but, come on. I'm not gonna mention something like that?"

Cora grimaced and flicked her fingers at her friend.

"So no inspiration at all, then?" Sandra asked her, more seriously. "I would have thought you would have so much to draw from, honey."

"To be honest, I've not played any music at all, since I came back from the tour."

"But you told me that you knew it was time to write your opus, Cora," Sandra fussed.

"I do think it's time," she admitted. "More so now, I think. I do feel that something is ready to be captured, so maybe soon. But it won't just be written overnight, even if I start it today. Something like that has to breathe and develop. It takes time, which I guess I suddenly find myself with plenty of."

"Okay, well maybe that's a God thing, instead of a sad thing," Sandra pointed out.

"Maybe," Cora agreed. "I think it could be."

Sandra rested her gentle eyes on Cora's face and reached to touch her hand.

"Was it hard, honey, to go to Jane's viewing?"

She lowered her head a moment before looking back up to meet Sandra's gaze.

"I had no idea Jane was so beautiful. That was probably the hardest part for me because she looked as if she were only sleeping, and it just didn't seem fair for her to die so young. I could never have guessed that her death was so violent. I mean, it would have to have been violent, wouldn't it? That kind of fall?"

"Maybe not as much as it could have been, not if she were willingly falling without fear, Cora."

She lifted her emotional eyes to her friend.

"How do you mean?"

Sandra leaned back and pressed her lips together.

"I guess I mean that the Jane I remember, seemed to have some sort of other-world thing about her. It was as if she were only just passing through, not this town, but life. She never seemed to have a tight grip on it. Instead of thinking of it as dying, Cora, maybe Jane was just leaving us, because it was time for her to let go."

"Maybe she was wiser than the rest of us, then."

Cora swiped at a single tear. "I didn't see Morgan, of course, and I guess I'm glad about that. I don't think I could have borne the kind of tragedy I would have found in his eyes."

Sandra sat thinking quietly about that. "You know," she began slowly, "in spite of the sad way things seem to have ended between the two of you, and I say 'seem' because I'm not convinced that things have really ended, there's something about that man that is fundamentally decent."

She nodded toward Debra who had come in to reach under the counter for something and then head back into the kitchen. "She could tell you about that beautiful, new Dodge truck that her friend Harley is driving around in.

"Harley got a call from the local dealership after Morgan went back up north. They told him to come pick out anything on their lot and take the keys. They said it was all paid for.

"Harley told Debra that Morgan had said something about finding a way to thank him, but he didn't really take him seriously. He said Morgan didn't have to follow through, and he wouldn't have thought any less of him."

Cora smiled down at her coffee. "I'm not surprised."

Sandra glanced over at Walt, who had stood up and was leaning against the counter by the register, grinning at her.

"He just does that to make me get up," she declared, looking back over at Cora was raised brows.

"He waits until Debra is in the back and then moseys over to the register, just to see me hop."

Cora smiled and watched Sandra do a little two-step on her way over to him, causing him to look at her with laughter in his eyes. He held his hat in his hands and she got ready for him to ask his usual question.

"Sandra, when are you gonna marry me?"

"How about next Thursday, Walt?" she offered.

"Works for me."

She lifted her hand to wave him out the door then stopped and stared at him. She looked over at Cora, who was also staring, with wide eyes and her hand over her mouth.

"If you get your chores done." Sandra prompted him, just in case he'd forgotten how their little routine went.

"I seem to be all caught up," he returned, continuing to look at her with a bit of amusement.

Sandra narrowed her eyes and inspected him closely.

"Walt Emmons, you better be careful, or I'll think you're serious." She took the receipt he had laid by the register and rang up his lunch for him.

Instead of putting his hat on and giving her his usual little wink, he continued to stand there, as if he were waiting.

"So, we're on for next Thursday, then?"

Sandra put her fingers over her lips and paused, trying to read him. He held her gaze without flinching and she began to look a little flustered.

"You're not serious, though, right?" she asked him, leaning close, in order to keep her voice down.

"I expect I am. Next Thursday sounds about perfect."

"Walt Emmons! Are you honestly asking me to marry you?" She was incredulous.

"I'm not asking you to play dominoes," he returned, with a little wink. "So, next Thursday here, then?"

She tried to stare him down, but a little smile hovered around her mouth and she drew in a deep breath.

"Fine. Next Thursday at five o' clock in the afternoon.

"That gives me time to get someone to cover for me on Friday and Saturday and we can get back from wherever you plan on taking me in time for me to open up on Monday."

He leaned over and dropped a light kiss on her cheek.

"Well, alright, then."

Walt strolled out with a happy little grin on his lean, handsome face while all of Sandra's customers who had long stopped eating and talking in order to eavesdrop, began to gasp collectively and chatter in wild excitement.

She watched him go, then made her way back to Cora's table with a pleased little expression on her face.

"Sandra, do you realize that Walt Emmons thinks you're going to marry him?" Cora demanded. Her pretty green eyes couldn't get any wider.

"He'd better," she shrugged, still smiling.

"You mean you're serious?" Cora was shocked.

"Honey, I've been waitin' on that man to finally propose to me and mean it for over eight years, and I'd just about given up on him! Yes, darlin', I'm serious."

"Is he?" Cora just wanted to be sure.

She glanced toward the door her rugged cowboy had just walked out of. "Oh, yes ma'am."

Sandra looked back at Cora with a lift of her brows.

"I don't suppose I could talk you into playing any music for the wedding?"

"If you don't at least try, I'll never speak to you again," she promised, with a little laugh.

Sandra slapped her hands together.

"There's that, taken care of then. Now I need a cake."

She stood up and scanned her eyes for someone she'd seen earlier. "Margrete! Can you whip us up a wedding cake for Thursday?"

The elderly Danish woman, famous in their small town for her beautiful confections nodded in delight.

"There!" Sandra looked at Cora triumphantly. "There's that, taken care of! This wedding planning stuff is easy!"

She stopped and sat back down reaching for Cora's hand.

"Oh, honey, that was just insensitive! I'm so sorry!"

"Nah!" Cora waved her apology away. "Not everyone is meant to be married, but I do think you and Walt are. I'm actually beginning to be a little excited about this."

"Are you sure?" Sandra searched her pretty face carefully.

"I absolutely am! So, piano or cello, for the wedding? Or violin? I'm good with whatever you choose."

"I can't see you lugging a piano through these doors, honey, so we'd better go with B or C," the happy bride-to-be declared, unable to keep from laughing.

She looked around and leaned closer, confidentially.

"I actually already have a dress."

Cora couldn't seem to come up with a facial expression that didn't require her to open her eyes wider and wider.

"So, we just need to get a license," Sandra mulled. "I'll call him about that tonight."

She pushed up from the table. "I better go see if I can still fit in my dress. Like I said, I've been waiting eight years."

She trotted into the back to take off her apron and grab her truck keys, passing Debra who was coming out of the kitchen with the same shocked look on her face that everyone else was wearing.

Cora leaned back in her chair and looked around Ingleside Fare with a warm feeling beginning to settle around her heart. She loved this weird little town.

✳✳✳

Morgan had been going through Jane's personal belongings for the past few days, alternately smiling or sighing, and sometimes laughing or crying, depending on what he found that had special meaning.

He was stunned to find Floppy still intact, since Jane had loved the old stuffed rabbit practically bare. He placed her old security bunny into the keep pile, then moved it back over to the pile intended for some other person to discover something to find some joy in.

Once again, he told himself that he had to be willing to let go. Letting go was hard, he silently admitted, picking Floppy up and putting him back in the keep pile.

Jane had quite an odd collection of trinkets and things that seemed to have obviously meant quite a lot to her. Morgan had even found her journals, but something kept him from looking through them.

He was still struggling with the feeling that he would be violating her privacy even though, after he'd sat in the car with Lily, while she told him what had happened to Jane at church camp, he wished with all his heart that he had been much more willing to have read his sister's diaries.

He felt that somewhere in all these, especially in one that he thought he might remember seeing her with, when she was quite young, she must have chronicled her feelings about that, although Lily felt it was unlikely, since Jane's experience with the eagle seemed to have been divinely appointed to save her little heart and mind from being destroyed.

Morgan asked himself why there hadn't been a divine appointment that stopped that wretched excuse of a human from being able to molest his sister, but he had no answers. Still, he did know enough about living in a fallen world to realize that just as God uses people for His purposes, so evil does, as well.

He pushed these thoughts away, as he continued to sift through his sweet Jane's simple, modest possessions. He flipped through a sketchbook, and stopped, quickly drawing in his breath and feeling a familiar surge of emotion as he saw a drawing of him and Cora that Jane had been working on. He suspected that she had looked for images of Cora to draw her inspiration from, and would have given this to them at the wedding she thought she had missed.

It was a simple depiction of Cora's head on his shoulder, with her eyes gazing up at him, as he looked down at her, with a tenderness between the two of them that Jane had somehow been able to capture.

Morgan closed the sketchbook quickly, but laid it in the keep pile without second guessing himself.

He finally decided to take a break and wandered into his kitchen to make a quick cup of coffee with a single pod, only because it was fast, but not necessarily good.

He stood waiting, looking out his kitchen window at some hummingbirds that insisted on fighting and dive-bombing each other, even though Morgan's gardener had put out plenty of feeders for all of them.

Morgan heard the loud sputtering noises of the coffee maker and reached for his cup, then came over to rest at the table, his mind both blank and cluttered at the same time, as it had been for days.

He was still feeling a strange sense of disappointment at arriving at Cora's hotel too late to speak to her. It was true that he had no idea what he would have said to her or even what his demeanor would have been toward her, since he was still feeling the sting of what her conductor had said to him over the phone, and particularly over the way she hadn't even tried to take her phone away from him and explain.

He had just talked to her a couple of days before that and she had never said one thing to him about possibly extending her tour until May, which was an important thing for her to have failed to mention, since it obviously meant changing their wedding date. The fact that she hadn't bothered to tell him or to correct Andrew Holland when *he* told him is what had confused Morgan and angered him more than anything else.

All she'd been able to talk to him about was how much she was looking forward to the first week in April, so why shouldn't he have been rocked by learning that she had agreed to stay with the tour through May?

Morgan sat staring down into his coffee vacantly. Then, what had Cora meant in her note, by saying that she didn't understand why their wedding never happened, or why he hadn't been able to tell her that he couldn't marry her, after all? It almost sounded as if she had been there, waiting for him.

Morgan ran his hand roughly up and down the back of his dark curls and finally pulled his computer over toward him.

He was hoping to just mindlessly surf in order to become distracted enough to stop camping out around all of this.

He logged into his social media page and was touched by all the posts offering condolences over Jane's passing. There was no way he could possibly reply to hundreds of posts, so he simply wrote a new post thanking everyone and expressing his regrets at not being able to personally reply to each message and pinned it to the top of his page.

He clicked on his notifications and idly clicked on first one person's page and then another.

He noticed that Ingleside Fare had posted and assumed it was just some special that Sandra Birch was running. He began to pay more attention when he realized that it was an actual informative post and not just something about her menu.

There was a picture of Walt Emmons, who Morgan had seen but didn't personally know, and Sandra Birch together in an embrace and a wedding announcement scheduled for the next coming Thursday, at the restaurant.

Morgan smiled as he remembered the running gag Cora had told him they had, always starting with Walt proposing and Sandra offering him "next Thursday", only to have Walt cite the need to finish his chores and then see.

"It looks like ol' Walt finally got caught up on his chores," Morgan murmured to himself.

He continued to read and wasn't surprised to find that Cora would be playing the music for the ceremony. He felt sure that Sandra and Walt had to know that they were getting a top tier, classically trained virtuoso, but it somehow was just like Cora to not think of herself in that way and gladly agree to play her instrument in the middle of a small town restaurant.

This time, Morgan didn't try to push back a level of admiration and appreciation for this fascinating woman.

He didn't understand what had happened to change things between them, but he did know that Cora was the woman Jane had described as being gentle and merciful.

He had tried to make himself believe that he had let her go, but if he really had, why was her absence more keenly felt with each passing day? The only thing he was sure of was that continuing to tell himself that he no longer loved her didn't make it true.

He looked down at the picture of Cora seated at her usual table at the restaurant and giving Sandra Birch's paparazzi antics an impatient smile, then reached a finger to touch her lovely image, before softly whispering to himself.

"Letting go is hard."

Chapter Twenty-Four

Cora sat on the front porch of her cabin, slowly rocking and cradling a cup of hot coffee in her hands. She had actually had to go back inside and bring one of the throws on her sofa back out with her to snuggle up in, since the morning air was chilly.

Night had brought down the curtain and when morning raised it, summer, which had persistently refused to get off the stage and allow autumn to play its role, had finally relinquished its claim, and the first few leaves of color had begun to flutter around, as if hesitantly responding to their cue.

Perhaps it was playing for Sandra and Walt's wedding that had caused Cora to begin to feel music start to live and breathe inside her again, but she reached for it, and had begun slowly weaving the tapestry of what showed every indication that it was not merely another composition to add to her body of work.

One of Cora's most revered music professors had once taken her aside and informed her that the writing of an opus magnum represented the crowning pinnacle of an artist's body of work and that he felt she had the ingredients of such a milestone already resident within her.

He had told her that many composers waited too late, fearing that if they gave in to their inclination to write such a composition, then they would be accepting their presumed fate of having nowhere to go from there.

He was quick to point out that he considered such a caution to serve no purpose other than to ensure that no masterpiece was ever achieved, and implored Cora to write her opus magnum when she felt it awaken inside her, regardless of the number of years she had lived, or had not yet lived.

"When it asks to be released, child, you must let it go. Keeping it a prisoner will slowly kill it."

Now she sat thinking of the early hours before daylight, when music came to gently wake her and call her to the piano.

For the first time in a very long while, Cora was playing for herself, and certainly not to satisfy the demands of an ambitious, self-seeking conductor.

Even now, Cora had no knowledge of the scheme Andrew Holland had conceived to ensure that his star would not be allowed to marry the man she loved. She had no hint that he had done anything other than simply complain about her intention to become Morgan Robert's wife, or that he had actually taken deceitful measures to stop their marriage from ever becoming a reality.

All she knew is that Morgan no longer loved her and that once he had returned to his life in Washington, to his business, and his responsibilities, he must have managed to convince himself that what he had found with Cora was a pleasant romance, exciting and perhaps even comforting while he was being emotionally tested, but at the end of the day, not something he could permanently invest a commitment in.

Although she loved him still, it was time to let him go, but not without a final farewell. The music that came to draw her from her bed in the early hours of morning had urged her to write her closing words in the form of haunting, irresistable tones that rose and fell like the tide.

Other farewells soon came to lend their musical voices, and Cora's heart broke across the pages for the beautiful, irrepressible, tragic, childlike Jane Roberts, whose great shame and exploitation were still unknown to Cora in the realm of the natural, but in the unseen spiritual domain around her, were broken and poured out like an exquisite fragrance.

Cora had risen during a moment of stark silence and had quietly gone to her room to lift Jane's painting of the trees from her wall and to bring it to rest near her piano, so that she could look into it, and listen to what Jane was telling her.

The message was so humbling that she stopped and cried softly into her hands, but felt a sense of relief that she had remembered to record the moment, in an effort to preserve it.

The tonic note, both literally and metaphorically, seemed to act as a sort of gravitational point, drawing all of the melody and pitch and structure toward it. That source of stability, gently insistent, began to identify itself to Cora as the underlying element around which all of her opus resolved.

She had begun to feel engulfed by what the music was doing to her and had made herself get up from her piano and come out to the porch, where she now sat, watching the shy approach of autumn and somehow knowing that when she next joined her piano, the culmination of her body of works would begin to meld into what gave every indication of being her crowning achievement, her opus magnum.

She knew that even though the mysterious tonic note was multifaceted, as it collected the streams and movements of her music back to itself, it was consistently leading her to a place of closure, merely by sounding the solitary, tender, reverberating cadence of letting go.

It was the gentle blowing of a delicate dandelion. It was the lighting of a paper lantern and releasing it into the dark night sky. It was allowing a much loved, yet caged bird to go free. It was the scattering of ashes. It was, as Cora rested her eyes on the trees before her, the floating away of leaves never more beautiful than in their death.

The whispering sound of the deceiving, dancing wind could be heard, as he beguiled the lovely trees and convinced them to give their beauty to him, only to carelessly scatter it on the ground and ask for more.

Cora slowly stood to her feet, a melancholy smile brushing her lips, and returned to give her hands and her heart to the now silent piano, that was longing for her to continue their journey.

She rested on the bench and once again allowed her eyes to gaze on the beautiful painting that always seemed to beckon her. As she steadily watched, she could see the hint of a red plaid shirt moving among the thick of the trees and toward her.

They were the clothes of a dark haired, dark eyed man who first challenged her presence, then declared his love for her; a man who resented her, then adored her; a man who pledged himself to her, then took himself away.

Cora knew that the way to rightly hear what the music was saying was to refuse to protect herself, to remain vulnerable, and to expose herself to injury and humiliation. There could be no safe place, no night light, no rewriting of the ending. Honesty is not always beautiful, nor is it always joyful.

Once again, and hours upon hours into the night, the sounds of pleasure and sorrow could be heard wrestling for dominance, before attempting a tenuous truce to allow sleep to do its restorative work.

Cora would rise tomorrow, and once again yield herself to become the conduit to express the painful truth that holding too tightly to the desire of ones heart carries the inherent risk of destroying its beauty, simply by controlling it.

She would reveal that the fingers of hands that will not let go serve as the bars of a prison that cause its captive to become diminished in value and despised in the eyes of its jailer.

She would return to the tonic note that will encapsulate the chords, and tempo, and timbre, and motion of her composition, bringing it to the quiet conclusion that the act of cherishing something by releasing it and granting it the freedom to leave, is the art of letting go.

Cora sat in the control room of the studio with her conductor on one side of her and her producer on the other.

She had asked a very delighted and honored Victor Reitzell to serve as the conductor for the recording of her composition, never even considering Andrew Holland. She had only agreed to the tour that Andrew had conducted for the sake of the tour, not because she held him in high regard for his skill.

Victor had sought the abilities of Phillip Granger as a producer, to oversee the technical aspects of the recording process, as well as to offer feedback on performances, and provide input on artistic decisions.

It was Victor's responsibility to lead the musicians to interpret and perform Cora's work accurately, and in alignment with her vision.

He had carefully chosen the musicians based on their expertise and was himself highly respected and able to achieve even the most subtle nuances from his orchestra.

The three of them relaxed at the console with the audio engineer and listened to the playback of the first portion of Cora's opus, which was a symphony.

Throughout the remaining studio sessions, she would transition from it with a series of seven movements, weaving together different textures and moods, before ending with yet another reflective symphony to provide a sense of closure and contemplation, inviting the listener to introspect and ponder, and leaving a lasting emotional impact.

Cora had asked for a playback of the opening symphony with the orchestra, without her piano in the mix, and then for a second playback with her piano added. She and Victor traded a look of pure bliss when they realized how beautifully the musicians had interpreted her score.

"So when we proceed to record the movements..." Phillip Granger flipped his sheets over, appearing to be searching for something. "Are you naming these movements, Cora, or simply numbering them? I had expected them to be named but I don't see anything here."

She drew in a breath and seemed to hesitate. "Well, I've named them for my own purposes, of course, but I'm a bit reluctant to name them publicly, due to the very personal nature of the music."

She glanced over at Victor with a look of concern. "I suppose that will come back to haunt me, though, won't it?"

"I suppose it might," he replied honestly.

"I mean, Cora, the entire opus is so very clearly personal. The very name of it is about as intimate as I've ever known you to be willing to be. If you simply number the movements, you may end up drawing unwanted attention to that fact and create a distraction from the overall work.

"You need to ask yourself if that's really what you want to have to answer questions about."

She seemed to be mulling it over, then reached for Phillip's scores and a pen and scribbled the name of each movement where it occurred.

He peered at what she'd written and after a moment simply said, "That's beautiful. I can't think why you would have wanted to hide something like this."

Victor nodded in approval. "Let's just put it out there for what it truly is, Cora, and not try to cover anything up."

She stared ahead for a moment, before looking over at her conductor with teary eyes and a slight nod. He reached a hand to lightly pat her arm and smiled in agreement.

"Shall we continue to record the orchestra as a whole, then, rather than work with sections?" Phillip wondered, deferring to the composer.

"I think so. They seem to need each other in some of the more fragile places. If that makes sense," she added, with a little laugh, causing him to smile.

"Why did I just get the image in my head of one candle in the dark tilting to light another, that tilts to light another, building in intensity until the shadows retreat into the corners?"

Victor Reitzell laughed at his producer's elaborate depiction with pleasure.

"Now you see, Cora, why I chose this man to produce your opus. In the words of your generation, he clocks it."

A ripple of laughter escaped her, surprising her and relieving her. She'd forgotten that she could laugh.

There was an hour or so before the next session, but rather than leave and come back, Cora opted to stay in the lounge area and stretched her legs out on a sofa, to look back over the notes she'd made for the next session.

She took out a pencil from her canvas bag and flipped back through the entire score, writing the names of the movements for herself, as she had for the producer, then sat studying them, as if seeing them for the first time.

"First movement," she whispered, as she wrote, "The Encounter."

Something about the first movement caused the faintest smile to hover around Cora's lips, before she continued naming the rest of them.

"Second movement, The Nurturing." She had questioned that one, but decided that it only needed to make sense to her, and that anything could be open to interpretation. In the end, she remembered the wound to her hand and the unexpected embrace of a hurting man and told herself that she would not change it.

"Third movement, The Discovery." Another smile came with the naming of this movement, and it was perhaps the longest one of the series.

"Fourth movement, The Yearning." Cora had again whispered the name, looking around as if hoping it hadn't revealed too much.

"Fifth movement, The Brokenness." As she heard herself say the name of this movement, she struggled for composure and felt the threat of tears that would be hard to stop, once they began to flow, and because they were not tears for herself, they came from a place of compassion.

"Sixth movement, The Remission." It was not a hard choice to make for the naming of the sixth movement of Cora's opus. The sixth movement was birthed out of the need to both forgive and to be forgiven. It was about the laying aside of heavy weights and the releasing of disappointments.

"Seventh movement, The Release." Cora felt a rogue tear break free and steal across her skin. She hurriedly sat up and straightened her music, then wiped at her cheeks impatiently.

Again, she heard the insistent articulation of the tonic note and resigned herself to accept the echoing theme of truly loving by letting go.

Chapter Twenty-Five

Paul Hartmann smiled at his beautiful daughter with forgivable pride and reached for a second cup to get her day started with some fresh coffee. She returned his smile with a sleepy one of her own, as she padded into the kitchen in her sock feet.

"I could smell it through the door," she claimed, reaching to give her father a morning hug. "I knew, if I lay there long enough, you'd be the one to have to make it."

"Oh, were you already awake, then?"

"I was. The problem with spending so much time around music is that it's constantly playing in my head. I was lying there reworking parts of the opus, although it's a little late. That ship has sailed, now that it's being aired. Or parts of it, I guess," she corrected herself. "I suppose if a person wants to hear the entire hour and fifty minutes of it, they'll have to catch a concert."

"Oh honey, don't you dare let a sleepless night make you think you need to change a note of it!" Professor Hartmann chided. "That has to be the most perfect composition I've ever heard, as is. You've got to let it go."

He followed her over to the table and pulled out a chair for her, before settling down in his.

"Let it go. See what I did there?"

"I do, you're already brilliant this morning."

He chuckled at that and reached to give her hair a playful tousle. "Good to know, since I have a lecture at eleven."

Cora warmed her hands around her cup and stifled a yawn before lifting it to breathe in the steamy aroma.

"Well," her father began, with a bit of teasing, "how things have changed. My daughter has had to hire an agent!"

"Oh, my goodness, don't remind me," she protested. "I've already had to pull back on the reins. She's sitting on G, waiting on O, and I'm afraid she's going to make a few false starts, if we don't get some ground rules established."

"Is she trying to accept invitations for every interview that's requested, then?"

"Yes! I understand that this is how agents make their money, but I told her that I'll pay her myself, if she'll just take a breather."

Cora's father laughed heartily at that. "Who would have thought that Amy Vanderhorn was such a 'full steam ahead' personality? She stirs up so many clichés, it's entertaining. She strikes while the iron is hot, she pulls out all the stops, she makes hay while the sun shines, she has the pedal to the metal, she pushes the envelope, she fires on all cylinders."

They both had to laugh at the herculean efforts of the normally quiet, discreet woman who had been a friend of their family for many years and worked mostly as a literary agent, but happily accepted the offer to work with the daughter of her dear friend, Paul Hartmann.

"Well, if she begins to wear you out, honey, I'll be happy to talk to her," Professor Hartmann offered.

"Oh, I think things will slow down. This morning talk show she's booked for today airs from the west coast, so I have a two hour time zone cushion before the remote crew arrives here. That's at least a relief."

"And it gets me a visit from my girl. So, you're fine with Amy handling your official social media page?" her father asked.

"Sure. I mean, I wouldn't hand over the keys to my personal page, but for that one, I'd feel weird tooting my own horn." She leaned over close and looked up at her dad with a grin. "Tooting my own horn. See what I did there?"

He pushed back from the table and stopped to drop a kiss on the top of her head. "Surely, we are dazzling, this morning! Onward and upward! Gung ho!"

Cora let him know with a little eye roll that it was okay to put the clichés away now, causing him to laugh again.

"I'll be able to watch you this morning," he let her know, as he prepared to go get dressed. "Your interview airs at ten here, so I'll be watching from the faculty lounge, before my lecture. If anyone has commandeered the television set in there, I will not be held responsible for loss of limbs and subsequent bloodshed."

He strolled out humming a few notes of Cora's opus and she smiled down at the book of devotions he had left on the table and pulled it around to add scriptures to morning coffee.

�֎ �֎ ✖

The hosts of the syndicated live morning talk show that originated in the Pacific Standard Time zone returned from their commercial break with an air of excitement.

Amy Vanderhorn had posted an announcement of the scheduled interview on Cora Hartmann's official social media page several days in advance, since Cora had been showing a reluctance to grant interviews, and people were breathlessly waiting to see and hear her, many for the first time. In fact, it was because Cora's father routinely watched or recorded this particular show that Amy was finally able to get Cora onboard.

Cora knew that she had to become more willing to allow publicity if she intended for people to hear her composition, but she still lacked the proper enthusiasm.

As much as Paul Hartmann and his daughter liked to joke about her agent's tendency to hit the ground running, she actually did defer to Cora and had issued far more apologetic declines than acceptances so far, on behalf of her star client.

She was understandably excited for this particular success and had arrived at the Hartmann residence well before the remote crew, to help Cora with last minute wardrobe decisions and advice.

In addition to the director, camera operators, sound and lighting technicians, the producer and his assistant, a makeup artist, and a stylist also arrived.

When Cora finally emerged from her room to meet with them in front of her father's very beautiful stone wall and massive fireplace, where he had also been interviewed from time to time, after the release of a new book, both the makeup artist and the stylist realized that they would have an easy day.

Cora was a naturally beautiful woman and needed nothing more than subtle touches for the cameras and lights.

The stylist also coordinated the wardrobes for these remote interviews and had brought options, but was quick to approve the simple, olive green, crepe, sheath dress that Cora was already wearing. Its simple three-quarter length sleeves hugged her slender arms and the tailored lines flattered her willowy form, the hem stopping just below her knee and displaying slim, shapely legs.

"Your dress is an exact match for your eyes, Miss Hartmann," she informed her, with satisfaction. "Your hair's highlights really pop against the color. I didn't bring anything with me that would be any better."

Cora smiled graciously and thanked her, before taking a copy of the page from the media packet that her agent had provided to the show's producer in preparation for her interview.

"This is a general idea of the questions you'll be asked, Cora, but also just know that they may stray a bit from this. That's not unusual." Amy Vanderhorn gave her a bracing pat on the back, stepping away as the director called for last looks and the makeup artist checked the need for any touch up.

Just prior to cutting away to their live feed with Cora, a portion of her opus, taken from the last symphony, was played and allowed to reach its poignant final note, before one of the hosts said simply, "It is our distinct privilege to have with us the composer of this masterpiece, Miss Cora Hartmann."

Mark Garrett and Anne Nolan welcomed Cora to their show with noticeable enthusiasm, especially since they had both been furnished with a full-length recording of Cora's opus magnum and each had the pleasure of hearing it in its entirety the evening before.

"Cora, all of us are so excited to finally get to speak to the creator of what has now been revealed as your opus magnum," Mark Garrett began.

Morgan Roberts was impatient for the camera to finally capture Cora's image. He had seen on her official social media page that she would be interviewed remotely today, and had simply told his secretary that he had no wish to be disturbed.

Now, he rested against the arm of his couch, glancing up at the large television in his office, well aware of the adrenaline coursing through his body, as he waited to see her face. He couldn't understand why he would want to put himself in harm's way like this, but he seemed unable to resist.

As Cora's beautiful face appeared, Morgan drew in his breath and immediately began to struggle.

"Cora, what is your response to the notion that you're actually very young to already be turning in your opus magnum and, before you answer that, let me just explain to our viewers that a composer may write many opuses in the course of his or her career, but an opus magnum represents the peak of a composer's entire body of work."

Cora simply nodded and waited.

"So with that in mind," Anne Nolan continued, "how do you address the question of your already deciding that what you've just released is, in fact, your opus magnum? Or does that not necessarily negate any future inspiration?"

"It's not that I don't expect to ever compose again," Cora replied gently, "because, in fact, I hear music consistently inside me, and I do intend to continue to try to capture what I can.

"But touching on your question about my being willing to identify this work as my opus magnum, I suppose that every composer has an innate sense that they are being driven by a profound vision that demands to be realized and distilled into what they hope will be a monumental work of art."

"Are you able, Cora, to identify your inspiration that seems to have been your guiding force for this creation?"

Mark Garrett did stray a bit from the list of questions, just as Amy Vanderhorn had warned Cora, but she simply gave him an enigmatic smile that Morgan had seen many times.

He knew that it presented itself as ambiguous, but that it hid many things.

"I am," she cautiously admitted. "I will simply say that my opus magnum has been written as the most pivotal, important, meaningful, and profound year of my life reaches it's first anniversary mark.

"I was told long ago by one of my instructors that when I felt it stir and awaken inside me, I needed to write it, regardless of the number of years I had lived or had not yet lived; and that when it begged to be released, I was to let it go, because holding it as a prisoner would be to slowly kill it.

"It was wisdom for me, and I heeded his words."

"It does sound like wise counsel," Anne Nolan said. "But it was inspired by a year in your life? Not by, say, a person?"

"A year brings who it brings and what it brings," Cora replied lightly, refusing to be baited.

"Did you write your opus magnum all at once, Cora, or does something like that evolve over time?" Anne asked, still unable to believe the level of mastery she had easily recognized in this young, beautiful composer's masterpiece.

"I had begun to feel a little over a year ago, that I would soon write it," Cora said slowly. "I came off my last tour at the end of March, but personal circumstances caused me to be unable to play music anymore. In fact, I wasn't sure I'd ever be able to play again."

The hosts shared a look of shock between them, as Cora continued. Morgan moved forward onto the edge of the couch, forgetting to breathe, as he listened to Cora in disbelief.

"But when I was asked to play for the wedding of one of my very dearest friends, it seemed to remind me that music was still inside me and needed to come out."

Mark Garrett noted the flushed color on Cora's cheeks and very kindly steered the interview back to the opus, itself.

"Anne and I both were thrilled to take home copies of your entire opus magnum last night, and I must say, I have never heard anything so arresting, so thought-provoking and reverently done. It was almost spiritual."

His co-host nodded in silent agreement, as he continued.

"If I'm not mistaken, Cora, Anne and I have a very distinct honor today. Up until now, we've been told, that the name of your opus magnum has never been made public. Our producer tells us that you have consented to finally tell us all what you have titled your masterpiece. Would you share that with us now, and would you also tell us about its structure?"

They sat waiting and Cora glanced off to one side in a way that only Morgan recognized as an effort to fight off tears. He had not only caused her to have to battle them many times, but he had kissed them away when she would ultimately lose her ability to restrain them.

When she spoke again, it was in a soft, reflective manner.

"The name of my opus magnum is 'The Art Of Letting Go.' Its components are an opening symphony, a departure into seven distinct movements, and it resolves in yet another symphony. These components are the structure of the work.

"I was able to follow the call of what seemed to be a consistent tonic note, although an allegorical one, that was dedicated to bringing me to some kind of closure and kept me faithful to the message."

"You mentioned seven movements, Cora, and I was able to clearly recognize those as I listened at home," Anne Nolan ventured. "Have you also named those movements? I realize that some movements are merely numbered, but I would think in a work of this magnitude, that those very beautiful movements that are clearly inspired, must surely be captioned."

Cora drew in a breath and glanced down, then bravely looked into the camera with a calmness in her bearing.

"Yes, I would agree that the movements which are the actual framework that everything is built on are inspired, and I did caption them.

"At the risk of repeating myself, there are seven, and for anyone out there taking notes," she said with a sudden little grin that made Morgan smile sadly in response, "the movements are named, one through seven, "The Encounter, The Nurturing, The Discovery, The Yearning, The Brokenness, The Remission, and The Release."

"The Release," Anne repeated softly to herself, "which brings the listener full circle to what is now known as The Art Of Letting Go."

"I do hope so," Cora replied with a sweet smile.

Another portion of Cora's composition was played and then Mark Garrett and Anne Nolan thanked Cora profusely for granting them this interview, as the show went to a commercial break, ending the segment.

Morgan could feel hot tears burning his eyes. He sat speechless, before suddenly pushing himself up from the couch and over to his desk, where he pulled open the drawer and began frantically searching for the padded envelope from Paul Hartmann that he had stubbornly never opened.

As he read it now, the look on his face mirrored the agony in his heart. It wasn't the angry, hurt tone of Paul Hartmann's words that stung him.

It was learning that Cora had continued to hold out hope for Morgan to come, even up until the time of their wedding.

She had been there, as she had promised to be. She had waited for him to fulfill his promise. She had been abandoned.

"Dear God," he gasped, in a harsh, ragged voice.

Morgan turned to look out of his windows, lifting a hand to rest over his mouth and allowing more tears to express the grief he was suddenly consumed with.

"What have I done?"

Chapter Twenty-Six

He couldn't bring himself to simply call her. For one thing, there was an odd sort of serenity about Cora that Morgan felt might indicate that she really had let him go. He understood that. He deserved it. But he couldn't accept it, not without her looking into his eyes and telling him so.

He rushed into his house, pulling his tie off and shedding his business attire, then hurriedly changing his clothes.

Of course, Morgan knew that his pilot was hardly likely to take off without his boss, but he continued to rush, throwing things into his bags with the same frantic sense of urgency as he had when he had gotten the call from Lily that Jane had died.

He grabbed up a small carry on and moved swiftly around his room, opening drawers and cabinets, and tossing what he found into it, then looking wildly around, trying to force himself to slow down and think.

Morgan had placed a call to a friend of his who was affiliated with the talk show that hosted Cora's interview. His friend told him where the remote originated from and Morgan was able to figure out that Cora had been at her father's house.

He had no idea if she was still there or if she had flown back home, so he stood wavering a moment, unsure of how to instruct his pilot.

Finally, he decided that if she wasn't home, he'd just wait for her there. She had once given him a key to the cabin and even though Morgan knew that he had hurt her deeply, he also knew that she was unlikely to have had the locks changed.

Just making a decision seemed to spur him into action again, and he grabbed his things and headed to the airport.

Once his plane was airborne, only then could Morgan begin to breathe and of course, reconsider his rash conduct. He knew that the impulsive behavior that urged him to hop on a plane and take off in search of Cora was completely foreign to his usual method of having a plan and following it.

Now, he was besieged by doubts. For all he knew, Cora might be completely cold and hostile to him. In fact, he fully expected her to be, and who could blame her?

He sat back in his seat and folded his arms, letting his dark, troubled eyes reflect his misgivings. He had heard it with his own ears. Cora had clearly said that she had left the tour at the end of March, not May.

Then why had Andrew Holland told him that she had committed to staying with the tour?

Something dark began to stir in the back of Morgan's mind and a stern, rigid set to his jaw indicated the level of anger he was beginning to feel.

He was slowly discovering the motive behind Andrew Holland telling him that Cora was staying with the tour. It was the same reason that he had clearly addressed Cora as "darling" and "sweetheart" and it was also the reason Morgan had heard no response from Cora in the background.

The entire call was manipulated, and obviously staged to do exactly what it did do; to make Morgan believe that Cora had changed her mind about marrying him.

He closed his eyes, having difficulty controlling his emotions as he saw the words penned in Cora's beautiful script.

I don't know if I'll ever understand why our wedding never happened or why you couldn't tell me that you weren't able to marry me, after all. It doesn't seem like you, somehow.

How could she have been so gracious in the note she had written him when she had come to Jane's viewing?

Just as he had done on his flight to recover the body of his beloved Jane, Morgan once again gave way to private tears, leaning forward, resting his elbows on his thighs and running his hands through his hair in frustration, before rising to go run cold water and wash his face.

It seemed to him that his flight would never arrive but when his pilot finally landed the plane, Morgan told him that he didn't have to remain, and that he would call him when he was ready to return, or just book a commercial flight.

He gathered his belongings and hurried down to secure a rental car for the hour long drive to the cabin.

The rental agent looked up at the well-known Morgan Roberts in dismay, when he asked for a vehicle.

"Oh, Mr. Roberts, I'm afraid nothing is ready to rent out. There's a huge harvest festival underway this week, and the football team is playing their biggest rival at home. People have been arriving and grabbing up cars, left and right."

Morgan stood looking around, rubbing the tense, strained muscles at the base of his neck.

"When you say nothing is ready to rent out, what exactly does that mean?" he asked, trying to remain calm.

"Well, it's our post-rental vehicle prep, sir. The only cars here are the ones that have been returned but not checked or serviced. A car could be fine or it could have issues. There's really no way to know until our employees check."

"And how long will that take?" Morgan asked, after drawing in a deep breath, his impatience beginning to show.

"I doubt it could happen for several hours, Mr. Roberts. There's the exterior inspection, the interior cleaning, the mechanical check, the maintenance service, sanitizing."

The agent stopped as Morgan held up a hand.

"And you're the only car rental counter open, as I look around, am I correct?"

"I'm afraid so, and we were just closing. There aren't any cars to be rented anywhere around, I'm afraid."

"Are you the manager?"

"No, but I'd be glad to get him for you."

Morgan wasn't any happier when the manager came to the counter. His agent had told him what Morgan was wanting, but the manager explained that no reputable rental company would rent a car that had not been prepped, even if the customer were to sign a waiver.

"I'm wasting my time with you people," Morgan said through clenched teeth.

"But Mr. Roberts..."

He held up his hand again.

"No, I get it. It's not your fault; policies are in place for a reason. It's fine. I'll just have to figure something out."

"Could we call you a cab, perhaps?"

"Please."

Morgan waited out in front of the airport until his cab arrived. He couldn't help making the mental observation that apparently the cab company did not adhere to the same strict car prep policy that the rental agency did, not that it mattered, since the driver wasn't willing to drive him as far as he needed to go.

He spotted a car lot and asked the driver to let him out there. He gave a sigh of relief as the car lot's owner hurried out.

"Is everything here used?" Morgan asked abruptly.

"Well, yes sir, that's all we sell, unfortunately. We do have some nice vehicles, though, if you'd care to look around."

"Just sell me something," Morgan returned dryly.

The man opened his eyes wide. "A car? Truck?"

Morgan scanned the lot quickly. "Just whatever you'd consider to be reliable."

The owner walked him over to a mid-size sedan but when he began to use words like "this little beauty" and to concoct some sort of one-owner story, Morgan stopped him.

"I'll take it, fine."

"You will? Now?"

Morgan looked at him wearily. "I do hope that you're not about to tell me some long, drawn-out story about needing to prep this car before you can sell it to me. I'm tired, I'm aggravated, and I still have a long drive ahead of me."

"Why, no. I'll just have one of my workers check the fluids while you and I head to the office."

"Thank you."

Morgan shifted the weight of his bags and waited for the car lot's owner to lead the way.

He stopped to point the car out to one of his employees and instructed him to get it ready to go, then led Morgan into his small, prefabricated office to draw up the bill of sale.

Morgan took the keys and tossed his bags into the trunk, and was finally on the road to Cora's cabin.

As he drove, he thought about the biting things that Paul Hartmann had written to him, even though he certainly didn't enjoy playing them over in his mind.

I wonder, since you are so obviously capable of such heinous behavior, if it gives you some sort of morbid pleasure to know that my daughter still, up until the time that the ceremony was to have begun, kept hope alive that something, somehow, would bring you to her. Yes, she would have married you that very moment, even after the way you treated her.

Morgan blinked back more tears, and pressed his lips together tightly.

Of course Cora's father was angry! Why shouldn't he be, when his only child had been humiliated by a man who had made promises to her, and then was never heard from again?

He had mentioned the recording that was on the flash drive in the envelope. Morgan still hadn't heard it, but he knew that it was from the concert that Thomas Delcourt had given such a glowing review in reference to.

Two days after that, it was over between them, and all because Morgan had believed what Andrew Holland had told him, and wouldn't even take Cora's calls.

What was he thinking, having the nerve now to drive up to the cabin, as if he actually expected her to even look at him, let alone speak to him? What had possessed him to be so foolishly impulsive?

"You've come this far," Morgan muttered to himself. "She'll either see you, or she won't. But you will have tried."

His pulse began to accelerate as he realized that he was very close now to the cabin. Just when he had begun to express silent relief that he had overcome the difficulty of obtaining a vehicle, the car in question gave a loud pop and began to veer to one side.

Morgan grappled with the wheel and brought it to a stop on the shoulder. It didn't take him long to realize that the front passenger tire had blown out.

He mumbled something inappropriate and went around to remove his bags from the trunk and search for the spare. When he located it and lifted it out, his vocabulary took another hit.

The spare was as flat as the tire that had just blown out.

Morgan was so put out by the kind of day he was having that all he could do now was smile bitterly and shake his head. He stood with his hands on his hips and mulled over what to do.

Finally, he threw all his things back into the trunk and locked the car, then began to make his way on foot in the direction of Cora's cabin, deciding to just cut through the trees, since the driveway was still a good way on down the road.

Cora brought her cashmere throw out of the house and wrapped it around her shoulders, to sit and wait for the sun to begin to drop behind the trees.

It had been a long day. She had left right after her interview to fly back and then drove herself to the cabin. She wasn't that tired when she arrived, but it had been so silent in the cabin and she had been so affected by her first interview since her opus magnum had been released, that she had begun to feel fatigued, or maybe just depressed. It was hard to tell which.

Now she settled into her rocker and rested her head back and allowed herself to reflect on where she was in her life and career, and where she might be headed. She had no plan.

She smiled faintly to herself as she realized that the view ahead of her must be very near to what Jane had sat looking at. The trees were growing more colorful with every passing day, even though their beauty was fleeting.

The sun had now begun to filter its way through the limbs of the trees, almost as if apologizing for the reckless behavior of the wind, that had taken what it wanted, and then tossed it about on the ground, in wild abandon.

Cora couldn't resist feeling sorry for the way the trees were being ravaged, and thinking of the irony of her once letting Morgan Roberts know that she was not a tree.

"Well, maybe I am a tree, after all," she sighed.

She continued to stare absently into the beautiful hardwoods before narrowing her eyes and feeling the oddest sense that she had become trapped in Jane's painting.

After a moment, Cora tried to focus and look more closely, as a flash of red began to emerge from the thick of the woods. Cora held her breath and raised a hand to her face, then rested it at the base of her throat.

She watched a dark-haired pirate come closer and closer, until he stopped and lifted his eyes to hers.

She slowly rose from her chair and they stood facing each other in silence, both of them unsure of what was real. After a long moment, Morgan dropped his gaze and lowered his head, silently accepting that she had nothing to say to him.

As he stood staring down at the ground, the softest touch of a gentle hand brushed his cheek. Cora had silently stepped down from the porch and slowly approached him. While his head was bowed, she was overcome with the need to look into his eyes and had silently coaxed him to look at her.

When he raised his eyes to hers, they were filled with tears.

Cora said nothing but reached her arms to gather him close and he crushed her to himself. She could feel him trembling, holding onto her with desperation, having no words but clinging to her for as long as she allowed him to.

Morgan laid his forehead against hers and Cora caressed his face, strongly effected by the amount of pain she was witnessing. She whispered his name and he looked down at her, with a sense of urgency.

"Cora, have you let me go?" he asked, unable to keep the emotion out of his shaking voice.

She gazed at him with the same look in her eyes that arrested him on the night they sat talking in his vehicle, when he had realized that this woman was his very lifeline.

"Yes, I have. But letting go isn't always giving up."

Her words told him that there still might be hope and that it might not be too late for them. He slipped his hand up into her hair and kissed her as he had never kissed her before.

It was a long time coming and neither of them were willing to be rushed. Finally, Morgan pulled Cora into his arms and breathed out a sigh.

"There are reasons, Cora, but there are no excuses."

She stroked his brow, then reached to take his hands.

"Come and tell me," she whispered.

She started to lead him into the cabin, but he paused and pulled lightly on her hand.

She looked up at him, wondering.

"Even if you tell me that we have no future together, will you still forgive me?" he asked.

"Morgan Roberts, can you really not see that I've forgiven you? Must I write you another opus?"

They shared a long tender look, before she tugged once more on his hands.

"Come and tell me."

Chapter Twenty-Seven

The way that the two of them immediately gravitated to the sofa and nestled close together, staring into the fireplace and thinking their thoughts, was as natural as breathing. It had always been their instinct and the way they drew from each other's comfort.

Cora rested her head on Morgan's shoulder.

"I'm so sorry, Morgan, about Jane. I can't even tell you how much I have grieved for you."

"I saw you, Cora, as you were leaving the chapel," he said softly. "I wanted so much to call out your name, but my heart was already hurting and I could only handle so much grief, that day, I'm afraid."

He was holding her hand and began to caress it. "I missed you so much during the service for Jane. I kept imagining the way your hand would feel on my arm, and the way your eyes would talk to mine."

She said nothing but pressed herself closer to him, letting him know that she was listening.

Morgan expelled a heavy breath. "We'll come back to Jane in a bit, but there are things that need to be said sooner, rather than later."

He absently lifted her hand and opened it to kiss her palm.

"I'm so sorry, Cora, that I believed Andrew Holland."

She drew her brows in confusion, then looked at him in complete bewilderment.

"Do you know Andrew Holland?"

"We've never met," he admitted. "It was what he said to me on the phone."

"You called him?" She was perplexed.

"I called you. But Andrew answered."

Cora shifted her body to face him and pulled her legs up onto the sofa, tucking them underneath and giving him a searching look.

"How did that happen? I've never told Andrew Holland that he could answer my phone."

"He said you were both at a reception."

Morgan waited, watching realization dawn on her as she worked through the timing of which reception he meant.

"I checked my phone with my coat and other belongings when I arrived, because you had already let me know that we probably wouldn't be able to talk until much later."

She continued to try to work through it. "I do remember seeing him on a phone, over near the entrance. I just assumed someone had called him and he was trying to stand where he could hear. It was a bit loud in there."

She began to display a brewing indignation. "He answered my phone? The coat check employee just handed him my phone, then? Seriously?"

"Apparently," Morgan replied. "He led me to believe that you had no problem with him answering your phone and told me that you also knew that you could answer his. He told me that you had decided to stay with the tour until the end of May."

Cora's face was a storm. "The tour didn't continue after March, and I wouldn't have stayed with it, even if it had! If anyone knew that, he certainly did! He knew our wedding was the first week in April."

"He said that you had never mentioned having a fiancé, then began to imply that you could hear him talking to me. He called you 'darling' and 'sweetheart' and asked if you had only been toying with him. I couldn't understand why you didn't stop him, or take your phone away from him, if you could hear him."

Cora gave him a stunned look, then reached her hand to touch his face.

"Morgan, I'm so sorry!" she whispered.

"No, sweetheart, I'm the one who's sorry. I have no defense for simply believing what he said. That's inexcusable."

She shook her head.

"Maybe if you knew Andrew, it might be inexcusable, but you didn't know him at all. Why should you think that the tour's conductor would be lying to you?"

She took in a deep breath, still angry.

"I've only ever tolerated Andrew Holland, for the sake of the annual tour. Not only do I not consider him to be especially capable, but he's about as despicable and self-serving a person as I've ever met, which is why I never even considered him to conduct my opus."

Morgan allowed a faint smile, but continued to stare into the flames with a sadness resting on his face.

"Morgan," Cora said, getting him to return his attention to her.   "I see how all that played out.   I'm just so sorry."

He leaned his head back and raised his eyes to the ceiling and Cora reached a finger to stop a tear from escaping.

"Your father's letter broke my heart," he said, "even though I refused to even open it until this morning."

"My father wrote you a letter?"

"Back in April. Don't be angry with him," Morgan replied, in a dull voice. "It showed how much he loves his daughter and how deeply he was hurting for you. He didn't say anything to me that I didn't deserve. In fact, I think he exercised great restraint."

He turned his face to hers. "You were there, waiting for me at Ingleside."

She rested gentle eyes on him.

"Morgan, we have to move away from that day. We can't change any of it."

Her calm words discouraged him, and he began to tell himself that he had squandered his one chance to marry her.

"You didn't have to return the ring, Cora," he said in a whisper. "I wanted you to have it."

"But I did," she whispered back.   "Besides, if the man didn't come with the ring, I could just buy my own ring."

She managed to laugh softly, and caused him to smile, if only sadly.

"I suppose I should confess that when I read your note and saw which hotel you were staying in, I tore off in a mad rush to get to you before you left, but you were gone."

Something deep in her heart reacted to that.

"Why were you trying to get to me, Morgan?"

"Because I was confused when I read your note. You said you couldn't understand why I wasn't at our wedding."

She nodded and looked at him steadily.

"And you thought there was no wedding to come to."

Morgan closed his eyes to shut out the vision of his beloved Cora waiting in vain, trying to keep hope alive, but finally realizing that he was not coming, as he had promised.

He lifted her hand to his lips and grimaced with the pain of regret, and she laid one arm behind him and drew his head to her shoulder.

She quietly soothed him, then gently said, "Let's not stay in that dark place, Morgan. We have to get beyond it."

"Does getting beyond it mean that marrying me is something else that you've let go of?"

She studied him with soft, expressive eyes.

"I'm not sure how to explain this to you," she began slowly. "I do much better revealing myself musically, than I do by trying to verbalize what I feel.

"When I speak of letting go, I don't mean discarding, or pushing something away, or even cutting myself off from it, even though some of the imagery that came to me as I wrote my opus suggests otherwise.

"It isn't about me removing a source of pain, in an effort to spare myself. That's not what letting go is for me, especially when I began to realize that pain is not my enemy."

She saw the way he carefully watched her, taking in every word and the slightest nuance in her expression and touched a fingertip to his face.

"Love is not about possession. I couldn't allow myself to continue to hold onto you, even secretly in my heart, if you desired to be free.

"The uncanny nature of the emotional whirlwind that brought us together in the first place, wasn't lost on me, Morgan, and I had to face the fact that once you returned to your real life, it was natural for you to begin to doubt that what we had was ever real and to decide that it wasn't a stable foundation to build a future on.

"I accepted that, because it was much more sensible for a man like you to view us through that filter, rather than clinging to what we found together. I thought it probably seemed like a fantasy to you once we were apart, and that you might even have become embarrassed by it. You're a highly visible businessman, and your reputation is not that you're led by your emotions.

"I had to let you go. It was the only way to truly love you. I also had to be willing to expose myself to the pain of releasing you. I do believe that there's an art to letting go, and I knew I had to learn it, in order to heal."

Morgan sat silently processing her words, and she gave him the time he needed without adding anything else. Finally, he looked at her with eyes that still held questions.

"You based letting me go on the assumption that I wanted to be free, Cora. Does any of that change at all, if I tell you that being set free by you will destroy me?"

He sat up straight and shifted his position on the sofa, lifting an arm to lay it behind her and fixing her with a sober, intense gaze.

"You talk about my being a highly visible man, and I suppose that's true, but being highly visible makes me a target, as much as it makes me a success.

"Women come and they go, but when it's all said and done, I would never trust my heart to any woman but you. I told you, back in the beginning, Cora, that you own me.

"You say that you've let me go and I suppose that's your way of telling me that you no longer own me, but what if I have no wish to be free? What if I delight in your owning my heart? Is there no recourse? Do I have to accept the sentence you're passing on me, and become some sort of exile, when all I want is to be with you?"

Cora felt both an exhilaration and a warning for her to not simply lay hold of his words.

"You're still hurting," she pointed out, lifting her eyes to his. "Our relationship grew out of the need for comfort, and our clinging to each other kept us close, during uncertainty.

"Those elements are still very much present, Morgan. How do we know that if our lives suddenly shifted out of these painful conditions where we still have this need for each other, and into places of happiness, where we begin to thrive separately, that we would still love each other in the same way that we do now? How do we know that our love for each other isn't actually just our need for each other?"

Morgan sank back into the sofa, folding his arms and staring straight head. "Why does it sound as if you've already determined this to be the case, Cora?"

"I guess it does sound that way," she admitted, faintly. She moved to settle back against him and shared his vacant look at the fireplace.

"For me, I can only say that I wasn't the one dealing with the kinds of fear and pain that you were grappling with, when we first met. All I could do at that time, was to try to help you through it and be some sort of constant for you.

"But I'm who I told you I was, in the beginning. I've always been a focused individual with no time for romance and no desire to even look into such things. So, for me, I wasn't going to throw around words like 'love' as if scattering bird seed. That's why, when we met upstairs to pack up Jane's paintings, I told you that I felt like an idiot, and that I wasn't a tree."

"That's the day we admitted that this is love," he reminded her quietly.

She nodded. "For me, it was."

"Is it no longer, then?"

She knew it was only a matter of time before she gave in to tears and her time was up.

"Cora..." Morgan put his arm around her and pulled her close, in a way that allowed him to cradle her and watch her face carefully.

"Are you the kind of woman who would tell me that you no longer love me, just to convince me to leave? Would you lie about something like that? Because if there's any chance at all that you do love me, I am begging you to be honest about it."

"It's not whether or not I love *you*, Morgan."

"Yes! Yes, it is whether or not you love *me*. I'm sorry if you insist on calling what I have for you in my heart nothing more than the need for comfort, Cora, but there's absolutely no truth in that.

"Do you think I've lived all my life confused about what I feel and what I don't feel? Do I seem like the kind of man who *does* toss around words like 'love' carelessly? What would I gain from that?"

He was becoming frustrated.

"I can't undo how completely stupid and foolish I was to just blindly accept what your conductor told me. I can't change the fact that I believed that there was no wedding. I can't take back the reality that I wouldn't even take your calls. It's all there, Cora, a testament of one man's idiocy, and I'm ashamed of it.

"I can't force you to believe me, when I tell you that I love you with everything that's in me and that all I want in this world is for you to take back my ring and be my wife.

"You've let me go, and it was beautiful and generous on your part, but if you refuse to allow me to come back to you, when I have no wish to be let go, when all I want in this world is you, how is that not discarding me?"

Cora caught her breath as the force of his words impacted her. She held his gaze for a long moment, before a slow smile found its way to her lips.

"Morgan Roberts, you'd better be telling me the truth!"

His answer was to capture her mouth with his, in a slow, steady series of kisses that left no doubt.

"Tomorrow," he finally whispered, when he gathered her back close to his side and relaxed with her in front of the fire.

"What's tomorrow?" she wondered looking up at him.

"The day we get our marriage license."

Cora smiled peacefully and snuggled closer.

"Is your father likely to start out marrying us and then interrupt the ceremony by being the one to object?" Morgan wondered with a little grin.

"Maybe," Cora laughed. She glanced up at him.

"No, my dad will understand, Morgan. He knows how much I love you. He'll be happy for us."

"We should call him and schedule a date. If I recall, an intoxicatingly beautiful woman once put her lips next to my ear and assured me that she wanted a marriage, not a wedding. I wonder how she feels about that, now?"

"She'll take whatever she can get," Cora muttered, causing him to laugh.

"We'll enlist Sandra's help," Morgan suggested. "If anyone can rally the troops, it's that woman."

Cora nodded then looked around the room with a bit of confusion.

"Where are your things? Wait... how did you get here?"

Morgan laughed and dropped a kiss on her cheek. "All this time, and you just now wonder that?"

"Well, I mean..." She blushed and he wondered what caused her to.

"I used to sit and stare at Jane's painting of the trees. In fact, when I wrote my opus magnum, I brought it to the piano, and drew from it. But even back when we were first separated and had nothing but video calls, I would concentrate on it and sometimes, I could see you coming through the trees to me.

"So this evening, when I looked up and saw you coming through the trees, I had to struggle to make myself realize that you were really here."

She wrinkled her brow. "But why didn't you just drive up? You're the one who ordered that impressive driveway."

"And I would love to have driven up it," he said dryly. "But the only way I could get here from the airport, since apparently there are so many things going on in that city that there were absolutely no rental cars to be had, was to buy a clunker at a used car lot and just hope it could get me here.

"It almost did, but about a half mile from your driveway, it blew a tire and I guess someone had already blown the spare. So, I locked everything up and came walking through the trees, all for the purposes of fulfilling your dream, apparently."

Cora stood up and reached for his hand. "Let's drive back and get your things."

He happily agreed and took the keys she held out to him. They rode down the drive together, then turned to get back to where the humble car was still sitting. Cora took one look at it and reached to grab Morgan's handsome face and plant a firm kiss on him.

"What was that for?" he wondered.

"If I ever doubted that you love me, I'm convinced," she declared. "There's no way, Morgan Roberts, that you would be caught driving around in something like that, if you weren't a desperate man!"

"That's all I'm saying," he grinned, closing the trunk of the car and tossing his bags into Cora's vehicle.

They let themselves back into the cabin and Morgan took his bags to the guestroom before joining Cora again in front of the fireplace.

They stood warming themselves and he loosely wrapped his arms around her.

"Can we talk about Jane?"

"Are you up to it?" She looked at him with concern.

"I am, with you," he replied. "I'm sure you've heard all the conjecture and rumors flying around about the manner of her death. It's true that she fell off the top of the gorge in West Virginia. It wasn't a suicide attempt, though.

"She was camping with that bunch of hippie friends of hers and one of them talked her into drinking a tea brewed with a hallucinogen. She willingly leaped from the top."

Cora gasped and held her hands up to her mouth.

"Her friend Lily tried to stop her. But Jane was sure that an eagle had come to take her away to a safe place. Her jumping was her attempt to fly to it."

Cora wiped at her cheeks and kept her eyes on Morgan's sad face, as he recounted the demise of his sweet sister to her.

"Before she died, Jane told Lily about being molested when she was a little girl at a church camp. The word 'molested' makes it sound like less than what it actually was.

"While this was happening to her, she saw an eagle land nearby, outside the window and kept her eyes focused on it. Lily said Jane told her that the eagle had been sent to her and that as long as she kept looking at it, she couldn't feel anything.

"Later that evening, Jane had been dancing and getting closer and closer to the edge. Lily tried to persuade her to come back to her, and kept inching toward her, but she was afraid Jane would step backward. She was just hoping to get close enough to grab Jane's clothing.

"All the while, she kept begging Jane to come to her. Jane told Lily that the eagle had come back to the gorge to take her away to safety, and she willingly jumped."

Cora had to keep wiping at the corners of her eyes.

"Sandra told me that Jane seemed to have some sort of other-world thing about her. She said it was if Jane was only passing through the world, but not planning on staying. She said I shouldn't think of Jane as dying, but that she was just leaving because it was time for her to let go."

"It seems that she knew it was," Morgan sadly agreed. "She wrote me a sweet letter. I brought it in case you want to read it later."

He tightened his arms around Cora and gave her a squeeze and a slight smile. "I saw the necklace you left with Jane, Cora. Thank you for that, sweetheart."

"I was supposed to give it to her at our wedding," Cora said softly.

"Jane never did know that we hadn't gotten married," Morgan told her, brushing her hair back from her eyes. "I found a drawing she did of the two of us in one of her sketchbooks."

"We'll want to frame that and keep it," she said.

He rested his eyes on Cora's.

"I love you."

She touched his chin. "I love you, Morgan."

"Thank God, we've agreed on that!" he said with a grin.

"Off you go, and off I go, Cora Hartmann, soon to be Cora Hartmann-Roberts. Tomorrow is a full day."

She accepted his goodnight kiss and gave him one back, then headed off to her room to have one of the best night's sleeps that she'd had in many long months.

Chapter Twenty-Eight

Morgan's eyes were still closed but a smile flitted across his face, as he recognized sweet sounds being made by a very beautiful woman who was obviously trying to play her piano as softly as she could.

He could tell, just by venturing to barely open one eye, that it was still dark outside. He could also tell, by opening the other eye and sitting up in bed, that the very beautiful woman had also made coffee.

He grinned and reached for his robe, and shuffled out of their room to make an easy choice and head straight for his wife.

"While I admire your habit of rising early, I admit I'm still always a little startled by it," he murmured, sitting beside her at the piano and claiming his kiss.

"I woke you up."

"Is that a statement, a question, or an apology?"

She reached over to pick up her empty coffee cup and held it up to him with a little flirtatious raising and lowering of her brows.

"I see," her husband laughed. "It's a request for a refill."

"That way, when we go to Ingleside for breakfast, I'll just have one and that'll make Sandra happy."

"You little deceiver," Morgan said, standing up and reaching for her hand. "Come keep me company."

She let him escort her out to the kitchen and pour their coffee, watching him with her head tilted and a mischievous look in her eyes.

"What's that about?" Morgan asked, setting her cup in front of her and joining her at the table.

"You don't snore," she commented.

"Statement, question, or compliment?"

She rolled her eyes and he laughed.

"I'm not sure why I've never noticed your very succinct way of expressing yourself, before," he observed. "I'm trying to interpret these little short sentences of yours and correctly categorize them.

"So, I don't snore. Are you crushed? Shall I learn how?"

"I've just always heard women say that one of the hardest things to get used to after getting married is that their husbands snore. Sandra says Walt snores. My mom used to say that Dad snored. But you don't."

"So, we're not really married?" He lifted his cup of coffee and looked at her lazily over the rim, as he took a sip.

"I'm just saying that you don't snore."

"Next time I'm asleep, shove a pea up my nose and let's see how I get on," he suggested, with a little wink.

She fixed him with a pointed look, then came around to lean over him and wrap her arms around his neck.

"Our media pages are blowing up the Internet," she reported. "It looks like our getting married shocked almost everybody. Reports are that we have been flying under the radar. Did you know that about us?"

"I did not," he admitted. "Did you know that Morgan Roberts, well-known timber baron and business mogul, has taken a child bride?"

"I'm twenty-eight!" Cora exclaimed.

"I think it was a typo. Apparently, the reporter put '18' instead of '28', which is why one should always spell out ages when writing. That might have helped him."

"Do we demand a retraction?" Cora asked, coming around and hinting very clearly that she wished him to make room for her. He pushed his chair back and let her settle on his lap.

"I think not. Let's see how much mileage we can get out of the fact that one of the most gifted composers to come along in decades is only eighteen and married to a thirty-eight year old mogul. That should get us some nifty wedding gifts."

Cora screamed out with laughter and caused him to grin and rough up her hair.

They teased each other with an exaggerated long look, before Morgan lifted her hair back and tapped his lips. Cora bent down to see what she could do.

"Only married four days and we've run out of things to say," she laughed.

"Talking is overrated," her husband informed her.

"Not according to my agent," she replied with a little scowl. "According to her, I don't do enough of it."

"Well, honey, I know we're still doing our honeymoon thing, even though we haven't actually left for that yet, but do you not feel that you should remain visible and accessible on the heels of the release of your opus? You don't want people to quickly lose interest, do you?"

She twisted her mouth into a little grimace.

"The first interview was hard, I guess, but it was at least interesting. Now, it's like they just take that script and pass it around and keep asking me the same dull questions."

"Mix it up, a little bit."

"They have a set list of questions," she informed him.

"But do any of them have a clue as to what Mrs. Cora Hartmann-Roberts is likely to say?"

"Probably." She frowned.

"Then don't say that."

Cora gave him a confused look.

"Here," Morgan said, reaching over for a banana and holding it up to his face like a microphone.

"Cora, could you tell us more about the seven movements of the main structure of your opus?"

Cora drew in a deep breath and recited in a dull monotone, "Encounter, Nurturing, Discovery, Yearning, Brokenness, Remission, Release."

"Let's try that again," he suggested with a little grin. He handed her the banana.

"You be the host," he instructed with a little smirk.

Cora looked at him strangely, then obliged him.

"Mr. Roberts, will you please share the seven movements of your wife's recently revealed opus magnum?"

"Why certainly! They are 'Encounter: Crashing Into Flannel While Looking For Snakes', 'Nurturing: Having A Hand Bandaged By An Axe Murderer', 'Discovery: Squatters And Pirates, Bats And Rats', 'Yearning: Women Who Secretly Want To Be Trees Or Marry The Men Who Murder Them', 'Brokenness: What Happens To An Eight Thousand Dollar Sculpture When A Timber Baron Is Angry At The Woman He Loves'..."

Morgan stopped when Cora put her hand over his mouth and looked at him with wide, disbelieving eyes.

"Are you serious?"

"Quite. You owe me eight thousand dead presidents," he said, with a deadpan expression.

She continued to just stare at him.

"If you don't have it on you, I'm sure we can work something out," he offered generously.

"At any rate, as far as your tiresome interviews are concerned, you might trying making them more interesting on your end of things and see what that gets you."

"Probably banned in some countries," she sighed.

"Who needs 'em? We just won't go to those countries."

Morgan looked up at his wife with a less teasing look.

"Thank you."

"For what?" she wondered.

"For bidding on this house. For refusing to let me bully you into leaving. For not believing in Bigfoot." His smile came out of hiding. "For taking that ugly blue carpet out of here."

He opened her left hand and kissed her faded scar.

"For the careful, sweet, protective way you wrapped every one of Jane's paintings and saved them, and for not throwing out any of her things, even though you had a right to.

"Jane said that you had grace and that you were merciful. But I already knew that."

"Why are you being so sweet to me, right now?" Cora asked, resting her eyes on his.

"Because I'm about to ask you for a favor," he confessed with a little grin.

"I should have known," Mrs. Cora Hartmann-Roberts said with a bland expression. "And what would that be?"

"I thought maybe you'd be willing to come help me work on my snoring."

She giggled and made him laugh.

He tapped her leg and motioned for her to get up, then stood and looked down at her with quiet joy in his eyes.

"I do seriously have something in mind I'd like to do, and even though it's not necessarily within your purview, your help would be invaluable and it would mean more coming from you than from anyone else."

She realized he was being serious and simply stood gazing up at him and waiting.

"I'd like to display Jane's art. I thought of doing it up in Washington, and I'd have no trouble getting patrons onboard or reviewers to begin crawling around, simply because it seems that I can sneeze and they're all over it.

"But I'd like to do that here, I think. The downtown area is nice, but it really needs a jumpstart, as far as tourists are concerned. I think that if we're able to make this place our main home, I can either maintain a schedule for commuting or we can break our living arrangements up into seasons. This would be a great place to build a gallery to house Jane's work. I also think you're far more musically inspired here than you might even realize."

He slipped his hands around her waist and studied her.

"Give me your thoughts."

"Morgan, yes. Of course, yes! I don't know how I can help you; I mean, you're right when you say it's not necessarily within my purview, but I want so much to be a part of establishing Jane's legacy."

He lifted her chin and took a few kisses from her.

"Let's head down to Ingleside for breakfast then, and while we're downtown, we'll either find something that would already be suitable, or we'll renovate something."

Morgan gave her chin a tender stroke before heading off to grab a shower and get dressed, and Cora watched him go with a soft, sweetness washing over her.

She wandered back into the living room and stood looking down at her piano, absently reaching a hand to play a single note and let it fade away on its own.

Something passed through her thoughts and into her memory, and she lifted the lid of her piano bench to retrieve a small scrap of paper.

It had been tucked behind the edge of the cheap old frame that had been around Jane's painting of the trees, that now hung in their bedroom. Cora had found a more substantial, beautiful frame for the painting, not long before she had begun writing her opus.

When she brought the new frame to the cabin and carefully lifted the painting out of its old, cracked wooden one, the paper had fallen out of it and had landed at her feet. When she had bent to pick it up, she realized that it was something that Jane had written down and hidden in the frame.

She had tucked it into her piano bench and thought of it many times, during the tears that came with writing her opus.

She opened it now and read it again with eyes that were misting over with some sadness but much gratitude.

"A time to search, and a time to stop looking;
A time to hold on, and a time to let go."

Also by Rhonda Hanson

The Father Series

Father's Choice
Father's Wings
Father's Song

A linked novel

Father's Friend

The Master Of Hawthorn Manor
Buying The Farm
Once Upon An Altar
The Adventures of Pahwoo and Her Friends

Grace Under Pressure Publishing
P.O. Box 337
Bell Buckle, TN 37020

graceunderpressure.com

www.ingramcontent.com/pod-product-compliance
Lightning Source LLC
Chambersburg PA
CBHW050321160726

48002CB00001B/131